SPANISH MISSION

SPANISH MISSION

K.B. Spangler

A Girl and Her Fed Books

*For Allison and the staff of the North Carolina Zoo,
and in memory of Carmine the Roadrunner*

Chapter One

Fucking chupacabras.

All right, I know. I *know*, all right? I'm working on the swearing. The dead nun was pretty insistent about that. Besides, I'm past due to drop it as a filthy habit: nobody in the history of modern medicine has been wheeled into the ER and wanted to hear their doctor shout, "God-*damn*, son, I bet I could fit a beer can in that bullet wound!" And yes, yes, you're right, there's no such thing as a chupacabra. However, as I've just learned there are such things as ghosts who can take the form of a chupacabra, and since there are currently forty of these jerks chasing me across the Sonoran Desert, I think I'm going to double down.

*Mother*fucking chupacabras.

While I'm at it? The ghost of Thomas Paine is an asshole, too.

Put a pin in the chupacabras. We'll get to the chupacabras, but it takes a few days to go from when my buddy Mare learned about ghosts to the undead cryptid murder brigade.

We begin, as so many things have, with Thomas Paine.

(That asshole.)

A couple of days ago, Thomas Paine—yes, *that* Thomas Paine, American legend and Founding Father—appeared in Mare's kitchen. He did this in spite of the fact that the Founding Fathers had promised to avoid my husband's coworkers. Swore up and down they'd leave them alone. But no, that bloody Englishman decided he knew better. So? He decided to introduce himself to his great-great-great-etcetera niece.

Mare was certainly not expecting to meet her dead great-etcetera uncle in her own home. I'm not exactly sure what happened, but Mare got enough of the basics from Paine to learn that the dead still walk the earth, and that her boss, Patrick Mulcahy, knows all about it.

My part in this story began when I got home from a long day of exams and a longer evening with the usual meet-and-greets with doctors and my fellow med students. I found a note from my husband, the aforementioned Patrick Mulcahy, on the counter next to a bowl of dry cereal:

Emergency. Might be LBF-related. I'll call if you're needed.

I grumbled about our Little Blue Friends, ate the cereal, and went to bed with my phone on the pillow. I don't remember anything between that and when my husband shook me by the shoulder.

"Hope?" he whispered. "Hey, sweetie, get up. You're needed."

"Medical?" I mumbled. A medical emergency would—

"Ghosts," he said.

I rolled over, threw off the covers, and spend the rest of the journey to the living room trying to remember how to walk. Feet were involved, that was obvious, but there was an order to them which eluded me. When I finally got downstairs, I found Mare wearing a path through the cherrywood floor from pacing (figuratively), and clutching the koala to her chest (literally).

If you don't know about the koala, I'll get to him later. The short-short version is: he's very smart, very talkative (again, literally), and happens to think Mare is the bee's knees (again, figuratively).

Also? If you want to tap out now because of the talking koala, nobody'll blame you. He is by no means the weirdest monster in my life. See: horde of chupacabras. And there was that minotaur last year, but he's dead now. Deader.

Wait.

Chaos—this is *chaos*.

Deep breath.

Forget the chupacabras. The chupacabras will have to wait their turn.

Lemme start over.

Chapter Two

Ghosts are dead humans. I will never *ever* understand why living humans freak out over the "dead" part. We already know what we are, and dying doesn't change our essential natures. That's the part which scares the shit out of me—take a dead human who had high opinions of himself in life, stick a couple centuries of historical salesmanship on top of him, and you get the ghost of a Founding Father.

(Between you, me, and the wall over there? I'm sick of dealing with dead Founding Fathers.)

When I arrived in my living room, I knew at least one Founding Father had to be involved, because Mare was as white as a…sheet.[1] Mare panics easily, because brain chemistry can be a real bitch, but she doesn't *scare!* Except something had scared the crap out of her. She was pacing the room, and clutching the koala to her like a giant wiggly stuffed animal. The koala, who puts up with nonsense from Mare that he'd murder me for trying, let out a little "Ooof!" and gestured for me to come and rescue him.

Mary Murphy is a petite Irish-American women with red hair down to her knees. She'd be the first to tell you that she's not exactly beautiful, but she does have that rare kind of intelligence that can freeze you in your tracks with a glance. I met her through my husband; they're part of the same government agency.

OACET.

The Office of Adaptive and Complementary Enhancement Technologies.

Yes, *that* OACET. The one where its members each have a

---

1 Ghosts are blue. Usually a vivid dayglow blue which is bright enough to read by on a dark night, but as they can change their appearances at will, they can show up in whatever shade of blue their little undead hearts desire.

small cybernetic implant in their heads which links them into the same shared neural network. The one where its members can take control of any networked machine with a thought.

In other words? They're cyborgs.

Mare doesn't look like a cyborg. She looks like a bookish grad student who suffers from chronic sleep-killing anxiety. My husband doesn't look like a cyborg, either. He's tall, blond, and built like a sexy mountain in a suit. None of the three-hundred-plus cyborgs in OACET look the way you'd think they should. There's not a single RoboCop among them—they just look like your typical pack of healthy early-thirty-somethings.

Me? I'm Hope Blackwell. I've recently gotten my medical degree and am drowning in specialized exams and residency placements. I've got dark hair and brown eyes. I stand a little taller than Mare, and have an additional layer of muscles and scars from a lifetime of training in judo. I'm not a cyborg, and I'm not part of their collective. But I am a psychic,[2] which explains why my husband tagged me in when he realized that ghosts were involved. In our household, he handles all matters relating to technology and political intrigue, and I handle the undead. Not the most conventional delegation for chores, true, but it works for us.

Last but not least, the koala is named Speedy. He's the inevitable outcome when a mad geneticist tries to create a talking animal and forgets to compensate for linguistic relativism.

There. Is that less chaotic? Sometimes I honestly can't tell. Case in point: my friend Mare, the cyborg, holding my friend Speedy, the talking koala, while stomping around my living room and panicking about ghosts. This is normal for me!

But not for poor Mare.

She was so scared. Angry, too, but mostly scared. Who could blame her? Learning about life after death is always a hell of a thing. And Thomas Paine may be a rock star with the broad

---

2 I hate that word, by the way. Suggests I have occult knowledge and innate abilities beyond the ken of normal human beings. Well, I don't know shit about the occult, and any abilities I have are those I've worked my ass off to acquire, so go fuck a bunch of glorified innateness.

strokes, but he's always been a little sketchy on the specifics, so Mare was angry and confused and shaking a koala at me.

(That last one was mostly figuratively, although the koala was looking a little nauseated.)

"*You!*" she snarled.

Speedy rolled his eyes.

"Coffee?" I asked, as I shuffled towards the kitchen.

Mare followed, yelling about ghosts and historical figures and whatnot. She's prone to wearing sensible shoes, and all I heard beneath her rant was the **pwomp*pwomp*pwomp*pwomp** of a terrified woman in flat leather soles.

There was already a pot of fresh coffee brewing in the kitchen. I glanced at Mare.

"Not me," she snapped, pushing her hair back from her face.

I shouted, "Thanks, Sparky!" towards the ceiling. The kitchen lights flickered in acknowledgement as my husband heard me. The coffee was too hot to drink, so I let it play an active assist in the role of a ceramic handwarmer as I settled myself at the kitchen table.

Mare was still yelling. It took about ten minutes, but she managed to tire herself out. Once she had finished, she looped her koala-free hand around the back of a chair, dragged it away from the table, and sat across from me, clasping Speedy to her chest like he was a stuffed toy.

"What happened?" I asked. "Be specific."

Mare took a deep breath. Her eyes were getting a little wide, a little white around the edges. Her panic attacks don't happen as often as they used to, but if anything could trigger one, it'd be a Founding Father's questionable afterlife choices.

"I was reading," she said. Her breathing picked up speed as she spoke. "I was...This tiny blue man showed up. He had... he had wings... Patrick felt my panic and told me not to talk to anyone else and he came over to see...and...and...he said he was my uncle and... *And there was a **ghost** in my **kitchen?!**"*

"Who?"

"Patrick!"

"The ghost was also named Patrick?"

"Wha—oh! He said he was Thomas Paine!"

"Ah."

I wanted to bury my head in my hands and curse, but managed to stay upright and...not curse.

Thomas Paine.

Doing the exact thing he had promised not to do.

When I had first been pulled into OACET, I had done some rough genealogy on OACET Agents to try to prevent this very thing from happening. I had given up from sheer overwork—if your family has been in America for long enough, you're probably related to *a* Founding Father to *some* degree—and had instead gone straight to the source by throwing a nice dinner party and inviting everyone on the Declaration of Independence's Wikipedia page. I got the ghosts nicely tipsy on expensive whiskey, and made them all promise to stay away from OACET. Because, thanks to the cybernetic implant in their brains, OACET Agents can see powerful ghosts. So, if you want to keep the Afterlife a secret...

Damn it all, they had promised! It had been really nice whiskey, too.

"Thomas Paine," I said. "He came to you? Greeted you like long-lost kin?"

She stared at me with wide, frightened eyes, then nodded.

"Okay," I said. "First, the basics—ghosts are real."

"Got that part," she snapped. "Thanks."

"They're not horror movie monsters," I continued. (I wasn't talking over her, but you don't allow someone to derail the life-after-death speech. I've given this speech enough times to know that therein lies capital-S Screaming.) "They're human beings—dead ones, yeah, but they're still human. They're ordinary people with all the bullshit and baggage that every single person carries with them. And Paine wanted to meet you, I guess."

"Why him? Why not my—"

"Because your grandmother or your uncle or your favorite

dog didn't come back as a ghost. From what they tell me, it requires a lot of energy to return from the other side. Most everybody who dies doesn't have access to that much power.

"And lots of folks who die don't want to come back," I added, testing the coffee with my little finger. Still too hot. "I don't know why. They won't tell me."[3]

"You don't know?"

"Nobody does," Speedy said. He's got a deep, rich voice which sounds a little like James Earl Jones. "Nobody still living."

"Why not?" Mare asked.

Speedy hopped up from her lap onto the tabletop. "Ghosts don't talk about death," he said, as he dunked the claws on one front paw into my coffee.

I glared at him. He grinned, wrapped his weirdly dexterous paws around my cup, and took one hell of a long drink.

His eyes widened.

"Problem?" I asked.

"Needs milk," he said, and scurried down the table leg. I pretended not to notice how he was panting like a dog on his way to the fridge.

(If you didn't join us on our adventures with the minotaur, this is a very good time to mention that while the koala is one of my dearest friends, he is also a surgical-grade asshole and I treat him accordingly.)

"Hope, *please!*" Mare was twisting her hair into knots.

Ah, yes. I had allowed the koala to derail the life-after-death speech, and we were about to wander straight into deepest, darkest Screaming.

"It's okay," I said. "Listen, the world is exactly the same as it was when you woke up this morning. You just know a little

___

3 I'm *hoping* that ghosts don't talk about what waits in the Afterlife because there's really a Heaven, a benevolent higher power, all the chocolate swimming pools one can backstroke through and so on, and that telling us would lead to mass suicide as we try to beat the rush to the Fluffy Kitten Ball Pit. I'm *guessing* that ghosts don't talk about what waits in the Afterlife because they don't have the ability to convey such information in a manner that our tiny mortal brains can comprehend. And I'm *dreading* that they've escaped from a dimension of giant soul-sucking demon millipedes. All I know for sure is that when I die, I'm gonna punch everything I see until they either throw me back into reality or drop me into the Kitten Pit.

more about it, is all."

She blinked at me once, twice, and then broke down crying.

That was it for the night. I tried to get her to talk, but… you know. Massive mental paradigm shifts followed by panic attacks make for difficult conversation. It was easier to move her upstairs to the bedroom and slide her into bed between me and Sparky, and let her cry herself to sleep.

Note: regardless of what you may have read on the tabloid websites, Sparky and I are monogamous. But he and Mare are part of the same hivemind, and that tends to bulldoze any walls you've built around your own personal space. I knew what I was getting into when I married into their collective, so putting Mare between us and buffering her against the world for a few short hours? Not even a thing.

She woke up pissed.

"Ghosts," she said through gritted teeth.

I had been enjoying the lazy comfort of a late morning. My October break had just started, and I had a rare week off from everything. No classes or rotations. No formal dinner parties, or political events, or anything. No responsibilities. Nothing to do but catch up on my sleep and start studying for finals.

"Ghosts!"

Au revoir, sleep.

"Thanks, Paine," I muttered around a face full of koala fur. I prodded Speedy's butt until he rolled off my pillow and curled up into a fluffy beige ball next to Mare.

Sparky was gone. His side of the bed was cold. He likes to be at work before the sun rises, and had snuck out without waking us. I slipped out from under the warm blankets to use the bathroom.

I was not quite finished conducting my business when Mare opened the door and barged in.

"Ghosts!" she shouted again.

"Mare?" I said, as I tugged my nightshirt down over various exposed regions. "Privacy? Remember personal privacy? I do! It was amazing!"

"Ghosts!" She wasn't listening. "They've always been here?"

"Yup. They've been here as long as humanity has, for…Well, for obvious reasons." I gave up trying to hide my shame: most of the OACET Agents honestly didn't notice little details like nudity any more. Fucking hiveminds. I hopped in the shower; Mare followed. She had another good cry, because that's what showers are good for, and began to wash her hair out of habit. I parked myself under one of the rainfall faucets and waited for Mare to figure out which parts of this mess didn't fit.

It took a while, but life after death is a complicated concept. Plus, Mare has a lot of hair.

"How do you know about the ghosts?" she asked.

"I'm a psychic," I said. "And no, I can't see the future, or read your mind, or make plants grow, or…anything like that. All I can do is talk to ghosts."

She stared at the water as the last of the shampoo bubbles floated merrily down the drain. "How did you become psychic? Near-death experience?"

"Nah," I said. I wanted coffee. Badly. Water, water everywhere, and not a drop of caffeine. "Nothing that sexy. Someone tried to roofie me in college. When I woke up? Bam. Ghosts."

"Someone tried to roofie *you?*" Mare sounded slightly incredulous.

I shrugged. "He tried to slip it into a friend's drink," I said. "Special house blend of LSD and Rohypnol, and some other junk to mask the taste. I intercepted."

"Was there…um…"

"He got what he deserved," I said. I flexed my right hand; we had been in the shower long enough for my skin to turn pruney, and it was almost solid white over my knuckles. Another few years, and I'll be working on my third decade of scars. "I woke up in the Afterlife, I think," I said. "The details are fuzzy. There were dragons and a lot of dead presidents. Then Ben showed up, and he's stuck around ever since."

"Ben? Who's Ben?"

"Ah." I froze. This was when things always took a particularly interesting turn for the weird. I kept my thoughts away from my best friend and concentrated on making a decent lather with my soap. "Um. Benjamin Franklin."

"Um," she said, eyes going wide with fresh panic. "Benjamin Franklin. *The* Benjamin Franklin?"

"Yeah. Want to meet him?"

"I do not," she said, rather quickly. "No. Not right now."

"That's smart. He's a bit of a perv," I said. "He'd never peek in on me in the shower, but you might want to wait until you're wearing clothes."

Mare slumped to the shower floor and broke down crying again.

Listen, you might be getting the wrong idea about Mare. She's not a bundle of useless, weepy hair. Learning that there's life after death is…it's big. Really big. And Mare had this knowledge dumped on her out of nowhere, and she had come to me for help, and instead of helping her I just kept piling on strange realities.

She looked up at me with big green eyes.

I gave up. Goodbye, October break. Goodbye, sleep and studying and too much crappy network television. "C'mon," I said, as I snapped off the shower and handed Mare a towel. "Girls' weekend."

Chapter Three

In hindsight, we shouldn't have rented the convertible.

Sparky has a thing for classic cars. Muscle cars. Big ol' Motor City powerhouses with engines that roar like lions over their kill. When we got married, I gave him a 1965 Mustang as his wedding present. Cherry red. Flawless. I loved riding in that thing. So when we hit the ground in Las Vegas, I had a matching luxury rental all lined up. Except it was powder blue, not red. And the oldest one I could find was the 1969 model. But I thought that would be okay, especially since it had a little more horsepower under the hood than the original.

I didn't take into account that one of my travel companions had four-and-a-half feet of hair.

In the excitement of the moment, neither did she.

Speedy did: the koala started laughing as soon as he saw the car.

(We weren't having a girls' weekend after all. Speedy had thrown a fit and demanded to come along, so he did, because you don't leave a superintelligent koala alone when he's in a snit. I figured we could ditch him at the local zoo while we ran the Strip.[4])

Right. So. Picture it: two women, dressed to the nines and giddy for a week of escapism, donning stylish sunglasses and stepping into this gleaming blue convertible.

They take off down the road in a squeal of rubber.

They get about fifty feet before the passenger is gasping in

4 Not, you know, lock him in a cage or anything like that. Speedy doesn't travel well—koalas are territorial, and his primary territory is the arboretum attached to the back of my house. But he'll cozy up to any female koala he finds, and that improves his mood immeasurably. When we're on the road, I make sure to drop him at any convenient koala enclosure and damn the consequences. Which are considerable. But none of those consequences are as scary as a mad genius marsupial who isn't getting his strange on the regular.

oxygen deprivation because the wind has lashed her own hair around her neck and chair, and she's slowly being strangled.

The car stops. The hair is slowly and carefully untangled, and then pulled into a ponytail.

The car starts.

More gasping.

The car stops. The ponytail is slowly and carefully braided.

The car starts. It goes a little further this time, but soon? The gasping.

The car stops. Bobby pins are located. The hair is turned into a very large bun.

(The driver begins to worry that the entire week will be spent worrying about hair, being murdered by hair, or murdering someone as a direct consequence of being worried about hair.)

We finally made it to the Strip at sunset.

In the movies, the Strip is not stop-and-go traffic. There's a music backdrop, something fun and poppy, instead of the usual sounds of people shouting or laughing (or, later in the evening, barfing in the gutters). But it was a very pleasant autumn day, and the sun was just right, and if you didn't mind the traffic and the constant stream of obscenities shouted by, and then at, the koala, it was actually pretty nice.

We were staying at the Bellagio, as they had a last-minute penthouse opening. I'm not much of a penthouse person myself, but, hey, you can only have your entire comprehension of life after death rocked to its foundation once (fingers crossed!) so I was treating Mare to something nice. We pulled up at the curb and the manager was there to greet us. All smiles. So *nice* to have you stay with us, Dr. Blackwell! And this is Agent Murphy, from OACET? And...ah...I see you brought your...talking koala.

The talking koala flipped off the manager and waddled his way down the Strip. Alone. Pedestrians dropped what they were doing and began begging him for selfies, and I heard rubber against the road as cars swerved to catch a glimpse of him.

Fame, man.

The manager escorted us through the great black doors of the Bellagio's main entrance, and we were officially in Las Vegas.

I love Vegas. *Love* it! Every part of the city is done up in shock value, and the more exclusive the building, the more tasteful the shock. The Bellagio's main lobby is nothing but golds and creams, and would be as boring as your dentist's office if it wasn't for the colorful sculptures. Mare gasped as we walked under a field of glass flowers—hundreds of them!—the light behind their spun-glass heads casting rainbows across the room.

"Beautiful!" she said, her hands outstretched to let the colors paint her skin.

Heads turned as we crossed the lobby, but this was Vegas after all: you expected to see a celebrity or two. A flock of older women with Vulcan housewife hairdos swooped down on us. The manager held them off with a practiced song and dance, and took us straight to the penthouse's private elevator.

Private elevator? Hell yes! The penthouse had its own private elevator, private balcony, private everything. Mare and I wouldn't have to see another living human being for days. Not unless we made the effort.

Suited me just fine.

The manager opened the doors and offered to give us a tour of the suite, but Mare gave a little squeal of delight and vanished. There was the usual huff-and-puff of cyborg mutterings as she oriented herself to the new machines in her midst, and she reappeared with two cappuccinos.

"There's fruit and homemade ice cream!" she said. "And a plate full of cold cuts in the fridge, and chilled lobster! With champagne!"

She drank both cappuccinos, handed me the empty mugs, and disappeared again.

"I think we're good," I said to the manager. He nodded and left without a word.

I walked into the suite. The sound of running water was followed by the din of a dozen televisions bursting into life.

"Everything's on WiFi!" Mare shouted.

"There should be a Jacuzzi in your room!" I yelled back.

More sounds of water, this time hollow and booming as it crashed down into a large open space. "Found it!"

I settled down on the nearest couch and groped around for a remote control. Crappy network television is a universal constant, regardless of its service fees. I must have been tired: I thought I was invested in a sitcom about vague misunderstandings, but when I blinked, the sun had gone down and Mare was standing in front of me. She was carrying a wooden tray. Espresso this time, with a steaming carafe surrounded by even smaller porcelain mugs.

"Can we talk?" she asked.

"I dunno," I said, stretching. "Can we?"

"Yeah." Mare dropped down beside me in a cascade of red hair. She sighed. "Thanks for giving me time to process all of this."

"No problem." I took up one of the tiny mugs and poured myself a shot. Excellent flavor: cyborgs liked to master new gadgets as soon as they found them, especially if they had a computer in them. Seems like the Bellagio's espresso machines fell within their gadget obsession.

Mare stared off into space so long that I nearly drifted back to sleep—even a goddess of organization requires time to formulate a strategy for managing her newfound relationship with the Afterlife—but she started small. "You're psychic," she said quietly. "What does that mean?"

I laughed. "Nothing. Or almost nothing. There's the thing about talking to ghosts, of course. I can pick up other people's emotions, sometimes, but everyone can do that."

"You're... What are you? A witch? A...what?"

"Most everybody in the community just calls ourselves psychics," I said, and crooked a finger over the espresso mug. "It's a small community. Tiny. There's maybe three, four hundred of us worldwide, and I'm not in their address books. They don't like me at all, so if you've got any questions about what I am, or what they do, I can't answer them.

"Mike can," I added. Mike Reilly was a mutual friend, and the closest thing to a monk that we'd ever meet in real life. "He was born into that community. He's sort of like a prince to them. Just…try not to ask him about his family if you can help it. He's estranged. Got out of there as fast as he could and never looked back."

"Oh." Mare's fingernails tapped on the mug as she kicked this new data around. "Why don't they like you?"

"I might be psychic now, but I wasn't born that way," I said. "So I don't count as a real psychic to them. I'm more threat than asset. They like to keep their secrets, and folks like me? We come along and we Shirley MacLaine all over the news, and the next thing you know there're neck-deep in dumb people asking too-smart questions."

More nail tapping. It was a light, pleasant sound, like wind chimes made from pieces of sanded glass.

"How do the ghosts tie in to OACET?" she asked.

"That's a good question," I said. "You sure you want the whole story?"

She arched one red eyebrow at me.

"You asked for it," I said, and I started talking.

It. Took. Hours.[5]

Mare had sat there and absorbed every word, even the parts she already knew by heart. Even the parts that she had lived through. There was no weeping this time: she was angry but calm.

---

[5] Lemme give you the extra-short version. My husband, and Mare, and four hun—uh, I mean, the others—got roped into a top-secret government project. They were kids at the time. Babies, really, just out of college or whatever. There was some brain surgery, and some neurological implants, and then they were cyborgs.

Except this top-secret program was a back-end run around the government. A way to get access to world-breaking technology on the cheap, really: get the government to fund the program, make sure there was a failsafe that would prevent it from working, and swoop in to help give those poor malfunctioning cyborg kids a new start in life.

It was a really, really shitty time in those kids' lives due to the…well, you know. The criminal shenanigans and psychological manipulation. Sparky and I managed to put a stop to it, and he took over the Office of Adaptive and Complementary Enhancement Technologies. Mare is pretty high up in OACET. As far as the secrets and intrigue went, the only thing she didn't know about were the ghosts.

Scratch that: she was downright frosty.

"Frequencies," she said. "My implant operates on the same frequencies as ghosts."

"Yup," I replied. "Ghosts are just energy. If a ghost is strong—if they're made from enough energy to give it a powerful signature—it's likely that an OACET Agent can see and hear them. Since we're trying really hard to keep the ghosts a secret, the strong ghosts stay away from your collective so nobody thinks they've started hallucinating."

"Except for Thomas Paine."

"Yeah, well, Paine has always thought he's smarter than everybody else in the room. I'm kinda mad at myself for assuming he'd play by the rules."

Mare stood, collected the espresso setting, and left. I heard a cork pop; when she returned, she was holding the bottle of champagne. She offered me the bottle. I took a long drink, and passed it back.

"What does this mean for me?" Mare asked between sips. "What do I...What do I do now?"

"Nothing you don't want to do," I said. "Since the implant uses the same frequencies as ghosts, you can see and hear them, but it doesn't mean you have to talk to them—hell, most of them don't want to talk to *you!* They're pretty big about keeping the lines between the living and the dead closed. They'll talk to psychics if they need to involve a live body for whatever reason, but otherwise they're happy to mind their own business.

"This is why we didn't tell you," I said. "Not because we didn't think you had a right to know, but because you had a right to *not* know. Proof of the existence of life after death? It fucks with your mind. It changes everything, and not in a good way. I'm sorry they dragged you into this."

Mare sighed and settled herself on the couch beside me. She kicked her bare feet up beside mine, and the two of us stared out the windows at the Vegas night sky.

After a while, she said, "It's not your fault."

"I know," I said. "I'm still sorry."

"One last question," she said, as she handed the bottle to me again. "How did the people who developed my implant find those frequencies in the first place?"

"Oh, man," I winced. "Can we save that question for later?"

"No."

"All right," I sighed. "The way I heard it, the dudes who invented the tech got their hands on some weird data. They crunched the numbers and figured out it could be used to link a user into an untapped part of the electromagnetic spectrum."

"Where'd the data come from?"

"Showed up on their monitors, in their inboxes... Untraceable. We think we know who sent it to them, though."

I regretted those words as soon as Mare asked: "Who?"

Nothing to do but pretend to be lost in the champagne. Sadly? Mare was not to be dissuaded. One small pale hand wrapped around the bottle's neck, and she yanked it away from me. "*Who?!*" she snarled.

"Some ghosts might not be...as passive as others," I replied. The room was dark, but it was the dark of the mountaintop when light floats up from the valley floor below. Las Vegas was open for business. "Some of them might want to bridge the worlds of the living and the dead, but they don't have enough power to do it on their own. They're the ones who gave the data to the researchers, the ones who helped them discover those frequencies."

"The ghosts did this?" Mare's voice was weaker than it had been. She drank half of the bottle without stopping, then asked: "They...they turned us into cyborgs? Why?"

"We don't know," I said. "Not for sure. Like I said, ghosts are hard to pin down. There's an entire world on the other side of this one, and I'm not sure we're capable of understanding the rules."

(That was a hedge on my part, by the way. From what I've gathered about the Afterlife—or, at least the Limbo you visit before you reach the true Afterlife—it's basically high school with the jocks on one side and the nerds on the other, a hierarchy of punchings and kickings that will last throughout eternity. Would that cheer up Mare? Or anyone who remembers high school? No, most definitely not.)

"But—"

"Don't do this to yourself," I said, as we had a brief slapfight over the champagne bottle. I won, and I tucked the nearly empty bottle between my hip and the couch. "I don't know the answers, and it'll drive you bonkers if you overthink it."

"They're against us?" The edges of Mare's eyes were starting to match her hair. I didn't think she was about to cry. More like she was about to channel the parts of her heritage that drove her Celtic ancestors to run naked into battle. "The *dead* are against us?"

"No, but remember how I said that ghosts are just people?" I replied. "Well, some dead people are manipulative pricks. Just like living ones."

"It's not the same," Mare snapped.

"It kinda is," I said, as I pushed up my sleeve.

My left arm had seen better days. I had been kidnapped early last spring, and had fought off a second batch of would-be kidnappers a few months later. Both incidents had put a few more dents in my hide. The stitches from the second kidnapping attempt had come out just a couple of weeks ago. It hadn't ended well, and my arm was looking rather yuck.

Also? Both incidents were thanks to my involvement with OACET.

Mare hadn't paid attention to the scar when we were in the shower. The angry red in her eyes faded as she stared at the red line that wormed its way up my forearm. "Oh, Hope," she said. "I didn't know—"

"I'm not looking to trade traumas," I said, too sharply. Deep breath. The champagne bottle came out again. It was mostly empty; I drank half of what was left, then passed it to Mare so she could kill it. "Just know you're still playing the same game. What's changed is that there are more players, and the rules got super-weird."

She ran her hands through her hair. "God, Hope!" she said. "I just don't know what to *do!*"

"That's fine," I said. "That's why we came here. Let's go do Las Vegas."

Chapter Four

Gambling is fun. In its way. Which is to say, if you lose yourself in it and don't pay attention to how stupid it is, gambling's the greatest activity ever. There're all kinds of horror stories about gamblers getting lost in Vegas, what with the lack of windows and clocks in casinos, whole chunks of their vacations piddled away without even a stack of chips to show for it.

But gambling with a cyborg is fun in an entirely new way.

Mare and I changed clothes and rode our private elevator down to the lobby. She stepped into the lobby of the Bellagio like a tawny puma on the hunt, red hair falling in waves over a gold silk sheath. I was in black and white, a dark suit over the usual deep-necked blouse. Plus, black cowboy boots, because Las Vegas.

As her accessories, Mare had decided on a fresh champagne bottle and the thousand-yard stare of a woman who had just pierced the Veil. People saw her coming and *fled*.

Then they saw me coming, and swarmed back over us.

Lemme tell you what it's like to be famous.

Wait, no. Let me clarify—not just famous. A-list celebrity famous. The kind of fame where your first name is a household word.

It's a nightmare that never ends.

You've given your entire life over into a world that doesn't belong to you; you now belong to the world. When you're outside of your own four walls, your face isn't yours. How you walk, how you talk, how you dress… You think you've got some control over these, but you're lying to yourself. When you're in public, you're on display. I guess you can choose how you display yourself, yeah, but when you do that, you're submitting. To the press. To the public.

To your own peace of mind.

I never asked for any of this, by the way. I was simply minding my own business, hanging out with a famous ghost and dividing my time between day trading and an internship at a dying newspaper. Then, this handsome spy shows up with his talking koala, and we learned there were dead people at the bottom of his government conspiracy.

We've managed to keep the part about the dead people a secret. The conspiracy, though? We went public with that (and the talking koala, because really, once you've told the public that their government has created cyborgs that can take control of machines with their thoughts, a talking koala is not that big a deal).

Going public changed everything, and not all of it for the better. You know the freedom of being the only person on earth who knows where you are? Say you've gone out for a drive, and one road leads to another and you find yourself in a strange town, and you realize that you're the only one—the only one on the entire planet!—who knows where you are?

That's freedom. Anonymity is *freedom*.

I don't have that. Not anymore.

It'd be one thing if I had wanted to be a movie star or a sports personality. Someone who knows that fame is the price of the job. No, I went into an internship position at a newspaper when I got out of college, and that managed to land me in a government conspiracy. Once we went public with that, my life became a domino effect of public appearances and paparazzi following me in salivating hordes. Then there was a movie about me and Sparky, followed by a hosting gig on *Saturday Night Live*, followed by…

Never mind. Just believe me when I say it doesn't stop.

Goodbye, freedom.

But I do have money, and if there's one thing I've learned over these past few years it's that if you can't get what you want, you can at least buy its closest facsimile.

Tonight, we were buying the illusion of privacy.

There's a section of the Bellagio that has velvet ropes and large-shouldered men in dark uniforms standing behind them. The men saw us coming and smiled, and the velvet ropes were lifted. The typical casino floor is loud, flashy, and bangy. Serious cacophony. Vibrations kick up through your heels and force your mind to bobble around the room. The private rooms in the back? Those are another world of soft leathers and plush carpets, of polished wood and marble. There are people who will stare at you, yeah, and whisper to their friends about you, but it's usually, *"Why do those young women look vaguely familiar?"* instead of, *"For my birthday, Chad got me a fuckable body pillow with her face on it!"*

Mare went straight to the private craps tables, the ones made out of teak and mahogany instead of pressboard. The ones where the plastic dice felt a little too much like bone. The tables were busy, with men and women swirling around them in various shades of cocktail attire, but, like their middle-class counterparts in the Bellagio's main rooms, they saw Mare coming and gave her room.

I followed.

Mare picked one table at random and made a hole in the crowd to get to the Dealer and his Stickman. "Mary Murphy," she said, holding out one long hand to the Dealer. He shook it, bemused. Then, he glanced past Mare and spotted me, and froze.

(Mare's famous, too, but her groupies tended to haunt C-SPAN instead of Hollywood. I'm usually the one who gets recognized on sight, which is a shame as Mare's groupies are way more interesting than mine and usually have juicy gossip about the President.)

"I'm with the Office of Adaptive and Complementary Enhancement Technologies," Mare told the Dealer. "I won't be playing cards. Too easy for me to count them."

"Miss—" the Dealer began.

"Agent," she corrected him. "Agent Murphy, OACET. I'll be playing games of random chance tonight, unless you want to see me run an entire poker table."

"Which you do," I said to the Dealer. "You really do. It's pretty amazing."

The Dealer demurred, as polite as a sleepy baby kitten. He was good at his job, which was to make Mare (and me) happy. And Mare would only be happy with another bottle of champagne and a stack of chips waiting on the Come Out roll.

She made her bets. She watched. She waited. She placed chips like she was planting strategic landmines. She saw how the dice landed, how the Stickman would sweep them up and pass them to her, or to another player. That big brain of hers with its cute little cybernetic implant started to process raw data into usable information, and she began to win.

Bing, the dice would hit the table.

Bang, they'd bounce off the wall.

Boom, Mare would collect her payday.

People began to gather around her.

"Everything is math," she announced, as she made a cute guy in a tuxedo do the blowy-germs thing on her dice "Random chance is never truly random. There are patterns to everything, and if you learn those patterns, you can master the world."

The bets grew higher.

Mare tipped the Dealer and the Stickman, stepped away from the table with her winnings, and allowed the crowd to pretend they had become Agents with a mastery over numbers.

"Here," Mare said, and pushed a handful of chips at me. "This should cover me for the week."

I made a thousand-dollar chip dance across the backs of my fingers: she had given me twelve of them. "Mare—"

"I pay my own way," she said. "C'mon, let's hit the roulette tables."

More champagne. More cute men in tuxedos. Mare worked the roulette wheel until it sung her tune, and the crowd loved her for it. I was very much enjoying myself when I caught sight of the casino's manager at the fringes of the crowd.

He came around the roulette table, sidling up to me as quietly as possible.

"Dr. Blackwell—" he began.

"Agent Murphy's not cheating," I told him. "She's just very good."

The manager nodded, his posture made of manners and tight fingers. "Of course," he said. "Agent Murphy is following the rules, but... Yes. Dr. Blackwell, may I have a moment of your time?"

Ah. I recognized that look. I stepped away from the table, and could hear the tail ends of screams coming from the general casino floor.

"Right," I sighed. "Mare? I'll be back."

The manager escorted me through the room, past the velvet ropes and the broad-shouldered men. We moved through layer after layer of security, with the screams getting louder the entire time. The closer we got, the clearer the sounds—happy screams, really, with the high-pitched giggles of girls who were having the times of their lives—all of them threaded through with a familiar deep voice.

Speedy was in his element.

The koala didn't have Mare's standards. He set himself up on top of a poker table and was cleaning out the house. Blindfolded. I'm not lying: someone had tied a pretty pink scarf around his eyes and he was *still winning*.

The tables around him were packed. Just packed. Alcohol was flowing; the mood was high. There was even an eager-beaver film crew, sneaking their way through the crowd to get action shots of Speedy flipping a row of cards across his claws.

(Two thumbs, folks. Koalas have not one but two thumbs on each paw. Don't underestimate those dexterous sons of bitches. Or their brute strength. They've been climbing up and down trees for millennia, sometimes at rocket speed.)

"What's with the camera crew?" I asked. Casinos usually weren't okay about getting their infrastructure caught on tape.

"They have permits," he said, his nose pointed squarely towards the koala.

"Right," I said again. "So, Speedy's definitely cheating, but this looks like it might be good for business. How do you want me to shut this down?"

Relief poured from him. "Gently, please?"

I put two fingers in my mouth and whistled. The manager flinched.

"Sorry," I said. "The dirty version of getting Speedy to back down involves fire."

Over at the poker table, the blindfold came off. "Hope!" Speedy called. He leapt across the table, scattering cards and chips behind him. "Hope! Hey, kitten!"

Oh, boy. Not good. He was happy.

I knelt and scooped him up out of instinct: you only let a thirty-five-pound koala scurry straight up your legs and torso once, and then you've learned.

"Lookie!" Speedy was laughing, falling all over himself and nearly out of my arms. "Hey, Hope, look who's here!"

"Yeah, I can see… Oh."

The cameras had turned towards me. The nearest one was big, a pro model. Stamped across its hood was an outline of a skeleton, with the words "Spooky Solutions" scribbled across the bottom in a font made of femurs.

"Oh, lord," I sighed.

"Ghost Hunters!" he crowed. *"Paranormal Investigators!"*

"Trademarked!" A man peered from behind the larger of the two cameras. He was a couple of years older than me, with a round baby face covered in a scruff of beard. "Those names are trademarked. We're *Spooky Solutions."*

"What do you solve?" I asked.

The man stared at me, and then the camera went back up to hide his face. A second man, this one making a good attempt at being photogenic in his black jacket and jeans, stepped towards me. He seemed vaguely familiar, in his routine semi-athletic white guy way. "We've just encountered Hope Blackwell," he said to the camera. "Wife of Patrick Mulcahy, Head of the Office of Adaptive and Complementary Enhancement Technologies.

She's a famed judo master—"

"Student," I broke in. "You're lucky if you die a master. Who are you?"

"Eli Tellerman," Speedy said. He climbed from my arms and draped himself across my shoulders. "Public face of *Spooky Solutions*, the next big thing in paranormal explorations, encounters, etcetera."

"You do ghost tours?" I asked Tellerman.

His wry little grin sputtered at its edges. "Investigations," he said. "We investigate hauntings and get to the truth of the disturbance."

"Yeah, that definitely sounds like a revolution in the reality television department. And it involves five-star casinos, how?" I asked, and held up an entire fistful of fingers to a passing waitress. Whatever else this involved, I was darned sure it would require alcohol at various steps along the way.

"We're setting the story," came the voice from behind the camera.

"Keith Maples, my right-hand man," Tellerman said, waving vaguely towards the first camera. The baby-faced man's brown eyes bobbed up over the viewfinder, then back down again. "Over on the second camera is Oshea Price—"

There were introductions, five more of them. Tellerman traveled with an entourage of sound and tech guys, backup personalities, everything the budding paranormal ghost stalker needed to set his name in lights. Most of the entourage was college-age and male, except for a pair of African-American twins with bright, busy eyes.

The twins and I stared at each other for a thoughtful moment. I nodded to them; they each returned the gesture.

"This isn't a low-budget operation," I whispered to Speedy.

A koala's ears are better than anything. "Tellerman's stepmom is rich," he said, the whiskers on his muzzle buzzing against my ear. "And she's connected. That's why he's able to shoot in the Bellagio."

"Fuck," I muttered. Rich kids don't back off once they've got something juicy in their sights, and featuring the world's only superintelligent koala in his reality show would be a coup.

Oh, and me. And Mare, once she showed up—OACET Agents were commodities, and Mare and I are both easy on the eyes.

"You gonna be filming everything?" I asked Tellerman. "'cause I haven't signed a consent form and I've got a damned good lawyer."

"It's a private casino," he said, as easy as breathing. "Everyone here consents to being on camera when they walk through the doors."

"Okay then," I said, and turned to leave.

As I did, I caught sight of a bunch of dudes who set my spider sense to tingling. Four men. Casually dressed, even down to the shoes. But the way they watched me without watching me... The new scar on my left forearm began to burn, and all thought of camera crews and their baggage vanished.

After a quarter of a second, those thoughts came crashing back. "Wait!" Tellerman scooted around to put himself between me and the men; the camera followed. "You don't remember me?"

"Nope. Sorry." I tried to push the camera out of the way. By the time I did, the men had scattered in (suspiciously) different directions.

"You see them?" I asked Speedy.

He ignored me and pranced across my shoulders. Oh, he was in a fine mood. "Tellerman knows all about ghosts!" he giggled. "He knows how to hunt them and find them and—"

"Are you drunk?" I asked him.

"I'm not *not* drunk," he said, with a burp that smelled awfully like a eucalyptus martini.

"Hope Blackwell, could you tell us what brings you to Las Vegas?" The camera was back again, with Tellerman doing his best to maneuver an arm around my waist.

There was too much happening, and not enough time to regroup. "Enough," I said. "You want an interview? Fine. But we're not doing it here."

Chapter Five

INT. BELLAGIO CASINO, NIGHT

A private room in a restaurant. The room is empty except for the cast of Spooky Solutions, HOPE, MARE, KOALA, and hotel waitstaff. Participants are assembled around a table: waiters are serving drinks.

KEITH (V.O.): Ms. Black—

MARE: Doctor, please. Hope just started her residency.

KEITH (V.O.): Dr. Blackwell, what do you know about ghost ships?

HOPE (to WAITER): Thank you.

HOPE (to KEITH): Nothing.

KEITH (V.O.): You've heard of the Sonoran Desert?

HOPE: Down near Tucson? Yeah.

TELLERMAN: What would you say if I told you there was a fleet of Spanish galleons buried in the middle of the desert?

HOPE (laughing): Good one.

TELLERMAN: I'm serious, Dr. Blackwell, there're ghost ships—

HOPE: Hands off, bucko.

TELLERMAN (quietly, to HOPE): You don't remember me, do you?

HOPE: Nope. I meet a lot of people. Get to your sales pitch.

TELLERMAN: Congresswoman Laughran's party? Last August? My stepmother—

HOPE (groaning): You're Laughran's kid? Fuck.

MARE: Laughran? The same Laughran who sits on the House Intelligence Committee?

TELLERMAN (smiling, at MARE): My stepmother says hello.

KOALA (laughing): How's that for coincidence?

HOPE (to Koala): Goddamn it, Speedy!

HOPE (to TELLERMAN): What do you want? An investor? How much?

TELLERMAN: Hey, no, you've got me all wrong. This is a legitimate enterprise—

HOPE: —said no one ever, without some level of irony—

KEITH (V.O., nervous chuckling): If you're offering—

TELLERMAN (to KEITH): She's **not**.

HOPE (quietly): Goddamn it.

TELLERMAN: Could you not swear on camera? We're trying for a PG-14 rating.

HOPE: …what do you want?

TELLERMAN: Nothing special. Nothing that wouldn't take more than an afternoon of your time.

KEITH (V.O.): What? No, Eli, wait—

TELLERMAN (to KEITH): Shhh!

TELLERMAN (to HOPE): That trick you pulled in Greece last year? When you found the ancient library? If you came along with us—

HOPE: **What?!** That was an accident! It was… That was the koala's discovery. Take him with you.

KOALA: Hey, now—

HOPE: He's perfect for your show. Cute, cuddly…definitely better for television than me or Mare. We'll stay here in Vegas; he'll go with you to the desert.

KOALA: Hey!

MARE (to HOPE): Um, Hope? That's not—

HOPE: So, that's settled. Who wants to split the crab dip?

KOALA (to HOPE): Don't you even think about—

HOPE: Everybody? Crab dips all around?

HOPE (to WAITER): Cool, we'll order five for the table, thank you.

TELLERMAN: Dr. Blackwell, could you hear me out? This is a real opportunity to make history.

HOPE: Done that. Making history is extremely overrated. You do it once, people keep expecting you to do it again. It's a lot of pressure.

TELLERMAN (whispering to HOPE): Pirates.

HOPE: What?

TELLERMAN (quietly): In the desert.

HOPE: Like, pirate-pirates? Yo-ho-ho and bottles of rum?

TELLERMAN (nodding): Exactly.

HOPE: Oh for fuck's sake.

TELLERMAN: I'm serious. Dead serious.

HOPE: Right. Sure you don't want to pull another pitch? A lost gold mine would be more believable.

TELLERMAN: But it wouldn't be true. This fleet of Spanish ships? It ran aground during a flood. The pirates were chasing—

HOPE: Start over. If we're doing this, start from the beginning.

TELLERMAN: Okay. There's—There's King Philip III of Spain, right? Conquest of the New World. One of his projects was to find the Strait of Anián, part of the Northwest Passage that'd connect the Gulf of California to the Gulf of Mexico. In 1612, he put three ships under the charge of Captain Alvarez de Cordone. The real hero of our story is Captain Juan de Iturbe, who sailed the third ship—

HOPE: Three ships counts as a fleet?

TELLERMAN: They were a search party. But Philip also wanted to make a little profit on the side. So while these three ships searched the coast of Mexico, they were also fishing for pearls.

HOPE: Pearls. Okay.

TELLERMAN: Saltwater pearls were prized by royalty. Cordone had a team of professional pearl divers on his ships. Whenever they hit an oyster bed, they'd stop to harvest pearls. It's said they found millions of dollars in black pearls. News of what they were doing got out—

HOPE: Pirates.

TELLERMAN (nodding): Pirates. By that time, the fleet had shrunk to one: storms had claimed one boat, and Cordone was injured and had to turn back. Captain de Iturbe went on alone. His ship had no protection, but it was a caravel—

HOPE: Caravel?

KOALA: Fast boat with a shallow-bottomed hull. Could move in and out of tight places.

TELLERMAN (nodding): Exactly. As the story goes, Captain de Iturbe was pursued up and down the Coast of Mexico by William Hawley, a British privateer.

HOPE: Hawley? No clever nickname?

TELLERMAN: Hawley didn't need one. His name alone struck fear in the hearts of his victims.

HOPE: Uh-huh.

TELLERMAN: They say Hawley was all stretched out, like a scarecrow. He was nearly seven feet tall, with long legs and arms. His fingers bent like claws, and his toes were so long that he never wore—

HOPE: Marfan syndrome.

TELLERMAN: What?

HOPE: Lemme guess. Tall, thin, hollow-chested? Had buggy eyeballs? Maybe hunched over and gasped for breath as he spoke?

KEITH (V.O.): Uh…yeah! Yeah, he did!

HOPE: Pronounced Marfan syndrome. Poor guy. That's a death sentence if left untreated. His life expectancy was probably shit.

TELLERMAN: …just imagine, if you would, Captain de Iturbe and the pirate Hawley—

HOPE: The Dread Pirate Hawley?

TELLERMAN: Would you sh—Okay. Okay. Okay, there's Captain de Iturbe and Hawley in the Gulf of California. They've been in a battle of wills that's lasted for weeks. They keep to the coves, sneaking around at night, going ashore when they can to restock their supplies.

MARE: Quick question. Were they still fishing for pearls?

KEITH (V.O.): Yeah. Captain de Iturbe had to bring something back, or he'd never get another commission.

TELLERMAN: So we've got the heroic Captain de Iturbe versus Hawley. Back and forth, up and down the Gulf. But, finally, Captain de Iturbe made a mistake. A storm rolled in—a big one, the kind that only comes once in a century. Hawley used the storm as an opportunity to sneak up on the Spanish ship in the dead of night...but Iturbe realized this in the nick of time! The captain turned and sailed into what he thought was a shallow inlet, and hoped that his caravel would survive where Hawley's ship would run aground.

KEITH (V.O.): But instead of sailing into an inlet—

TELLERMAN: But instead of sailing into an uncharted part of the Gulf, Captain de Iturbe had accidentally sailed into a flood zone. The hundred-year storm had dumped enough water in the region to flood the valley connecting the Gulf to Lake Cahuilla.

KEITH (V.O.): That's where the Salton Sea is now. It wasn't the Salton Sea then, though, just a strip of desert—

TELLERMAN: Captain de Iturbe laid anchor and waited for the rains to stop, and when they did, he found himself—and his ship—landlocked in the middle of the desert.

HOPE: Then the pirates killed them all.

TELLERMAN (laughing): No, Captain de Iturbe and his crew lived. They abandoned their ship and walked out. They took as many pearls as they could carry, but left the rest. Captain de Iturbe wanted to go back but—

KEITH (V.O.): He could never find his ship again.

HOPE: But you can?

KEITH (V.O.): We can. See, we've got—

TELLERMAN (waving at the camera): We've got the advantage.

TELLERMAN (leaning towards HOPE): We can find the ghost of William Hawley.

HOPE: Sure.

TELLERMAN: Captain de Iturbe might have abandoned his ship, but Hawley didn't. Hawley sailed after him and his ship got trapped, just like the caravel. But Hawley couldn't abandon his ship—he was a pirate, and his ship was his life! When his ship ran aground, he tried to dig it out. As the water receded into the desert floor, it became obvious he was trapped.

Some of his men mutinied. They saw the fresh water running out, and decided to run. They waited until nightfall, then ambushed Hawley and the loyal members of his crew in their sleep.

KOALA: How?

TELLERMAN: Slit their throats. Ear to ear.

KOALA (muttering): Impractical. Poison's the way to go in a mutiny.

TELLERMAN: They say Hawley's ghost is still waiting, somewhere in the desert. In death, he and his crew have claimed two ships—his own, and Captain de Iturbe's caravel—each ship laden with treasure, lost beneath the sands.

HOPE: Treasure hunts don't end well. Trust me on this.

TELLERMAN: If we don't find the treasure, we can still find the ghosts. We've got state-of-the-art equipment; we can locate their EMF and track down their location. For Spooky Solutions, that's almost as good as finding two ships full of treasure.

HOPE: In the desert. You're going to wander around. Looking for ghosts. In a desert.

MARE: We're going with you.

HOPE: **What?!**

KOALA (laughing): Oh my gaaaaawd!

MARE: We're going with you.

HOPE (whispering to MARE): C'mon, Mare, this is—

HOPE (blocking Camera One with hand): It's bullshit. You know that.

Cut to Camera Two

MARE (whispering to HOPE): Is it? They're just kids, Hope.

HOPE (whispering to MARE): Half of these idiots are older than we are!

MARE: But the ghosts—

HOPE: Aren't. **Real**. Remember?

MARE: Do you want this on your conscience?

HOPE: Well, I'm not—

MARE: We're going.

Chapter Six

We were up hours before dawn, which makes sense, because if you're driving across the desert you want to be up hours before dawn. I was cranky. Speedy was cranky. Mare was also cranky, but the two of us weren't letting her have any of that, since it was her fault we weren't all comfy in our respective beds and sleeping off our hangovers.

"It's the right thing to do," she muttered, as we waited for the valet to show up with the Mustang.

I didn't reply. Instead, I watched the fountain in front of the building fold water over itself in slow methodological patterns. At this hour, even the fountain seemed sluggish.

Speedy slid down from my shoulders and landed on my gym bag. He scratched at the canvas to soften it up, and balled himself up with an irritated *huff!* I draped my jacket over him to keep off the spray from the water.

"They could get killed," Mare said. "They don't know what they're getting into. We're just…chaperoning. To make sure there aren't any real pirate ghosts. Right?"

"That's not how it works," I replied. My eyes weren't functioning. The corners felt as if they have been puttied over in slime. "If there are ghosts, they won't be strong enough to do anything. Maybe hide their keys, mess with the cameras. Little things."

"But Hawley was a killer! I did some reading last night, and he—"

"He's a nobody, Mare." I placed the bag on the ground and went to go sit on the curb. Mare followed me down. "If this were the ghost of Blackbeard or Long John Silver? Yeah, maybe they'd have some power, be some kind of threat. But Hawley? Nobody's cared about him in centuries."

"Long John Silver was a fictional character," Mare said.

"And a fast food chain," I replied. "If there were a real Long John Silver to go with either of those, he'd be worth something in terms of name recognition. Hawley's got nothing to build on. Even if he were dangerous, he couldn't do anything to the Ghostbusters."

"They're *Spooky Solutions,*" she said, turning a lock of her hair over and over in her hands. "Even if Hawley's almost powerless, how hard is it to cause a brain aneurysm? Or clog an artery, or crimp a spinal cord?"

I let her keep talking but didn't answer. Bodies are complicated. To the best of my knowledge, ghosts aren't a leading cause of congestive heart failure. Probably. All I know is there's a historical lack of corpses with handprints on the inside. If I could blindly reach inside a body, I'd have no idea what to do based on touch alone, and I'm a doctor.

Our rental car purred its way up the road and stopped before it reached us. I took a deep breath, then hauled myself back to my feet.

"It's the right thing to do," Mare said again as the valet handed me the keys. She didn't sound convinced.

We were about to get on the road when a large black touring van appeared. Or, it seemed black: as it followed the curve of the Bellagio's main drive, silver embedded within a layer of the van's graphic wrap caught the lights. A skeleton was clinging to the *Spooky Solutions* logo as if it were trying to keep from being blown away by the speed of the vehicle.

"Oh, no," Mare sighed.

"How important is Congresswoman Laughran?" I asked.

"She has line-item control over parts of OACET's operational budget," Mare replied, and threw a handful of her hair aside, as if it had said something nasty to her. "It's the right thing to do for a couple of reasons," she muttered.

"Ladies!" Tellerman came around the front of the van. "We've saved some seats for you."

I stowed the koala under my arm, and Mare and I shoved our

luggage in the Mustang's trunk. We slouched our way towards the van, casting wistful glances towards our car. Our lovely private car.

The van's sliding door opened, and three members of Tellerman's entourage fell over themselves as they tried to grab the keys from me. None of them looked to be over twenty-five.

"I got the insurance waiver, right?" I asked Mare.

"Yup."

I tossed the keys to the nearest crew member, and climbed aboard the van.

It would have been roomy if it weren't for all the clutter. Tellerman was driving (of course), with Keith banging away on a laptop in the back row. In the space between them was a mountain of luggage, electronics, and equipment, with the few voids filled by people.

The twins weren't sitting together. One of them had positioned herself behind Tellerman; the other had claimed the seat nearest the large sliding door.

Bingo, I thought.

The twin by the door—Oshea—looked up from her phone long enough to nod at me. There'd be no problems telling them apart: they may have been identical twins but they had gone out of their way to make themselves visually unique. Dina had a bodybuilder's physique and wore her hair close to her scalp, which let her to show off layers of stud earrings. Oshea had fewer muscles, and her hair was braided in neat, thick cornrows, each braid was tied off with a cowrie shell or a gold bead. They both had on jeans and tees, but where Oshea's outfit was the traditional blue and white, Dina's was black.

"Dr. Blackwell," called Tellerman, as he climbed into the driver's seat. "Come sit up here with me."

"Are you filming?" I asked.

"Always!" He patted the dashboard. There was a camera mounted to the vinyl, and another affixed above the rear-view mirror.

"Great." At least the passenger's seat wasn't full of junk. I climbed over some camera gear and squeezed my way past a soundboard, and hunkered down in the most spacious spot in the van.

The vinyl seat smelled like a strange man's sweat and was slightly damp against the backs of my bare arms. Whatever. I tugged the seatbelt tight and settled Speedy in my lap. The koala sighed in his sleep and moved to grip my thigh like a tree branch.

Tellerman leaned over and poked one of Speedy's ears. The koala flicked it in irritation.

"Just like on YouTube," Tellerman chuckled.

I grabbed his hand before he could do it again. "I'm telling you this just once as a courtesy," I said, as I released him. "Don't underestimate Speedy. He's an animal, and he's smarter than probably anything else on this planet, including supercomputers. The way he thinks? It's freakin' alien to us. So don't push him—he will fuck you up in ways you won't even realize until a monster puts an axe through your skull."

Tellerman laughed. "Sure."

"You've been warned," I sighed, and pulled my jacket over my face so I could sleep in peace.

Our route to the desert was fairly simple: drive south, then drive south some more. If you hit Yuma, you've gone too far. I dozed for most of the trip, and when I couldn't sleep, I laid my head against the window and watched the desert roll past.

It's not as bleak in the Sonoran Desert as you'd think. There's green against the buff, strips of grass and trees moving their way across the sand. A friend of mine who's a gardener says that plants are always in motion, and they claw their way through the earth like slow-moving animals. That's hard to see when everything's green; easier when there's a canvas of sand and stone, with life painted in dots along its surface.

For the most part, Tellerman left me alone. The only time he spoke up was when we passed the ruin of an old building, set a long way from the road. It tugged at me: there was a ghost inside. A weak ghost, but a ghost all the same.

"Abandoned church," Tellerman said quietly, as he watched me turn and follow the building until it vanished behind us. "They're all over the place down here."

I nodded, and tried not to think about the person who had chained their soul to the memory of a building.

We stopped once for gas, and that's when I got a chance to finally talk to the twins. Rephrase: they finally got their chance to talk to me. When I pushed open the door to the Ladies' Room, they were waiting for me, leaning against the sinks with their arms crossed.

"Who hired you?" I asked.

They exchanged a glance. The twin nearest to me—Dina—said: "The Congresswoman."

"Damn," I sighed. I had been hoping it had been Tellerman. It would have been the first sign that there was some sense in him. "What firm are you with?"

"Small one out of Los Angeles," said Oshea. "We do private security for actors and agents, mostly."

"Does Tellerman know you're here to cover his butt?"

Oshea chuckled. "No."

"All right," I said. "He won't learn from me."

"Thanks," Dina replied.

We broke off to use the facilities, which gave me about ninety seconds of uninterrupted think-time.

A security detail. No, a secret security detail.

I wasn't sure how I felt about that. The twins wouldn't come cheap, either: undercover security comes at a premium, since the security detail has to maintain a cover story in addition to performing their real jobs. If Dina and Oshea were on the Spooky Solutions payroll, they had multiple specialized skills.

Hiring them made a certain degree of sense. If my kid wanted to go crawl around in abandoned prisons or look for Bigfoot or whatever, I'd want somebody watching him.

(Well, I'd hope that my adult son would have the sense to not, y'know, do those things in the first place, but whatever. I've fought a minotaur. It's not like I can take the high road of normalcy here.)

The three of us regrouped at the sinks. I hummed "Happy Birthday" as I scrubbed up: I'm never going to be a surgeon, but there's nothing like a graduate-level course on infection to permanently alter your opinions on soap and fresh water. Yay, civilization.

Then, I had a thought.

"You notice those men in the casino?" I asked.

Dina nodded. "They showed up when you did."

"Not your security?" Oshea asked.

"I don't have a security firm," I said, and hoped they wouldn't press the issue.

Oshea's jaw dropped as her eyes moved down to the scar on my arm. "After what happened to you?"

"I'm fine," I said, as I snatched a paper towel from the dispenser. "The other guys aren't."

I didn't want—no, I didn't need—security. I had my ties to OACET, which kept most of the would-be weirdoes away with the implicit threat of summoning a horde of furious cyborgs. Benjamin Franklin was always a word away. And I had done so much damage to the last group of would-be kidnappers that there were lawsuits pending against me.

None of that prevented anyone and everyone from telling me that I should turn over what was left of my privacy to a bunch of hired thugs.

"You should really get one," Dina, professional hired thug, said.

"Do you want our firm's number?" Oshea asked.

Dina handled the opening statements, while Oshea stuck the landing with the questions. Interesting. But I decided to sweep the leg on this conversation before I got stuck with a bunch of strange dudes following me around forever.

"Y'all spar?" I asked.

They exchanged another one of those twin-glances. "Yeah," Dina said. "Mixed martial arts, mostly."

"If you think you can practice without Tellerman catching

on, lemme know," I said. "I'm always looking for new partners."
  They grinned.

Chapter Seven

When I woke up again, we were in Slab City.

I had never been there before, but I knew it at first sight. Which was, basically, concrete. Concrete as far as the eye could see, with the desert peeking over its edges where it bumped into the horizon. Graffiti ran up and down the sloping landscape, with drifts of blown sand covering the low points.

Tellerman drove slowly, peering left and right. Keith had filled the space between the front seats, and was doing the same.

"Where is everyone?" Tellerman asked. "This is supposed to be the local flavor segment. If we can't interview them, we don't have a piece."

"Still too early in the year for the snowbirds," I said, stretching. "And the locals aren't going to show themselves for yet another camera crew. Why are we here?"

"You know about Slab City?" Keith asked me.

I did. Slab City played right into my recent obsession about places with no cameras. Places where the residents just want to be left alone. Places where a sufficiently motivated person could, hypothetically speaking, disappear into thin air.

Instead of opening that can of wormy conversation, I shrugged and said, "Camp Dunlap? It was an old military base. Decommissioned, most of the buildings bulldozed in the Fifties. After that? Squatter paradise."

(By the way, if you ever find yourself in Slab City, don't call the permanent residents "squatters." They think of themselves as free. Free from laws, taxation, government supervision... that's what they want. That's why they moved to Slab City. I couldn't live there—No bathrooms, and 120-degree heat in the summers? No thank you.—but I respect those who can.)

"Nice," said Keith. "Could you say that again, but do it while looking out the window? Maybe with your chin on your hand? It'd be a great lead-in to the segment."

I glared at him through blurry eyes.

He waited until I realized he was serious.

"Hold him," I said, as I pushed a sleeping koala into Keith's arms.

Then I opened the door and jumped out of the van.

Tires squealed, but I was already coming out of my roll, and it was easy as anything to walk away, to disappear into the piles of scrap metal and broken concrete which lined the main drag. I ignored Tellerman's frantic shouts and vanished into Slab City.

(I had my phone, and Mare could always find me via my husband if there was an emergency. I'm never truly alone. Not anymore.)

My first impression of Slab City was the heat. It was hot. *Really* hot, and this was October. Living here during the summer must have been like living inside an oven. I set out towards a bright patch of color a goodly distance away. I wasn't sure what it was, at first, with the heat haze beating it into a bunch of different shapes, but nothing in nature was that particular shade of purple.

The purple resolved itself into a motor home, surrounded by sculptures of…birds? Sure, if birds could be made from sloping lines of iron. They flapped, in their way, metal balanced across metal that moved slowly in the still air.

The closer I got, the taller the birds became. By the time I reached them, they towered over me on their long, thin legs, with razor-sharp beaks aimed towards the sky, or straight down at the top of my head.

"My husband made 'em."

I glanced over to the puddle of shade cast by the motor home. A woman was lying on a weather-beaten plastic patio lounger, a cold drink in one hand. She was easily in her late seventies, and was completely bare-ass naked except for a pair of oversized sunglasses.

"He's an artist?" I asked.

"Was." The woman sucked on her drink through a green curly straw. "He's dead."

I nodded.

"Not gonna say you're sorry for my loss?" She sounded angry, but there was a laugh lurking behind the words.

I shrugged. "Death's a weird thing with me."

"I know. You got the look," she said. "Of someone thinkin' about jumpin' ship."

"I don't give up," I told her.

"Wasn't talkin' 'bout suicide," she said.

"I wasn't either."

The laugh came out. "Pull up a chair," she said, gesturing towards an old tire parked beneath a giant heron.

I looped my fingers beneath the tire's rubber rim and dragged it over the concrete. It was dry inside, the first old tire I had ever seen without a gazillion mosquito larvae swimming around the well, and I said as much.

The woman nodded. "Love it. We moved out here from Georgia," she said. "Here, the critters stay on the ground where they're supposed to."

I dropped the tire next to her, did a quick search of its interior for scorpions or spiders or whatever they had in this part of California, and sat down within her forest of giant squeaky birds.

She passed me her drink. It was, as best as I could tell, straight whiskey. The glass was none too clean, but I took a long swallow before I handed it back to her.

"Thanks," I said.

"What's your story?" she asked.

"You watch the news? Read the papers?"

"Not since Clinton was in office."

"Which one?"

Her eyebrows went up.

"Never mind," I said. "Let's just say I got roped into a road trip, and that turned into another road trip because some assholes want to look for pirate treasure in the desert."

"Ah." She gave an old woman's whiskey giggle. "Hawley's lost ship."

"You know the story?"

"Everyone around here does," she said. She stood up. "C'mon."

I followed her into the trailer. She had been outside for a good while; the weave of the plastic chair had stamped a complex pattern into her butt.

The interior of the trailer was decorated in more abstract metal birds. Most of them hung from wires strung along the ceiling. I recognized a few distinct outlines—woodpeckers, geese, and eagles—but the others blended into songbirds.

And there were books.

Books in shelves that took up most of the trailer. Books spread open across the counters. Books stacked in piles so high that some of the dangling birds scraped their stomachs on them. Books across half of the couch, and tumbling over themselves on the chairs and tables.

"Nice," I said, as I ran my hand across the top of the closest pile. Books—actual books with spines and ink and printed on chewed-up spit-out trees—were no longer a thing for me. With Sparky in the house, most of our personal library had gone the way of the Cloud. Even my medical textbooks were digital.

I've never been a big reader. Don't have the attention span for it, to be honest. But looking at those books? I felt the same kind of nostalgia that we must have felt for horses once Model Ts had swallowed the roads.

"They're not mine," the woman said, as she knelt in front of an ancient minifridge. She stood, holding a bottle of whiskey, and refilled her cup. "I'm one of the local libraries. Books come in, books go out."

I nodded. It made sense. Entertainment options in Slab City were different than those in downtown D.C.

"This way," she said, and led me down the book-lined hall to a closed door.

She opened it to a bedroom that was neat as a pin! Just super-clean. The walls, the furniture…everything in the room was freshly painted. There were more books in here, but they were arranged on sturdy white shelves by size and color. There was a small cut-glass chandelier overhead, free from even the smallest speck of dust and turning the light streaming through the windows into rainbows.

A small table set to the side of the door held a dozen magazines in the home goods and interior design genres. I flipped through them; they were mostly tiny house pornography.

The old woman shrugged. "I'd give an eye for a composting toilet."

She moved off to search a bookshelf, and came back with a thin paperback. The cover was an awful homemade Photoshop job, with *Ghost Ships of the Desert!* printed across the top in Papyrus font.

"Ships?" I asked. "Plural?"

"Hawley's lost ship is famous," she said. "But there are other stories. Or the same story, told different ways. My favorite is the one with the ghost of Marie de Borromeo. She's a Wailing Woman. You know about them?"

"A banshee," I said.

Lemme tell you about ghost stories.

If you read enough ghost stories, like I do (ghost stories and monster folklore are perfect for me, by the way, about three minutes of content and done), you begin to see patterns in them. Different cultures, some of them separated by a boggling amount of time and space, churn out the same kinds of monsters. Some of these are a wavy form of logic—dragons are just big lizards, mermaids are half a woman glued to a fish, that sort of thing. Others...

Take the Woman in White.

Not the Wilkie Collins novel. The actual Woman in White— the apparition who mourns and cries and sometimes tries to drag the living away with her. There's a variation on her in the Middle East, the Far East, Europe, and the Americas. In Mexico, she's *la Llorona*, a ghost who cries for her dead children. In Europe, she's the White Lady who haunts the ruins of castles as the last memory of murder. In the Philippines, a modern version haunts taxi drivers who have dropped off female passengers in situations they knew were sketchy as fuck.

In Ireland, she's a banshee. And if you see her, someone you love is going to die.

So. Ghostly woman plus tragedy equals death omen. This is nearly a universal truth across cultures.[6]

I might not know much about ghosts, but I'm learning. If the same story resonates across multiple cultures, there's a hell of a chance there's something to it.

The old woman flipped the book open to a dog-eared page and held it so I could see the picture. It was a poorly Xeroxed copy of a black and white photograph. Very blurry. It appeared to be a landscape with multiple human figures gathered around a pile of stones. The only two figures I could make out were that of a man who had fallen to his knees before a pale, vaguely woman-ish shape.

The white shape had a black hole where her mouth should be.

"That was taken in the 1940s," she said. "Some historians were searching for the ruins of Spanish missions, somewhere to the west of here."

I looked at the photograph again. Sure enough, the man was kneeling in a pile of cut stone. If I squinted, I could make out what remained of a building after a few centuries of earthquakes.

"What's Maria's tragedy?" I asked. "How'd she die?"

"Suicide."

"Ah," I said, nodding. "Lost a husband? Kids? Threw herself from the mission's roof?"

"She was a Jesuit nun. Everyone she knew was killed by pirates."

"Huh!" That was a new one. The ghosts of massacres tended

---

6 This also says something sharp about those societies. Think about it: their dead women are consigned to an afterlife of weeping and handwringing and occasionally tricking people to their deaths, instead of becoming old-fashioned slaughterghosts.

I'm not sure how I feel about this. On the one hand, I'd like to think that here in America, gender equality has progressed to the point where women have achieved slaughterghost status after we die. But on the other hand, this will probably just cause problems for me since I'm the one who'll have to hide the bodies.

to be children or old men.

My butt vibrated. "One sec," I said, as I reached for my phone. An image of a green cartoon pony dominated the screen. "Mare?"

"Hope? Hi." Mare sounded grumpy. "They're ready to leave."

"This soon?"

"They can't find anybody willing to talk to them about the local ghosts. They're fed up."

"Hang on," I said, and covered the mouthpiece. I turned to the woman and asked, "You wanna make some money?"

Chapter Eight

EXT. TRAILER, NOON.

An elderly woman in a heavy bathrobe is standing in front of a purple trailer, smoking a hand-rolled cigarette. She is being interviewed by TELLERMAN.

TELLERMAN: We're here in Slab City on our way to the shipwreck, and we've just met…may I call you Margot?

MARGOT: Full name, if you please.

TELLERMAN (sighing): Saint Margot, Mother of Turtles, Founder of the Church of Holy Poultry, Divine…uh…

MARGOT: Divine Priestess of Calamity.

TELLERMAN: I thought you said you were the Divine Priestess of Armageddon?

HOPE (V.O., laughing): She said Calamity. I heard her.

MARGOT (exhaling smoke at TELLERMAN): Yup. Calamity.

TELLERMAN: So…um…Margot…um…you have information about William Hawley? How did—

MARGOT: You don't know what you're getting into, boy.

TELLERMAN: What?

MARGOT: Hawley was a killer. Murdered near everyone that crossed his path. But he got rich doing it. You looking for his treasure?

TELLERMAN: His ghost, but if we find—

MARGOT (sniffing): Huh. His ghost. That might be a way to get around it.

TELLERMAN: Get around what?

MARGOT: The curse, boy! The one Hawley laid on his treasure, where any who look for it are doomed to die.

TELLERMAN: We haven't heard about a curse.

MARGOT: That's your own damned problem, then. All pirates curse their treasure. Good and proper, curses are, for pirates.

TELLERMAN (to HOPE): Could you **stop laughing?**

TELLERMAN (to KEITH): Put a hard stop in here, maybe a cut to a map of Hawley's territory.

MARGOT: Oh, everything near the Gulf was Hawley's territory. The Americas, Mexico…you name it. He liked the Colorado River—they say he hid his treasure as far up the river as he could go. The water was different, back then, before we put those goddamn dams across 'em, drained 'em dry. The Colorado was big and beautiful, even up here.

Hawley went inland, too. Not many pirates did that—they liked the sea for the clean getaway. But he'd raid inland when he thought he could get away with it. That's where your real ghost story comes from, boy, the time when Hawley burned down Marie de Borromeo's mission.

TELLERMAN (to camera, grinning): So, what can you tell us about Hawley and the ghost of Marie de Borromeo?

MARGOT (pointing): Not too far to the west, there's the *El Camino Real*. The highway, the one for the tourists? You can drive it, see some of the old Spanish missions for yourself. But not all of them. No, not all of them. The large ones survived. The small ones—the churches, ones built near settlements, or at the edges of the desert to attract settlers—most of those were abandoned two hundred years ago or more.

TELLERMAN: Were there any near the Salton Sea?

MARGOT (laughing): There are some **in** the Sea, boy! Back when they were building the missions, there was no Salton Sea. But Marie de Borromeo's mission? Go east, into the desert. 'bout a hundred miles. There's a patch of land that looks like a red river was burned into the sand. Follow that about a mile to the north, and you'll find what's left of the mission. Look hard—it's easy to miss. There's not much there anymore.

TELLERMAN: What destroyed the mission?

MARGOT: Hawley, boy. Hawley and his crew.

TELLERMAN: How?

MARGOT: Hawley and his men, they left the ship and went inland about twenty miles. Followed a river up to a small town. Spanish settlers, led by a Jesuit priest and three nuns.

TELLERMAN: Four people? I thought there'd be more. That's not a lot of—

MARGOT: Don't confuse tragedy with statistics, kid. The only thing that changes is the amount of blood.

Now. Marie de Borromeo was born to Spanish nobility. Don't be thinking of her as a tiny young thing. No, she gave birth to seven children before her husband died, saw them grown and married off in turn, and decided to go on one final adventure to the New World. She pulled some strings, and it was agreed that she could go if she pledged herself as a nun. So, in 1682, at the ripe old age of forty-eight, Marie de Borromeo arrived in California.

HOPE (entering frame): Question?

TELLERMAN: Hey, we're in the middle of—

MARGOT (smoking): Yeah?

HOPE (scrolling through phone): The dates don't line up. William Hawley and Captain de Iturbe had their duel around 1615, right? If Marie de Borromeo showed up in 1682, there's no way she would have met them. She wouldn't have even been born when they—

MARGOT: Pirates are monsters, kid. One murdering sea rapist is just like another. It might as well have been Hawley.

HOPE (shrugging): 'kay, that's fair.

MARGOT: With that said? This version of the story always has Hawley in it. And you know why?

TELLERMAN (excitedly): Because…because he committed the murders as a ghost!

HOPE (walking off-camera): Oh for fuck's sake.

MARGOT: (nodding, to Tellerman): Yup, even after his own death, Hawley was a killer.

MARE (V.O.): I knew it!

HOPE (V.O.): That's not how any of this works!

MARGOT: Marie de Borromeo had five good years in California before Hawley arrived. She, like the others at her mission, had heard rumors about the ghostly pirates in the area—

KEITH (V.O., eagerly): Holy shit!

MARGOT: —but they were more concerned with getting their territory under control. Colonization's hard work, especially if the natives have begun to realize they don't want you around. Marie de Borromeo was better than most. She was there for the adventure, not the preaching, and she liked to spend time with the children of the local Cahuilla tribe. She was the first Westerner to make contact with the Cahuilla, did you know? They stuck that title on a man, but she beat him there by—

TELLERMAN (interrupting): Are the Cahuilla important to this story?

MARGOT (continuing): The tribe was a day's walk from the mission, and she'd usually travel between the Cahuilla and her village once or twice a week.

MARGOT (inhaling on cigarette): On her last trip back to the mission, de Borromeo saw...

MARGOT (exhaling smoke & twirling cigarette through it): ... and she began to run.

TELLERMAN: Did she get there in time?

MARGOT: She got there in time to see the head fly off the body of the last surviving nun, if that's what you mean.

TELLERMAN: Oh.

MARGOT: Yeah. She looked up to the mission's high tower, and saw her friend murdered. The survivors said she screamed.

TELLERMAN: I would, too.

MARGOT (nodding): The mission was burning; her friends were dead. And she didn't know why!

HOPE (entering frame): Wait, what?

MARGOT: You can't see ghosts with the naked eye. You can only see what they do. So she saw her friend murdered, but didn't understand—

HOPE (quietly): Fuck.

HOPE (walking off-camera): Fuck fuck fuck fuck **fuck**.

TELLERMAN (to KEITH): Hard edit. Get rid of the swearing. We'll use this as a point to introduce the tech toys. EMF readouts, spectral photography—

MARGOT: You wanna hear about how de Borromeo died or not?

TELLERMAN (adjusting equipment): Right, right. Wait… one second… Okay, ready. What happened after Marie de Borromeo arrived?

MARGOT: The Cahuilla have the strangest creation myths, you know? Their god, Mukat, turned on them. He was benevolent, but he decided his own creations were getting uppity, so he taught them how to kill each other. The Cahuilla rose up and killed their own god, and then declared all life to be sacred. They believed if you killed another in cold blood, you would be transformed into a demon, and these demons killed in evil ways. Magical ways. Ways no normal human could accomplish.

TELLERMAN: That's what de Borromeo thought had killed her friends?

MARGOT (nodding): The survivors said she took out a willow switch and charged into the burning building, shouting the name of a Cahuilla demon. No one could stop her. The roof of the mission—it was a tile roof, but held up by wooden supports—was on fire, and was about to collapse.

MARGOT (smoking): But that wasn't the last of her. They saw Marie de Borromeo in the mission's high tower, fighting with something they couldn't see. The willow branch was gone; her hair and clothing were on fire. She was screaming in pain—Oh! How she was screaming! And her hands were wrapped tight around…something. Something only she could see.

TELLERMAN: And then?

MARGOT: Then the roof caved in, with de Borromeo beneath it. They say she took the demon with her when she died, to make sure he couldn't hurt anyone else.

(long pause)

MARGOT: But you go look for Hawley's treasure, and tell me how that works out.

Chapter Nine

We left Saint Margot, Mother of Turtles and Many Other Nouns and Adjectives, and followed her directions until the GPS told us we'd be goddamned idiots to go any further since the vehicles needed roads. Tellerman and Keith started arguing. The rest of us made eye contact and raced to get out of the van.

Mare and I walked off into the beaten path to explore. We found ourselves on a little offshoot of dirt that may or may not have been paved, once upon a time. There were the ruins of buildings around us. Stone husks, mostly, filled with stray bits of garbage left by careless tourists just like us.

"Where are we?" I asked Mare.

Her eyes unfocused: she was online. "Picacho, California," she said. "It was a mining town during the Gold Rush. Got flooded out when they built a dam. Those are…" She pointed towards the buildings. "…what's left of the gold mills."

"What's a gold mill?"

"Um…" Mare's eyes darted to the side as she followed a new link, then bounced back to center, "They processed ore and made it easier to extract the gold."

"Ah."

The deep voice of an angry koala came from the van: "We're not going *on foot* into a *desert*, you bone-dry fuckholsters!"

Mare and I headed towards the nearest ruin, and the profanity blew away behind us on the breeze. When we got close enough, she climbed onto a low wall and began to walk along it, arms outstretched to keep herself centered.

"What did you think of the de Borromeo story?" Mare asked.

I hopped up onto the wall behind her, and used it as a vantage point to look at what was left of the old mining town. There was a thick ribbon of water not too far away, shining bright in the sun. The banks of the river (or was it a reservoir?) were green—lush green!—and stood out like an enormous oasis. Or maybe a portal to another world.

"Margot's story…" Mare began.

"Yeah." What Margot had said about Marie de Borromeo had been on my mind, too. It had the hallmarks of a ghost story that involved actual ghosts, instead of the woo-woo jump-scare version. "Want me to call Ben and get his opinion?"

"Ben? Who's—*oh!* Um…"

"You'll meet him eventually," I said. One of the stones in the wall wobbled under my boots, and I moved on to the next one. "Might help, you know. Just have a normal conversation with him, and it'll put things in perspective."

"Hope?" Mare was staring at me. "You just suggested that I talk to Benjamin Franklin. *The* Benjamin Franklin. A man who's been dead for centuries! None of this is normal. You realize that, right?"

"Yeah." I abandoned the wall and jumped to the ground. Little puffs of dust flew up and rained down on the dry desert floor. "Except—again—this *is* normal for me, and from now on, it'll be normal for you. Since we can't turn back the clock, you've got to get used to that. Sorry."

Mare turned, and looked towards the reservoir. "Not now," she whispered. "Maybe later."

"Okay," I said, even though I knew she wasn't talking about Ben. Even though I didn't agree. "We'll take it at your own speed."

"Thank you." She knelt and picked up a small piece of garbage that someone had jammed between two stones, and tucked it into the pocket of her skirt to throw away later. "How about Mike? Would he know?"

"Good idea," I replied, and went for my phone. I flicked my thumb over its surface, and came up empty: no signal. "Would you mind?"

Mare nodded, and my phone bumped itself up to five full bars.

Cyborgs, man. So convenient.

I keep Mike's number on speed dial. If we were lucky, he wouldn't be teaching…

beep

…we weren't lucky.

Mike's voice, slow and thoughtful, rolled out from his voicemail. "Good afternoon, you've reached Michael Reilly. I'm not available to—"

I hung up and sent a text instead: *Mare met Thomas Paine. She has questions. Call her when you can.*

Mare read the text as it passed through her brain on its way into the mid-autumn sky. "Should you be committing that to writing?"

That's OACET for you: security-conscious even when the threat was non-existent. Or downright implausible. But if I had been brainwashed for five whole years as part of a government conspiracy, I'd be pretty jumpy, too.

"It'll be fine," I sighed.

There was a loud crash from the general direction of the van. Mare and I glanced over in time to see Tellerman hurl a black equipment case at a running koala.

"Oh, Jesus," I snarled, as I began to run. "He's gonna kill him!"

"It's okay. He didn't hit Speedy!" Mare called after me.

I wasn't worried about Speedy.

I was close enough to snag the koala as he skidded to a stop and turned to lunge at Tellerman. Which would have been amazing to watch, by the way—koalas are fast. And Speedy was…well, he is what it says on the tin. Once you convert the digestive tract of an adult male Queensland koala so he can sustain himself on wheat instead of eucalyptus, you get a creature with a ground game that's faster than that of most humans. Oh, and Mike? He's been teaching Speedy some Aikido. An extremely bastardized version of Aikido due to joint placement and an absurdly low center of gravity, yes, but Aikido nonetheless.[7]

"Don't," I said, as I held him like the owner of a cat that was _going into its carrier,_ whether *it wanted to or not!*

7 What I'm saying is, if Speedy decides he wants to get his claws in you? You're fucked.

"Lemme go!" he growled, and twisted to aim some of his pointier parts at me.

"Nope," I said, putting one hand behind his neck.

He relented: he might have been picking up some Aikido, but he's not stupid. "Did you hear what he called me?!" he said instead, the fur on his hackles sticking straight up.

"No, but yeah, I know," I said. I took my hand away from the back of his neck, and let him scurry up my arms so he could perch on my shoulders. "Do it on camera."

"What?"

Speedy's claws were digging into my flesh, which was worrying. He was always careful about keeping his claws pulled, because: (a) he talks a good game but he doesn't want to really hurt me; and (b) when he does hurt someone, you can be damned sure it wasn't by accident.[8]

"We're not here because we want to be," I reminded him, and turned so he could see the van. "When you take him down, make sure it's on camera, and make sure it's his fault."

The claws relaxed: Speedy loves a challenge. "Fine," he muttered.

"And for fuck's sake, don't get him killed." My face suddenly felt sticky as the memory of—Nope. I used the palms of my hands to scrub the imaginary blood and brains from my cheeks. "Just...don't. Okay?"

"Sure."

"Or maimed. Or...psychologically ruined. Nothing permanent. Not this time."

"You coulda left me in Vegas."

"Just do it," I said. "His stepmom—"

"Yeah, yeah," Speedy huffed. He sprawled across my shoulders like a chubby fur stole, and sighed.

"You're the reason we're here. Don't forget that."

He snorted. "You realize I had to get you out of there, right?"

Right. The bucket of burly men who had stalked me and Mare through the casino. "I thought you didn't see them."

"Oh, please."

---

8 See aforementioned reference to: "You're fucked."

"We would've been okay."

"Yeah, sure." He put his paws on my head and reared up like a meerkat to take in the desert. "Be kinda dumb of you to get assaulted three times in the same year."

"Their funerals." I shrugged hard enough for him to dig in with his claws again.

(I don't recommend being kidnapped, by the way. It's intensely boring, and when you end up hospitalizing the guys who did the kidnapping, the police, who should be asking you things like, "You poor dear! Can we get you more ice cream?" are instead focused on other things like, "Why can't this man see in color anymore?")

Gravel crunched underfoot as Mare reached us. She made soft comforting noises at Speedy, who allowed himself to be scooped up and cuddled. Mare then stormed off, koala tucked under her chin in a ball of fluffy self-righteousness, to shout at Tellerman.

Tellerman shouted back, which was…strange.

This was interesting, in a scary sort of way. Mare doesn't shout. Not really. She's an adult and she's freakin' brilliant, so when I say she's "shouting" at Tellerman, that's obviously a figure of speech. What she's doing is standing in front of him, arms crossed, using carefully chosen language to express her displeasure at seeing him hurl heavy items at a small defenseless (hah!) animal.

Tellerman, on the other hand, *shouted*. And his arms? Those *waved*.

I took a step closer to Mare.

The twins slipped into position behind Tellerman. Dina shook her head at me.

"No hard feelings," I told them.

Tellerman thought I was talking to him, and this shut him down. "You're leaving?" he asked.

Oh! For a brief glimmering moment, we had an out. No one would expect us to stick around after this. The penthouse at the Bellagio waited, along with bad television and long days by the pool. I stuffed my hands in my pockets to keep from grasping at that fragile straw.

"Don't see why we should stay." I said. "Not after you threatened our friend."

But Tellerman yanked himself together. "I'm sorry," he said. "I let my temper get the better of me. It won't happen again."

Damn. I bid a fond goodbye to the penthouse and sunbathing. Out of Tellerman's direct line of sight, the twins exchanged a bewildered glance: apparently, Tellerman wasn't big on apologies.

"Promise?" I asked, as Keith swung the camera between us.

"My word," he said, all smarm and graciousness.

We shook hands, and that settled that, except for Speedy staring at him with angry feral eyes.

Then we tackled the problem of how to navigate a desert.

Well, the rest of them tackled it. I left: there was nothing I could contribute to the conversation beyond swearing. Tellerman and Keith believed they could leave the van and the Mustang in the parking lot at the Picacho State Recreation Area, and then wander around from location to location like they usually did. Brief jaunts into the desert and all that. Speedy—along with me and most of the others—thought this was among the stupidest ideas ever had.

And, because I am dumb, I walked into the desert.

But not too far, because I'm not that dumb. Just far enough away from the others so I could get a feel for the place.

I'd never been to a desert before. I'd been to some rough places. The Chin Hills in Myanmar can be especially angry, with land rising and falling from wet to dry almost at whim. It's hard to plan around that, and you need to go with a local if you go at all.

A desert, though...

The ground rolled away from my feet, browns and greens and rock and sand. As I walked, it blended into sameness: days could go on, just like this, and the only thing that would change would be me. I felt the land sucking at the water in me: if I fell, it would drink me dry.

I knelt and laid my hands on the ground, and closed my eyes.

Years ago, I met a man on the summit of Nat Ma Taung. He wasn't a psychic, or any other flavor of supernatural. He was just an old white dude who liked to travel and spent a lot of time outdoors. He said that nobody takes the time to listen to the world around them. He had a lot of opinions about living in buildings and cities, and why we had lost track of the rhythms of nature.

He also smoked a lot of hash, but he was generous with it so I didn't hold that against him.

Anyhow. He did say something that stuck with me. We—humans as a species—have learned we can go where we want, and we can shape the land around us. Sometimes this is easy; we're more likely to settle near good farmland, or by warm sandy beaches with plenty of fish. But the days of settling in the easy spaces are over, and as our population grows, we have to chip away at the edges of the hard places to make room.

That old white dude on the side of the mountain? I remember him taking a big puff on his pipe and saying the hard places might hate us for that, but we didn't care enough to find out.

Ever since I learned I was psychic, I've at least tried to introduce myself to new spaces. I've never gotten an answer, but I still try. All other freaky possible psychic abilities aside, the one thing I can do is talk to the dead, and all life on earth is built on the bones of itself. Our planet is one gigantic teeming bowl of life…and what had to give way to make room for it.

If there's life, there's death.

If there's death, I can talk to it.

If I speak the language.

I don't think I'm capable of speaking the language of an entire land, but damn it, I can at least try to listen.

I let my mind go blank and tried to listen.

Nothing.

Mike says that when you listen—really, truly listen—you focus on what you are, and what you want to be, and what you *don't*, and you set all of that aside to hear the heart of what's being said.

I'm trying to listen, I swear.

How does a desert talk? All I heard was wind and sand and teeth. The twitch of things scuttling across the stone. Birds, a long distance away. Heat on my back, heat beneath my hands, heat beneath my feet.

Beneath *that*...

Something stirred.

Chapter Ten

I won't lie: I immediately noped out on the creepy shit and turned to rejoin the world of civilized (hah) humans. Besides, that's when the cargo helicopter passed overhead. I had kinda expected it, or something like it.

Lemme tell you about Mary Murphy.

Mare was born and raised in Alaska. Downtown Anchorage, by the way, not some rural community on the corner of nowhere. I say this not to shit on dinky rural life—which I sometimes fantasize about with the same passion I reserve for my erotic fantasies about Vin Diesel—but to point out that Mare's father was the head of freight management at the enormously busy Anchorage International Airport. When Mare was a kid, he used to take her to work with him on the weekends. Not for fun, or for daddy-daughter bonding time, but so she could *improve the shipping logistics of an international airport!* Mare would go over schedules, cargo, you name it, and tweak the details as she went. She says it was fun as anything, until it got old. Then her dad moved her over to the main terminal so she could improve the logistics of passenger flights, too.

Illegal as all hell, yeah. But when she went off to college, the airport suffered an immediate decline in efficiency which lasted until Mare came home for Christmas and used her newfound knowledge of input-output models to permanently restructure their operations.

That's Mare. She's an organizational specialist, but she doesn't clean out closets—she cleans out systems. In the private sector, people like Mare are the backbones of multinational corporations. When they go into civil service, presidents and generals use them to win wars.[9]

---

9 My husband uses her to keep OACET running. When I called to tell him that I was stealing Mare for the week, he said, very quietly, "…shit."

So, by the time I finished my brief jaunt into the desert, Mare had made a few calls and had assembled the following:

- Twelve soldiers (Army);
- Two small surveillance drones (also Army);
- Five Jeep Wranglers (also also Army);
- One ATV large enough for two people, if they were friendly;
- Four portable pop-up shelters (with air conditioning), size small;
- One portable pop-up bathroom (with showering facilities);
- A whole mess of provisions; and
- The aforementioned giant-as-fuck cargo helicopter!

I didn't think the helicopter—or the soldiers dropping off Mare's acquisitions—would be staying. It was certainly an impressive sight to see, tho'.

I meandered through the soldiers to where Mare and Tellerman were talking to Head Soldier and Head Soldier's Buddy. Head Soldier was a white guy, hurrying towards middle age, with the traditional flattop haircut. Buddy had the same haircut, but was much younger, taller, and lankier, and when he spotted me, he went to salute. This earned him a glare from Head Soldier that could be tried in court for assault.

Great.

Mare was deep in the politest of arguments with Head Soldier. "—not necessary, thank you," she said, her hands resting on the nearest drone. It was larger than the average consumer model, about the size of a kid's bicycle, and soft dove gray. It was cradled in its shipping crate, powered on and ready to go: the drone's high-pitched whine, similar to that of a dentist's drill, was burrowing its way into the soft meats of my brain.

Head Soldier's Buddy heard it too, but it was bothering him more than it did me: he kept shaking his head and clapping his hands over his ears.

I glanced over at the second shipping crate. Speedy was lying prone on the other drone, soaking in the sun while Dina petted him.

The noise wasn't bothering him at all? Weird. Speedy has a better sense of hearing than a wolf.

"I'm not releasing these without sending one of my men along," Head Soldier said. "You aren't trained to operate them. These are specialized machines, Agent Murphy."

Mare laughed. "Some would argue that I am, too," she said, as the second drone lifted from its crate.

The soldiers froze. Speedy squalled, then realized he was airborne and began to chortle like a madman as he held himself steady on the drone in a tight bear (sorry) hug. Mare took the drone on a slow loop around the camp before settling it back in its crate, snug as a robotic bug in a synthetic-blend rug.

Speedy waited until the rotors stopped turning before he leapt from the drone and scurried over to my legs. I scooped him up so he could perch on his usual place on my shoulders.

"Flying!" he whispered, as he pressed his forehead against my neck.

I smiled and gave him a quick scratch beneath his chin.

Head Soldier did the Army equivalent of throwing up his hands and going to lie down with a towel over his eyes: he nodded at Mare and gave an inch. "I see your point," he said. "But I need to follow protocol. Sergeant Fleishman goes with you, or I can't sign over the equipment."

Buddy— Sergeant Fleishman—grinned at Mare and said, "Call me Fish. Everyone does."

I'm not completely fluent in Armyspeak, but Head Soldier gave the type of slow blink which was best translated as: *Get this man away from me before I murder him. Just seventy-two hours of peace. That's all I need.*

"I don't want the Army involved," Tellerman said. "They could pull my footage if they don't like it."

Hard to argue with that, but Head Soldier tried. "Fleishman will stay off camera as much as possible—"

"I don't want him along," Tellerman said, as if his opinion mattered.

Head Soldier gave another slow blink. This one was aimed at Tellerman instead of Fish, and translated to: *Son, I have been stationed in this desert for years and I can think of at least eighty places where they'll never find your body.*

I liked Head Soldier.

"Can we compromise?" I asked him. "Fish comes with us, but he's off-duty?"

That started a round of "Well, actually" in which several different arguments fought to the death. TL:DR version is that Head Soldier won, Fish would be coming with us, and no, he'd be on-duty and in uniform the entire time.

(Oh, and when we returned the equipment? Mare would report to Head Soldier's base at the Yuma Proving Ground to help them perform a full inventory.[10] She said she would be doing it out of the kindness of her heart, but as Head Soldier said he was lending OACET this gear so we could run a routine field test, we all knew everyone was doing their best to keep the system rolling via quid-pro-quo.)

In the background of all of this polite politicking, Fish kept touching his ears.

I empathized: that buzzing whining noise seemed like it was everywhere. And there was no Doppler effect, either—I tried turning my head every which way, but the sound didn't change. It was the same low *bzzzzzzzzzt!* no matter which way I faced.

"Nobody else hears that?" Fish asked. His voice was louder

---

10 Mare was just gleestruck about this, by the way. She had never organized an entire Army base before, let alone one with storage facilities the size of those at Yuma. In her spare time, she'd grill Fish about the specifics of Who was responsible for inventory, What protocol were followed for the organization process, When the last inventories were conducted, Where specific classes of items were kept, Why certain protocols were followed instead of others, and How the entire base at Yuma was structured in respect to management and access.

I learned three things from overhearing these discussions. Item One: Fish paid attention to a metric fuckton of trivial details, which (at first) I thought was a huge red flag for Team Keep-Ghosts-A-Secret. Item Two: journalism as an industry suffered a profound loss when Mare decided to pursue a career in public service. Item Three: Yuma was about to be struck by the organizational equivalent of a nuclear warhead, and I hoped they had a lot of clipboards handy.

than polite, as if he thought he was pitching his words to carry through the noise.

"I do," I replied.

"Dr. Blackwell!" Fish grinned at me and held out his hand. I got the feeling he spent most of his time with that same goofy grin on his face. "I'm a fan!"

I smiled back—I like the goofy ones, to be honest—and reached to shake his hand.

A small electric shock, no stronger than a pop of static electricity, passed between us. And that noise like a dentist's drill? Gone.

Fish blinked, then moved his free hand to touch his ear. "It… stopped?" he asked.

Ah.

Lemme tell you about the first time I met Mike Reilly.

It was at a martial arts tournament, of course. I was a little bit hyperfocused that day—I had placed high enough to get on the Olympics team (again), but noooo, the coach was all "The thing is, you've got a reputation…" (again) and "You'd be representing our country…" (again) and I knew I was benched.

(Again.)

I was also a little bit angry.

By that time, I had already acquired Benjamin Franklin, but I still didn't believe he was anything other than a hallucination. I put up with him mainly because Ben is cool as cats, but there was a decent side dish of me thinking I just didn't have a choice in the matter.

(Trust me, when Ben first showed up, I got my doctor to put me on every kind of medication in the book, and when that didn't work, *he took me off of my Adderall!* That was a fun twelve weeks. Whee.)

No. Medication—whether too much or not enough—wasn't causing my hallucinations. Because they weren't hallucinations. I was just an ordinary psychic. Which, obviously, was impossible as all fuck so I didn't believe the ghost of Benjamin Franklin when he told me otherwise.

So, back to Mike Reilly. Also a psychic, but he grew up in a family of psychics so he knew the rules. Such as: if two psychics who have never met are in close proximity to each other, they can find each other by their auras.

In other words? Psychics *glow.*

Everybody's aura is different. Mike says mine is shades of blue and black, all twisted together. His is a bright sparkly blue, with yellow around the edges.

Now, say you're a woman in her late teens who's just gotten some bad news (again). And you've left the arena where the tournament is being held so you don't accidentally-on-purpose punch somebody (again). And you've found a quiet hidey-hole in a part of the building that's under renovation, because nobody is working on the weekend and that means nobody is around to see you cry.

(Again.)

Then this big blue glowstick of a man appears. He's shouting about this and that, and none of it makes any sense because he's talking about stuff that sounds like magic. You're pretty sure he's not even real.

If you were like me, you'd run.

If you were me in particular, you'd also hurl a loose cinderblock at his head as you sprinted past him.

(I've mentioned that Mike's a saint for putting up with me, right? I should probably do that more often.)

Anyhow, Mike was the first psychic I'd ever met. Which makes sense, as we're pretty rare. Mike says that the glowing aura thing is a sort of psychic GPS so we can locate each other in crowds, and it's no big deal because it goes away as soon as you make physical contact.

Such as a casual handshake.

I'd never considered that auras could be audible instead of visible, but let's be honest—I'm a fairly lousy psychic.

Apparently, so was Sergeant Fleishman.

But he didn't know it. Or if he did, he had never met another psychic in the wild before.

All of this put me in the worst position, by the way. I'm not much of an ambassador for anything, and if Fish didn't know a ground rule that even I had managed to pick up?

I wasn't about to go rampaging through his worldviews on the basis of a *sound*.

So I shook his hand and welcomed Fish to the party, and then went to leave a lengthy message on Mike's answering machine.

Chapter Eleven

We headed into the desert as the sun went down. Which was just super-dumb, if you ask me: we should have set up camp where we were, especially since we had learned that we were within spitting distance of the Yuma Proving Ground, and what they proved was that things blew up. But no, Tellerman said we were here to work, and that meant doing bonkers stuff in the dark.

So we loaded up the Jeeps, locked the cars (I threw a tarp over the Mustang and prayed for both its paint job and my security deposit), and into the dark we went.

We drove slowly, with our headlights burning like big ol' spotlights moving in front of us. Fish made us drive in single-file, convoy style, in case of sinkholes or other dangers lurking in the desert.

Every hour or so, Tellerman would call a halt. We'd all get out, the film crew would assemble, and Tellerman would talk about this and that and the other while gesturing towards interesting rocks.

When this happened, I'd slip into a quiet spot between the cars, close my eyes, and try to meditate on the facts.

Margot's story was bothering me. Banshee tales are usually wham-bam-thank-you-ma'am, in which a Wailing Woman appears as a death omen. Instead, we had Marie de Borromeo, a nun who was Spanish nobility, fighting an unseen foe.

Fact: the Old Families who interact with ghosts? They're often related to nobility. Not on the level of kings and queens, of course but definitely the rich landowner class. I had asked Mare to put OACET's research team on the de Borromeo family tree to see if they could turn up anything odd, although I didn't expect anything to come of it. It's hard to tell people to look for evidence of ghosts without tipping your hat to the existence of ghosts.

Fact: If Marie de Borromeo had been a psychic in life, she was a strong ghost in death. Psychics make a heavy imprint in the Afterlife.[11] She wouldn't be anywhere close to Ben's class—probably not even on par with Thomas Paine—but she'd probably be strong enough to kick some ass if the ass presented itself.

Fact: Ghosts are only whiffy puffs of vapor when they want to be. Mostly, they're solid. Or at least solidish. Ghosts have the same muscle memory that the living do, where we can train ourselves to act and react without conscious thought. But! Ghosts have body memory, too—they spent a lifetime in their skin and bones, and once those are gone, they're haunted by them. It's easy to forget the details of what it's like to have a body, maybe, with the irritations of rashes and pooping. Not so easy to forget that your consciousness is stationed within physical matter. Ghosts tend to carry this assumption around with them, and it affects how they define themselves in relation to the rest of us. Extra-strong ghosts like Ben? They feel as solid as if they were made of neurons and circulatory systems and all that related cytoplasmic goop. So while we might not be able to see ghosts, that doesn't mean they aren't there.

Fact: How many ghost stories have you heard where the living human straight-up starts beating on a monster? And *wins?* Zero. Hell, even Mike and I didn't stand a chance against the minotaur, and we're two of the best martial artists in the world. If Marie de Borromeo fought a ghost to a standstill and died in the process, that's still a win. Personally, I'd choose the option where I got to walk away from the fight while still breathing, but I'm picky like that. She chose to go down in battle. Let's pour one out for the old warrior nun.

---

11 There's a very good chance that when I die, I'm going to be one scary-ass powerful ghost. There's the fame thing, plus the psychic thing, meaning whatever imprint I leave in the Afterlife will probably be a Hope-shaped hole through time and space itself.

I should note that this is just guesswork on my part, by the way. None of the dead folks I hang out with will say one way or the other, even when I ask them all direct-like. But they do go out of their way to make sure I stay alive, so there's that.

Fact: Mare put OACET's research team on Hawley, too, and they've told her that the pirate was famous. Or, to be extra-specific, he was famous at the time he died, which made for great ghost stories within the Gulf of California. This fame has all but dried up by now, but back in the day, he was probably a semi-powerful ghost.

Fact: I was not looking forward to any and all experiences which would require me to reevaluate my opinions on undead serial killers.

Cut to me sitting between two Jeeps as I allowed my mind to drift out over the desert.

I don't know what I was doing. I guess I was hoping I'd sense the general direction of any undead presence, and steer us the fuck away from that. Kind of like how I sensed the echo of that ghost in the ruins of the Spanish mission.

Problem is, I'm a lousy psychic. No training. And I was very aware that my attempts to keep us out of danger might yank us straight to it—I've learned from experience that if I'm looking straight at something, there's a good chance that it can look at me.

What was I going to do? Nothing? No. But maybe I could do as little as possible, and keep us out of danger that way.

Sparky says that when he sends his senses out, he can feel the world around him. Our buddy Rachel can do this and so much more. Me, I kept my eyes closed and…sat.

Feeling nothing.

Nothing until…

…*gold*…

…*a man with a gold front tooth, grinning at me, a knife in one hand*—

"—nope," I whispered, pressing my right hand against the scar on my left arm. "Not tonight. Sorry, buddy."

I opened my eyes and looked up at the night sky.

The desert at night? Miles and miles from cities or towns or any light pollution at all? Now, there's a show. No moon yet, but a million stars running down that big white stripe of the

Milky Way. Flecks and specks of white dust, crashing through a blue-black so dark and warm that I wanted to wrap myself inside it like a velvet cloak. People always say they feel small when they look at the night sky, that the universe is *so big* and we're *so insignificant* in the grand scheme of things. But we're not, we're *here, now,* we exist in a world where there were things like dinosaurs and sugar cookies and, oh, let's say Margaret Thatcher, and that's so wonderful, so unique, so **perfect** that hell yes, we're small, but small doesn't mean worthless—

Across the desert, I felt that same vague something turn over in its sleep again.

No. This time it was *many* somethings.

"Aw, fuck," I muttered, as I yanked my mind away from the stars and back down to where a film crew was shouting—sorry, talking not-quite-loudly and definitely not waving their arms— at each other.

When I made the corner around the back end of the Jeeps, I bumped right into a camera. Two lights and a diffuser swung down and turned my face into what was likely a high-definition landscape of clogged pores and sweat.

"Dr. Blackwell! There you are!" Tellerman was in full showman mode, with Speedy riding his shoulders like a surfboard.

(Tellerman hadn't been forgiven. Not by a long shot. Speedy was *grinning.*)

"Oh, lord," I sighed. "Are we making camp here?"

"This is live," he said. "Tell our viewers about Hawley."

"Live?" I think I blinked a few times. "Like, *live*-live?"

Tellerman slipped an arm around my waist and turned me towards the camera. "The Dread Pirate Hawley," he said, his free hand moving towards the stars overhead. "The missing boat, the vanished sea! Tell our viewers why we're here!"

"Live?" I groaned. *"Fuuuuck!"*

I twisted out of Tellerman's creephold and stomped away. Keith was standing just behind the cameras, so I chose him first. "What does he mean, *live?!*"

"It's fine, swearing's fine," Keith assured me (yet still tugging me out of range of the microphones, hmm). "Don't worry about censoring yourself—we've decided to run this as a livestream on our website, not through syndication. You can say whatever you want, unfiltered."

"I didn't agree to be part of a live broadcast!"

"Actually, you did," Keith said. "It's part of the standard contract. Sometimes Tellerman decides to run with what he's got. Says it keeps the series fresh. We'll do an edited version for the show, too, so don't worry. You'll still be on television."

I wondered how hard it would be to rip Keith in half. Lengthwise.

The expression on my face must have gotten through to him. "It was your friend's idea," he said, pointing at Mare. "She said she could boost our signal to get it out of the desert."

Mare gave a sick grin and lifted her fingers in a very timid wave.

Cyborgs, man. So inconvenient.

I abandoned Keith and sidled up to Mare.

"I know, I know," she whispered. "One of the twins asked if I could do anything about her cell signal. Tellerman overheard us and asked what else I could do."

"Can you shut it down?"

"C'mon, Hope," Mare said. "Of course I can, but he knows that, too."

"This just gets better and better," I muttered.

The shadows across the scrublands changed as the lighting swung towards us. "Dr. Blackwell?" Tellerman called.

Mare gathered up her skirts, and the two of us ran into the desert.

We didn't go very far. Fragile ankles, loose rocks, poisonous snakes, and all that. But we went far enough so Tellerman couldn't catch us by swinging those lights around, as we were crouching in a ditch behind a pile of stones.

We peered over the edge of the ditch, and ducked down as the lights came around again. "Dr. Blackwell?" Tellerman called.

Mare giggled, both hands over her mouth to keep the sound

from carrying.

"This is the worst vacation ever," I whispered.

Her giggling grew slightly panicked.

And then I was laughing, too. We sat, shoulder to shoulder in the ditch, squeaking behind our fingers as Tellerman lost patience and entered the wavy-arms phase of shouting again. From a distance, we could hear Speedy egging him on. And, as Speedy was pounding on Tellerman's head and calling him all kinds of obscene names, this didn't help cure the giggles.

I was woefully unprepared for the bird.

I glanced up and saw a head peering down at us from the top of the ditch. Its feathered crest was highlighted against the stars. Definitely a bird, not a bird-adjacent dinosaur or similar. But from where I was sitting, it looked like one big bird.

I poked Mare, and pointed towards the bird.

"Oh!" Mare stopped laughing. "Hey, little guy," she said softly. "Shouldn't you be in bed?"

The bird hopped down onto Mare's head, then scampered down her body to rest on her knees.

Mare froze. The bird examined her, and chirped.

"You made a friend," I said.

Whatever the bird was? It was *ugly*. It was the kind of bird you'd get if a wizard found an old sock by the side of the road and decided to see what it would look like as a bird. About the size of a large housecat and lean, almost scrawny, with wings plastered tight against its sides. A tail nearly as long as its body. A pair of legs that would have looked at home on a stork. As best as I could make out by the light of the stars, it was mostly brown, with a white chest and white speckles cast across the brown of its back.

And its beak? That beak was as long as its entire head, and as thick around as one of its muscly legs. It was the kind of beak that performed serious bird business.

"It's a roadrunner!" Mare said.

"Roadrunner? Like, *beep-beep-zip-TANG!* roadrunner?"

"Yup!" Mare said. Her eyes were Wikipedia-distant.

"Interesting. Apparently, they enjoy hanging out with people."

"Pigeons of the desert, eh?" I asked, leaning towards Mare and the bird. "Maybe we should find it some moldy bread."

The roadrunner cocked its head to the side, then pecked me between my eyes. Three times.

"AW!" I shouted.

"They eat snakes," Mare said haughtily. "After stabbing them to death with their beaks."

"No shit!" I pressed the back of my hand against my forehead and pulled it away to check for blood. Yup, and lots of it. "Fuckin' asshole bird!"

"Don't be mean to her," Mare said, as she gingerly stroked the roadrunner's tail. The bird preened and made a warbling noise. "This is my first Disney princess moment, and I'll thank you not to ruin it."

I flailed at the three new holes in my head.

"She's very sorry," Mare said.

"I doubt that," I said. I squirmed out of my jacket and wadded up the sleeve to use as a bandage. It was soaked in moments; head wounds can be real gushers.

Mare sighed. "Okay, baby," she said to the bird. "We don't have any snakes for you. Hurry on home."

The roadrunner didn't want to leave. We spent a few minutes trying to shoo it away, but it kept climbing back onto various parts of Mare. We finally gave up and started walking back towards the vehicles. The roadrunner kept up with us, twining around Mare's ankles, only stopping when the noise and lights got uncomfortably intense. Once it realized Mare wasn't coming back, it started to bark, a mournful *arf arf arf*, like an abandoned dog.

This caught the attention of the film crew.

"Dr. Blackwell!" Tellerman came running. "Where did—"

I pulled my jacket away from my face.

Tellerman recoiled. "Oh my God," he said. "What happened to you?"

I stared at the camera behind him: it was difficult to see; the blood was making my vision all blurry and red.

"Here." Someone pressed a bottle of water and a strip of cotton cloth into my hands. This was followed by a sterile plastic packet of antiseptic. Fish, standing by with an Army emergency medical kit. "Roadrunner, right?"

"Is that a thing out here?" I asked, as I doused the cloth in water and went to work on my face. "Coulda warned us."

"They're jerks," he said. "But usually they're harmless jerks. There're a couple of families nesting around the base. Captain makes us treat them with respect."

I ran my finger across my forehead. Two of the tiny craters hadn't stopped bleeding.

"Here," Fish said, "let me."

I leaned against the nearest Jeep and let Fish take over. His hands were gentle as he scrubbed off the blood I had missed, and packed the holes with gauze. We both ignored the black eye of the camera bobbing between us: he needed its light.

"Around here, roadrunners are a good thing," he said. "They're natural pest control. Mice, spiders, rattlesnakes, you name it. Captain catches anyone chasing off a roadrunner? They're gonna get a boot up their ass.

"That's probably why they're considered good omens," he added, as he taped off the gauze in neat squares. "Every desert culture has a roadrunner in their mythology. The stories are about how they help humans. Warding off evil, helping lost humans get home... Hell, they even help souls find their way."

"Souls?" Mare asked quickly. "You mean, ghosts?"

"I guess, but in the stories they're not haunting anybody. They're just dead," Fish said. He started to pack up the med kit. "And roadrunners are guides that help them get to where they need to go."

"So, they help ghosts." Mare stared at me.

I shook my head.

"Let's set up camp here," said Tellerman. The cameras swung towards the roadrunner, standing at the edge of the light and still calling plaintively after Mare. "I've got a good feeling about this place."

Chapter Twelve

EXT. CAMPSITE—NIGHT.

*The group is sitting around a campfire. HOPE, MARE, FISH, and KOALA are sitting on one side of the fire; TELLERMAN, KEITH, and cast of **SPOOKY SOLUTIONS** are on the other side.*

MARE: I want to hear one of those roadrunner stories. The ones you were telling Hope about.

KEITH: Me, too. Got any Indian stories?

FISH: Sorry, not really. Around here, most of the legends with roadrunners are about the First People. I can't tell those.

MARE: Why not?

FISH: They're not mine to tell. Most of the stories about the First People are sacred. Telling them is like…like singing hymns in church, I guess. There's something ritualistic about 'em. They're stories meant to praise their gods.

TELLERMAN: You can still tell them.

MARE (to FISH): If they're sacred stories, how did you learn them?

FISH (to MARE): Read 'em, or heard 'em told. I like to go to local ceremonies, if they're open to the public. They're beautiful.

MARE (to FISH): Really? I like that.

FISH (to MARE): Ah. Ah, thank you, Agent.

MARE (to FISH, smiling): Call me Mare.

HOPE (quietly): Oh lord.

HOPE (to FISH): Got any roadrunner stories that aren't sacred?

FISH: I can tell a Hohokam story. They're long dead, so anything I say is myth, not religion.

TELLERMAN (to FISH): You know about the Hohokam?

OSHEA: What are Hohokam?

FISH: The Hohokam are a who, not a what. The Hohokam are one of the three lost tribes of the Sonoran Desert. From what we can tell, they were farmers, artists, and engineers. They built some of the first large permanent communities in the Americas.

HOPE: What happened to 'em?

KEITH: Vanished. The name 'Hohokam' means 'used-up' or 'finished' in the language of the Indians who survived. Their entire civilization disappeared, and nobody knows where they went. We're still finding what they left behind. Petroglyphs, sometimes even their buildings! I mean, maybe we'll find—

TELLERMAN (quickly): Fish, you were going to tell us a story?

FISH: Right, right. How about a Hohokam teaching tale? There are several stories where the roadrunner goes to help its friends and gets hurt for its trouble. In others, Coyote uses it as his messenger.

HOPE: Can you tell those?

FISH: Yeah, they're...I guess you can call them public-domain stories, now that the Hohokam are gone. How does it start...I don't remember where I heard this one. Might have been a children's book.

TELLERMAN: You read kids' books?

FISH (to TELLERMAN): When I'm reading to kids, yeah.

MARE (to FISH): You read to kids?

FISH (to MARE): Yeah, I volunteer at the base's Child Development Center. We get a lot of kids from—

TELLERMAN (to FISH): What's the story?

FISH: Okay. Let's see... It goes....back when the world was new, there was Coyote.

TELLERMAN (to FISH): I thought this story was about a roadrunner?

HOPE (to TELLERMAN, quietly): Oh my **God** just shut up.

FLEISHMAN: When we—by **we**, I mean, people who aren't native—hear stories about Coyote, we think of him as a single individual. But among the native peoples, Coyote is different things to different communities. In some traditions, he's helpful. In others, he's jealous and greedy. But he's always a trickster.

There was a time when the world was new and full of life, but all of the people who were in it had suddenly died. Coyote was the child of the sun and the moon, and he had enjoyed having these people around him. For the Hohokam, Coyote was helpful but vain: he liked to be praised, and the people had done this. But the people had angered their creator, who struck them down with a great flood which covered the land.

Coyote was sad. The people who had praised him were dead! So he called Roadrunner to him, and told Roadrunner to run to the east, the west, the north, and the south, and find the edge of the water. Roadrunner did as Coyote asked. She returned to him, and guided him to the exact center of the dry land.

Coyote called on Earth Doctor and Siuuhu, who were as brothers to him. These three powerful beings decided to make new people from the clay that they found at this break between the waters. But Coyote was not good at making people. Siuuhu saw what he was doing with his pieces of clay, and hurled them into the ocean. They became ducks and fish, and Siuuhu told Coyote that his people were so poorly made that they would only serve as food for humankind.

Coyote was furious with Siuuhu, but his brother had great skill in making people, and he knew Siuuhu's people would be perfect. When Siuuhu put the first batch of people into the oven to bake, Coyote removed them before they were fully cooked. These underdone people were white; Coyote had Roadrunner take them far, far away to cold lands. When the next batch of people went into the oven to bake, Coyote distracted Siuuhu with jokes and stories. These people were overcooked and came out of the oven as dark brown; Coyote had Roadrunner take them far, far away to where the land was scorching hot.

But Siuuhu watched the oven and took out the last batch of people at the right time. These new people became the Hohokam. Coyote had Roadrunner take the Hohokam to where the land was at times hot, and at times cold, and at times dry, and at times wet. Then, he sent Roadrunner with them to help the Hohokam understand the changing faces of their new home.

TELLERMAN: Is that it?

FISH: No. Since the Hohokam disappeared, all of their stories were told by those who came after them. Some researchers think the Hohokam were assimilated by the Pima-Papago peoples. There's another story which tells of a battle between Coyote and Buzzard, where Coyote's a stand-in for the Pima-Papago, and Buzzard is the Hohokam. Well, Coyote ate Buzzard right up. So Coyote might have helped make the Hohokam, but he wasn't going to protect them for all time.

Those tales don't have clear-cut lessons—they're not Aesop's fables—but one thing to remember is that Coyote should never be taken for granted.

Sound of roadrunner calling, off-camera.

Chapter Thirteen

The next morning dawned red. I know this because Dina had gotten me in a headlock and I had a clear view of the sky from beneath her armpit. I was all set to break it in a basic *Kesa gatame* counter, but then Oshea came in low and pinned me by the knees.

I tapped out.[12] We separated, bowed, and the two of them closed on me again.

The twins had very different fighting styles. There were some similarities, but Dina was more of a grappler while Oshea punched and kicked like a deadly ballerina. They were decidedly bad-ass, by the way: I had accidentally popped Oshea in the eye when her head wasn't where it should have been (my fault, not hers—I should have been more careful with a new sparring partner), and she didn't even flinch.

And they knew how to work together. They had trained to work together, complementing each other's strengths and shoring up their weaknesses.

Joy!

Dina opened with a roundhouse kick quick enough to take my head off. I blocked, grabbed, and pulled her leg into a modified *Morote gari*, and Dina went down.

Oshea closed in from my left side, fast. *Osoto gaeshi* this time, an outer reversal that put the woman flat on her back, with me guiding her to the ground. But Dina was up and her fists were hammers: I blocked and countered, blocked and countered, blocked and grabbed and Dina was down again.

This time, I was ready for Oshea. She went high, a grab

---

12 Note: Martial artists get crap all the damned time about "losers" (or, more recently, "cucks") who tap out instead of fighting until their opponents lay prostrate before them as ruined puddles of tenderized meat. The high-minded among us say something like: "Sparring is used to develop skills with our partners, and is not conflict with an enemy," but I usually just ask if they want to go a few rounds.

destined for a headlock. I took her arms in a *Koshi guruma* over my hip, across the curve of my back, and bam! Down.

It went on like this forever. One twin attacked, the other recovered and looked for an opening. Two against one, but two moving almost as one. You didn't come across this kind of partnership very often. I fought this way when I teamed up with Sparky, and also with Mike, but I'd never been the odd one out. It was a whole new experience for me and was just about the best thing ever, until Oshea hurled me towards the ground and I happened to notice the giant glass eye of the camera on my way down.

"God damn it!" I tapped out, rolled, and came up right in front of a stack of rocks with Keith hiding behind them. He dropped the camera and scrabbled backwards as I came at him. "I did *not* sign away this part of my life! Give me the tape. Or the card. Or the…gimme the whatever!"

Behind me, Dina made a choking noise as she saw the camera in the dirt. "Come on, Keith," she said. "Not the Nikon. It took me forever to talk Tellerman into buying that one!"

"Dina, get her off me!" Keith was covering his head with both hands, flinching from an attack that never came.

"Oh, shut up!" I snapped, and grabbed the camera. I shoved it at Dina, who ran a quick systems check.

"He was livestreaming us," she said.

"Keith." Oshea sounded hurt. "We talked about this."

"Can we not do this on camera?" Keith asked, as Dina turned that shiny glass eyeball on him.

"Oh, *now* he doesn't want—" I was furious, but Oshea put a hand on my shoulder.

"We've got this," she said. "It's not the first time."

My hands had a clench-unclench battle with my head, but I nodded. For whatever reason, the twins were hurt, and hurt trumps a pissing contest any day of the week.

"Good fight," I muttered, and headed towards the showers.

(I hate having my sparring matches filmed. There's the ever-present crowd of backseat martial artists on YouTube, of course, all of them ready and waiting to critique every part of my performance. Add in the assholes who see me minding my own business in public and assume that I've left my house for no other reason than to throw down with complete strangers, and you've got my Tuesday run to the dry cleaner's.)

The bathroom facilities were set off to the side of our tiny pop-up camp. They were tiny, with just enough room for a standing shower and, on the other side of a translucent divider, a chemical toilet. Showers had to be kept under two minutes, so none of that highfalutin hair washin' for any of us, especially Mare. Tellerman did, however, insist on showering: we were on camera, after all, and blah blah blah photogenic equals ratings blah blah try not to look like the dusty bottom of a shoe and blah.

I used the toilet, and then swept the adjoining shower stall for cameras.

Being married to a sexy piece of state-of-the-art technology has taught me a lot about what is possible and what isn't. For example, despite living in an age of magic beeping lasers, it still isn't possible to get an awful tattoo removed without investing tons of time and money. On the other hand, it is possible to make a camera small enough to fit on a shirt button. Now, ask me if I thought that Keith or Tellerman were above such creepy shenanigans as hiding cameras in a shower stall.

I checked all of the usual nooks and crannies, and found nothing. Then I checked the unusual nooks and crannies. After I was satisfied that my naked jiffies wouldn't go on public display, I stripped, took a *(freezing cold argh help the solar heating system didn't get a chance to collect any energy during the night!)* shower, and got dressed in clean clothes.

The shower knocked some sense into me, which I needed. I hadn't slept well. Sure, there was a great popup miniaturized house set aside for just Mare, Speedy, and me. Not exactly the penthouse at the Bellagio, but it had air conditioning and beds, and exactly zero scorpions. Unfortunately, Mare and young Fish had snuck away from the campfire not too long after he told his story about Roadrunner and the Coyote Creation Bakery. Speedy and I hung back with the others to give them some alone time. When I opened the door to our house a good while later, we had visual confirmation that Mare couldn't resist a man in uniform. Or, more precisely, a man in half a uniform. The…uh…top half. Plus socks.

After that, Speedy and I went to go howl at the moon for another hour. When we went back, Mare was sleeping. She was alone, except for the roadrunner. Somehow, the bird had gotten inside, and made itself a nest on top of Mare's blankets. It saw me and Speedy, and hissed at us. Quietly.

We gave up and went to go sleep in one of the Jeeps.

(I found this to be quite weird. Not the part about the Jeeps, or the roadrunner. I mean the sudden change of heart in a vengeful marsupial who has made every single day since I met him a high-stakes game of sadism poker. I was all set to drop-kick the bird into next Tuesday, but Speedy? He stared at Mare and the roadrunner for a good long moment, then insisted we leave them alone. Go figure.)

The rest of the camp had woken up and was milling around the tables we had set up near the fire pit. I drifted over to where Mare was sitting, and fell into the empty chair across from her. Fish was there, trying not to hover over her and failing miserably; she did him a kindness and sent him to go get me some coffee.

I glared at her; she performed the hero's task of not bursting into flames from blushing.

"How old is Sergeant Fish, anyhow?" I finally asked, as I watched him douse my coffee with enough sugar to render it crunchy.

"Not so young," Mare said, her nose ever-so-slightly pointed away from me. "He's four years younger than you."

"*Eight* years younger than you? *Mare*. Is he even old enough to drink?"

"If I cannot have my pool cabana boy at the Bellagio as planned," she said, sipping her coffee. "I will make do."

I didn't reply.

"He's not bad in bed," Mare admitted.[13]

That settled that. "What happened to the roadrunner?"

She pointed at her lap.

I rose off of my chair and peeked over the edge of the table. The roadrunner was nestled in Mare's lap, sound asleep.

"So, what's happening here?" I asked. "Do you have a new pet?"

Mare stroked the bird's back. The roadrunner made a gentle peep, and nuzzled its head against Mare's leg. "Maybe. I don't know," Mare said. "No. No, she's not a pet, she's a wild animal. It's really sweet how she seems to like me, but I can't keep her."

"Why not?" I pointed to Speedy. The koala was deep in discussion with Keith and Tellerman at the next table. "We've already got one wild animal."

"Speedy is housebroken," Mare said. "And understands logical consequences, even if he chooses to ignore them."

"Not all of them!" Speedy turned away from his conversation to shout at her. "Only those that are bullshit!"

Fish returned with my coffee, placed the cup in front of me like he was delivering a shipment of gold bullion, and pulled up a chair to sit the exact proper distance from Mare. Not too close, not too far—the Goldilocks Zone of fumbling self-

13 Which, believe it or not, is extremely high praise. Lemme tell you about Josh Glassman. You know that one friend you have who's really into running? Seriously, almost alarm-bells-ringing into running? The guy who thinks ultra-marathons are a warm-up event? If he's polite, he'll never talk to you about running because he knows you don't appreciate it like he does. For him, it's not so much a sport as an art form, and if you don't understand that distinction he's not going to waste his time educating you. But! If you ever tell him you want to learn about running? You've initiated *hours and hours* of conversation. Will he discuss the physical mechanics? Probably. The health benefits? Definitely. This will be followed by an offer to go running with him to see if you enjoy it. And don't worry, he'll start out slow until you're up to speed.

Replace running with sex, and Josh Glassman is exactly like that.

I'd never met a competitive sexlete before I met Josh. Sex is fun, yeah, that's a no-brainer, but it's not just sex for Josh; it's an esoteric mashup of a cardiovascular workout and the *Kama Sutra* and tantric meditation and the occasional break for chilled towels and energy bars. Keep in mind he doesn't do pity fucks, either—he might be willing to introduce you to a different kind of sex, but if he thinks he's wasting his time with a partner who can't learn to play at his level? He will very politely sideline you, permanently.

Now, Mare? Quiet, docile, bureaucratic Mare? She sleeps with Josh *on the regular.*

conscious courtship.

About thirteen seconds later, Tellerman plunked his chair down beside me. "Today, we're taking the drones out," he said. "I want to chart the north and west. Scout around, try to find the old mission that the crazy lady in Slab City mentioned."

North and west. My internal compass wasn't the greatest, but I was pretty sure the patch of somethings that woke up were to the north and west.

The hum of nearby electronics crept into my left ear; I turned to see Dina with the camera.

Sorry, she mouthed.

I shrugged. North and west currently had priority in the screaming pit of my stomach.

"Agent Murphy, can you control both drones at once?" Tellerman asked.

"Yes," Mare replied, and I breathed a silent sigh of relief.

"What do you want the rest of us to do?" I asked, as I attempted to chew my coffee. I was no longer worried about north and west, not if Mare was flying the drones. She could loop them around to the south and east, tamper with the data, and we'd kill time over the next few days on the lamest of scavenger hunts.

"We'll go north today, northwest tomorrow, and west the day after," he said. "Check out some of the locations the drones have spotted. Makes for better television than just top-down shots from an aircraft."

Welp, so much for that.

In Mare's lap, the roadrunner fluffed its feathers in its sleep.

"Who stays here at camp?" I asked. "We can't leave all of this stuff unguarded."

That idea hadn't occurred to Tellerman. "I…ah…The sergeant should stay with his gear."

"I should stay with Agent Murphy," Fish said. "The drones are…um—"

"Expensive government property," I offered.

"Very expensive," Fish agreed.

"I don't mind staying behind," I said, as I crossed my arms

and looked at Tellerman.

(I did, actually—north and west and slumbering somethings and all that—but Tellerman was going to drag me along no matter what. Probably Speedy, too. World's only talking koala makes for good television. But leverage was leverage, even if it was petty of me.)

"Let me check," he said, and left to discuss the duty roster with his crew.

Which left me and Mare with young Fish.

"I'll...uh...go run an equipment check," he said.

Once he was gone, I quietly filled Mare in on the somethings. As I spoke, her eyes went so wide that I wondered if they might pop out and dangle a little on the optic nerves.

"It's okay," I said. "It's probably nothing. I'm pretty awful at all of this psychic crap. I just thought you should know."

Mare nearly folded in half. "Oh, *God*, Hope!" she whispered, her arms curling around the roadrunner. "What are we going to do?!"

"We lead them away from the hot spots," I said. "It's cool, Mare. You wanted to come along to keep these kids out of trouble, so that's what we'll do."

That got to her. "You're right," she said with a deep breath, and gathered up the roadrunner in her skirts. "You're right. Let's do this."

Chapter Fourteen

I couldn't help but drink in the freakin' *gorgeousness* of the desert. It was nothing but color. The greens of hard vegetation lay like paint over the reds and purples of the hills, all against a blue sky that had no end. It was hot, yeah, but I didn't care. I walked across the desert with the breeze at my back, and let my mind go.

Mare had found the best reason ever to make sure we didn't go north and west—at least, not in the Jeeps. Everything around us was protected land, some parts of it more protected than others, and as a federal employee and devout lover of nature, Mare flat-out refused to drive a heavy vehicle through such an ecologically fragile environment. So, if you wanted your precious drones...

The young kids who usually carried the heavy stuff had stayed back at camp to guard the gear, so the ATV puttered along behind us, carrying water and equipment. Keith drove. Speedy rode on my shoulders at first, and then on Sergeant Fleishman's when the Army man said he didn't feel balanced on long hikes without carrying a heavy pack.

The rest of us walked.

The cameras went away about an hour into the trip. Tellerman said a lot of nothing in the desert made for bad television, and he was worried the folks who were livestreaming the feed wouldn't bother to tune in when things got hopping at night.

About an hour after that, Speedy and I began to teach the others some traditional Scottish drinking songs. There might have been some whiskey involved, but not too much, because desert, dehydration, etc.

Along the way, Fish pointed out the intricacies of the local wildlife, its geology, various petroglyphs carved in rocks or left in caves... I was getting the impression that despite the Army fatigues and a pair of calves that could run for days, Fish was somewhat on the helpful bookish end of the personality spectrum.

Oh, and the roadrunner? It followed Mare like a puppy. A happy, well-fed puppy: every time we kicked up a critter, the roadrunner was on it like jam on toast. Giant spider? *Peck-Gulp!* Big lizard? *Peck-Gulp!* Five-foot-long snake that might or might not have been venomous? *Peck-Whack-Whack-Whack-But-No-Gulp-That-Thing-Was-Huge!* I highly recommend that anyone who wanders through the desert take along a roadrunner.

After the third hour of walking, I was sweaty and dirty and starting to feel that honest hunger that follows physical exertion.

Now, *this* was a vacation!

"What are you smiling about?" Mare asked. She was wearing a white linen shirt over a mint green skirt, with her hair braided up tight and tucked under a wide-brimmed hat. That, plus a pair of huge black sunglasses, gave her the appearance of a 1950s movie star on safari.

"Nothing," I said, as I watched a pair of large birds fly towards the purple line of the faraway mountains.

"Hey, look at this!" Fish had broken away from the rest of us and was waving at a tall rock. Speedy was standing on the sergeant's shoulders to peer at the rock's high points.

Mare and I walked over and joined them in looking at a whole lot of childlike scribbles.

"More petroglyphs," Speedy said.

"They don't look like dinosaurs," I replied. "That one looks like a dog."

There was a very satisfying sound of koala-paw slapping against koala-forehead. "Petroglyphs aren't dinosaurs, dipshit. They're—"

"You *know* she knows what they are," Mare said, shaking her head at me.[14]

---

14 It's totally cool if you don't know what petroglyphs are. I do because I hang out with Speedy, and Speedy is a professional linguist, including ancient languages. If you don't hang out with your own superintelligent koala, all you need to know is that petroglyphs

I grinned at Speedy. "Should you call one of your buddies at the Smithsonian?" I asked him. "Maybe the ones on this rock haven't been recorded."

"Human walking, human walking, human walking...river... setting sun." Speedy pointed a claw at the figures in turn. "This looks like an ordinary trail marker. We can register its location and send in photos, but nobody's gonna catch the next plane out here for—"

"Hope Blackwell has just discovered something *amazing!*" Tellerman shouted in my ear.

I turned so quickly that the camera beaned off of my forehead, square-bang right where the roadrunner had drilled its three holes. I stamped off in a rage, my hands pressed against my head, Tellerman shouting after me and Keith chasing me with the camera.

I swore at them until they backed off and walked away, laughing at me.

There was going to be a blooper reel out of this trip. There just *had* to be a blooper reel. Why not? Get some free laughs, some good publicity. It'll be at the expense of a woman who was a celebrity, and everybody knows celebrities aren't real people, so why the hell not?

As my self-pity reached a crescendo, the roadrunner scooted in front of me.

I swore again and jumped sideways to keep from accidentally kicking it. Animals are...well, they're animals. I've been trying to cram a moral compass into the one animal I know is capable of reason for years, and it's gone nowhere. Getting angry at a bird for acting like a bird? True dick move.

"Hi," I said.

The roadrunner ran up to my feet, then ran a few more paces into the desert. It turned to look at me.

"Go on, girl," I told it. "I'll tell Mare you said goodbye."

It ran up and paused by my feet a second time, but now it

---

are prehistoric rock carvings. Not paintings. Petroglyphs are cut into the stone and are more durable. Same general goofy damn-it-all-Todd-look-what-your-son-has-done-to-the-walls shapes, though.

made a burping *"Perp!"* of a sound.

"Honey," I said, as I kept my full body's length between my forehead and the bird, "I've already got one animal companion, and he doesn't like competition. Mare's the one having problems with life after death. She's the one you want."

The roadrunner peered at me with its odd black-and-brown eyes, and then sped off in the general direction of Mare. I followed. When I got back to the ATV, the crew had broken for lunch. Nothing fancy, just packs of tuna salad and trail mix. Fish and Dina set up a portable canopy, and we crashed in its shade.

Tellerman dug out his tablet, and he and Mare started going over data from the drones' flight. I tuned them out after a few minutes of steady eavesdropping: Mare had been keeping the drones away from anything that looked even slightly interesting, and my nap wasn't going to take itself. I fell asleep on the desert floor with a koala curled up on my stomach, secure in the knowledge that we had to turn back soon if we wanted to make camp before dark.

I woke up with koala claws digging into my gut.

"I will make you *eat* those," I muttered.

"Shhh," whispered Speedy.

I cracked my eyes just enough to see him gesture towards Tellerman with both ears. Tellerman and Keith had their backs towards the rest of the group, and their heads bent over the tablet. The two of them kept checking an image against a large crumpled sheet of yellow…paper? No, something heavier than paper. Something they were hiding as best they could with their bodies.

"They have a treasure map," Speedy said quietly.

"Well, of course they do," I whispered back. "Is it a fake?"

"This is the first time I've seen it," he said. "I'd say it's a fake, except it's printed on something heavier than paper. Probably vellum. I'll have to check it out to be sure."

"All right." I closed my eyes and tried to listen in, but the two men and their map were out of range of human hearing.

They were well within a koala's range, though. "They want to see something," he said. "Not the pirate ship, and not the mission…"

Interesting, I thought. *What would two ghost hunters be looking for in the desert, if not ghosts?*

"On the Nefarious Villain scale, this is a…?" I asked.

"We're still safely in Trustfund Tantrum range," he said.

"All right," I replied, and resettled myself to resume my nap. "Wake me if we hit White Collar Crime."

I've always been able to sleep on demand, which turns out handy when you're in your last years of med school and you're married to a spy-turned-politician. Weird life, weird schedule. Plus the occasional sleepblock due to errant roadrunner.

Doesn't mean I can turn off the dreams, though.

Which isn't as bad as it sounds. Well, not anymore. When I was in Greece, my dreams got hijacked by one hell of a powerful ghost. That was bad. After that, I started practicing lucid dreaming techniques. Yeah, I was sad to give up the complete whackjob spontaneity of dreaming, but the tradeoff was control over my own head, so there's that.

(Oh, and I found that if I had lecture notes playing on headphones, I could study in my dreams. Create walk-through structures in my own head, skeletons and lymph nodes and such. My grades went up almost immediately.[15])

I'm not great at it. Mike says mastering lucid dreaming is a pursuit that takes a lifetime. But I'm good enough to recognize when a ghost starts fucking with my dreams, and to put the brakes on that bullshit immediately.

Case in point: I was enjoying a stroll through a valley made of clouds. I had cotton candy—which actually tasted the way that

---

15 Which pissed off Speedy so ferociously that he shimmied up the inside of the chimney and refused to come out until I agreed to take him to the zoo. Which I *hate* doing, by the way, because taking a perpetually randy koala to the zoo has an entirely different—perhaps legally punishable—outcome than taking a fellow human being. But I owed him. The only way I've been able to make it through med school as quickly as I have is thanks to Speedy, the world's best/worst study buddy. I won't say you should find a superintelligent trickster monster to help boost your grades; I will say there's a lot of incentive in not knowing when or how he's planning to set you on fire for failing your Immunology exam.

cotton candy should taste, and not that normal sickly sensation of a mouth full of sugaryuck—and a pet armadillo. I knew, in the way you just know during an excellent dream, that Sparky was waiting around the next cloud corner, and that he was naked.

Then, the clouds parted to reveal the wide open colors of the Sonora, and a woman began talking.

"Jorguín —"

"God *damn!*" I snarled, as the whimsy of the dream popped. Goodbye, cotton candy. Goodbye, armadillo. Goodbye, memorable fantasy excursion involving my husband's undercarriage. "Who's there?"

"Jorguín, don't take the Lord's name in vain."

I sat on the illusion of the desert floor. "Lemme guess," I said. "Marie de Borromeo?"

"I am Marie...wait, what? You know who I am?" Her voice was an accentless classic from middle America, the kind of bland, characterless persona that an actress in a '90s sitcom would have killed to achieve.

"Yeah. Hi," I replied. I looked around, and saw nothing but the desert. "Come out so we can have a real conversation."

"I cannot. Your wards are too strong."

"Wards. Sure. What's a ward?"

"You don't know what a..." The overwhelming feeling of Oh Dear That Was A Stupid Question And I Think I Might Be Dealing With A Stupid Person washed over the dreamscape. *"Are you the jorguín? The...witch? The medium? The conduit between different states of being?"*

"I just call myself a psychic," I said. "You were one, too, right? When you were alive?"

"...I was, yes. How did you know?"

I sighed and laid down. Above, clouds floated in hyper-realistic shapes. I poked at their edges until they went puffy. "The signs were there," I said. "So, what can I do for you?"

"You must leave—you are waking what must not be touched."

"God damn it," I whispered. "Fucking Tellerman."

"Witch, I told you—"

"I know, I know, no cursing," I said. "Sorry. It's a bad habit. Listen, I can't leave. I wish I could, but it's complicated. I'll see what I can do to avoid the...uh...the waking. What do you suggest?"

If the dead nun had been allowed to finish her warning, things might have played out differently. But no, that's when the dream lurched like a set of stuck gears, and I woke to find Tellerman in full proclamation mode: he had found something Amazing! Astonishing! Unbelievable! on the drone's scans, and we needed to get moving.

Chapter Fifteen

EXT. SONORAN DESERT, NIGHT.

Seven people (TELLERMAN, HOPE, MARE, FISH, OSHEA, DINA, and KOALA) are walking; OSHEA and DINA are working the cameras. KEITH is driving the ATV. There is a ROADRUNNER following MARE.

HOPE (to all): We need to turn around and head back to camp. It'll be dark before we get there, and I don't want to be caught out in the desert at night.

TELLERMAN: Don't tell me the famous Hope Blackwell is scared of the dark.

HOPE: Forgive me for not wanting to step on a sleepy rattlesnake.

TELLERMAN (holding up a tablet): There's a rock formation that looks like the hull of a ship, about a quarter-mile to the west. We've got plenty of time to check it out and get back to camp in time for dinner.

HOPE: Or we can just go tomorrow.

MARE: We've already walked seven miles today, Hope. What's another—oh! Oh. Yes. Let's go back.

MARE (to TELLERMAN): Tomorrow. We should come back tomorrow.

FISH: Let's take a vote and—

TELLERMAN: This isn't a democracy! This is a production company, and our set is just over the next hill! C'mon, get moving.

Crosstalk among crew. TELLERMAN walks off; KEITH follows him.

MARE (to HOPE, quietly): What do you think?

HOPE (watching TELLERMAN): We follow him, but we definitely need to—

HOPE (looking at CAMERA): We need to get back before dark.

HOPE (turning to follow TELLERMAN): Yes. Dark. Real stupid to be out in the desert after dark…fucking…cannot even with these…the **stupidest** people…

HOPE'S voice trails off as she walks out of range.

OSHEA (off-camera): Is she okay?

MARE (quickly): She's fine. She didn't get much sleep last night.

Time lapse: CAMERA cuts to MARE and FISH walking hand-in-hand. HOPE is carrying the KOALA on her back.

KOALA (to HOPE, quietly): …know for sure.

HOPE (to KOALA, quietly): Yeah, we do. There's something out there and—

HOPE (noticing CAMERA): Keith, can we get a moment alone? Pretty please with sugar on top?

TELLERMAN (off-camera, excitedly): Look!

CAMERA turns to take in TELLERMAN, who is pointing at a large shape in the distance.

TELLERMAN: There's the boat! We've found it!

HOPE (staring): I don't think that's a boat.

Chapter Sixteen

It definitely wasn't a boat. It was a pile of old stones shooting up from the ground, or lying flat, kicked over by wind or time. The bones of a whale skeleton probably looked like that after a few years. These stones, though…

"How old is this place?" I asked Fish. "Gotta be a mission or a mine. Spanish colonists or later, right?"

"Hard to say," he said. "Lots of pueblo-builders settled a little further to the east, but they had a few structures out this way. Could be the ruins of one of those. Or something from the Spanish colonial era." I blinked at him, and he shrugged. "Deserts aren't empty. Nobody takes down the buildings when they're abandoned, and they don't rot like they do out east."

As we got closer, we could see that the building or structure or whatever it was stood on the far side of what had once been a river. The water was gone; a dry riverbed with pieces of wood jutting out of the earth had been left in its place. Layers of stone had formed the walls of the bed, a hundred colors of reds and browns that had stacked themselves over more time than I could comprehend. It was beautiful, in a murder-you kind of way.

I poked the riverbed's wall with a toe, and watched it crumble. Fifteen feet down. I could jump it, no big thing. Except I didn't know if the floor of the riverbed was solid. Hit an air pocket, break an ankle or worse…

I slung my pack to the ground. "Fish and I are going first."

Token protests and hand-wringing, and then Fish and I were hand-over-hand, all the way to the bottom. We hopped around a bit, but the ground stayed in one piece.

"It's stable," I called to the others. I pointed towards the far wall. "But don't come down if you don't know if you can climb up."

They all came down. Even Keith, the least athletic of the group, abandoned the ATV and slid into the gully on his butt. I sighed; down is *always* easier than up.

We crossed the riverbed. Fish yanked on tree branches when he could, testing how deep they were buried. None of them came loose, but some of them wiggled. He stopped and stared at the sky.

"What?" I asked.

"It's October," he said. "Been a dry summer. We're due for a wet winter, but that won't start until December."

I looked up. The sky was crystal blue, with high ropes of clouds. "I think we're good," I replied.

He shrugged and resumed walking. "Most dangerous place in a desert is in the flood zones," he said. "Never hurts to be careful."

The opposite slope of the riverbank wasn't as steep. Speedy ran up the wall easier than he could climb an old knotty pine. Same with the roadrunner (minus the tree analogy). Fish helped Mare up, and the two of them began scouting around with Tellerman while the twins and I took turns moving Keith and the cameras. For a moment, I had both cameras in my sweaty hands at the same time, with a convenient fifteen-foot drop—

"Don't," Dina said with a grin.

"You're killin' me here," I grumbled, but I set the cameras down and gave her a hand up. She was carrying two bags of film equipment, which damn near doubled her weight.[16]

Speedy was waiting for me at the edge of the standing stones. I knelt so he could climb up. When he reached my shoulders, he whispered, "Hang back."

I untied and retied my boots while he spoke. "Mare's new boy toy said he keeps hearing a woman scream."

"Fish said that?" I glanced over to where Mare and Fish were

---

16 This trip was teaching me a lot about the production side of television programming. I had assumed it was point-and-shoot with snarky eyerolls at the talent, but that was only about a third of it. The rest was work.

standing. He kept swirling a finger in his ear, then looking around, then swirling a different finger in his other ear, then looking around... Rinse, repeat.

"You hear anything?" Speedy asked, his beady eyes darting around the stones.

I closed my eyes and concentrated. I heard the others talking. Birds. Wind. Maybe—just maybe—an inkling of a scream, but between the birds and the wind, who could tell?

"Nothing," I said. I stood and hurried to close the distance.

I hopped a low wall and entered the ruins. There was a flattish surface underfoot that was different from the choppy rock of the desert. A courtyard? Whatever it had once been, it was long gone. Desert brooms were blooming through its holes in clouds of puffy white.

I stopped walking. The broken stones seemed familiar. I changed course and headed towards the largest stack of stones.

"Hey," Speedy said. "Where you goin'?"

"Do you recognize this place?" I asked.

"Yeah. I meet Digger the talking wombat here every other Tuesday," he snapped. "What the hell do you think?"

"Eat a dick." I made the jump to the first stone. I paused so Speedy could slide down to my waist and drop to the ground, and the two of us scrambled up the pile. I reached the top and looked around.

The Xeroxed copy of the photo that Saint Margot of the Coveted Composting Toilet had shown me didn't match this place. Sure, plenty could happen to a land within a hundred years (give or take), but there wasn't enough to set it aside as *that* monastery.

Still...

"You sure Fish said he heard a woman screaming?"

Speedy answered by wiggling his softball-sized ears.

"Right." I found a flat surface at the top of the pile and sat, legs crossed in lotus position, hands tented in my lap.

"Oh, lord," Speedy sighed. "Just take a nap."

"I'm trying it Mike's way," I said, and tried to clear my mind of distractions.

"You're not Mike," he said. "You're you." He curled against my thigh like it was a tree branch, and went to sleep.

Sleep.

Hadn't been getting much of *that* lately. A nap was appealing, but Mike was insistent about meditation and mindfulness. That to be *here* meant being *aware*.

The fresh scar on my arm itched.

"I'm working on it, okay?" I muttered, and tried to concentrate on nothing and everything at the same time.

The everything part of meditation is easy. I've never had problems with the everything part. It's attempting to hold onto nothingness that trips me up.

Wind. A hawk, far away. The smell of the desert before the evening...

...a man with a gold front tooth...

I opened my eyes, closed them, and tried again.

The man in my memory was smiling at me.

"Nope," I said quietly, and opened my eyes so I could take in the colors of the desert.

There was a quick and fluffy sound, like a small feather pillow shaking itself, and Mare's roadrunner hopped up on the stone beside me.

"Hey," I said. "Gonna peck me again?"

The bird made its *Perp!* noise and stared at me.

I leaned over so I could look the roadrunner in its eyes. Okay, one eye. Not the same eye, either: it kept turning its head to stare at me with its offset peepers.

"Talk to me," I said. "Who sent you? What are you?"

It cocked its head at me, as if it were thinking.

"Is there a ghost in there?" I leaned in as close as I could. "Are you possessed?"

The roadrunner stared at me, first with one beady black eyeball, then the other, and then speared its beak into my forehead before taking off in a small cloud of dust.

I slammed both hands against my forehead to rub out the pain.

It hadn't hurt as much this time. My head was still bandaged from where the bird had attacked me the night before, and the padding had absorbed most of the attack. "Beep-beep yourself, bitch," I muttered.

"I love that bird," Speedy said, his eyes still closed.

"Gonna freakin' *fricassee* it!" I vowed.

He rolled over and stretched, extending one forepaw at a time, like a cat. "Y'know, it keeps beaning you right where the third eye is supposed to be."

"Mystical horseshit." I checked my fingertips; no fresh blood. Thank you, bandages.

"Says an actual psychic. You sense anything?"

I did the now-normal up-periscope gesture to make sure there were no cameras around, and then said, "No. Nothing."

"Try taking a nap."

I stood, scooping him up as I went.

He sighed and climbed to my shoulders. "You're not Mike," he said. "What works for him might not work for you."

"I know," I replied. "Not gonna let my dreams become the information superhighway for strange dead people, though."

"That's fair," he muttered. "But what—"

"No. There's always gonna be a 'but what,'" I said, as I started to climb down the rocks. "But what about the minotaur? But what about the army of dead somethings waking up in the desert? If I don't put the brakes on now, then—"

"Hold up," he said. "Army of whatnows?"

"I told you about them."

"No, you said *'something'* was waking up," he said. "And now you're using the word *'army'*, so…"

"Figure of speech."

"Your subconscious is the most coherent part of you," he said. "Listen to it."

"Thanks, asshole." We hit the wide stones of the plaza. I could imagine what this place had been in its prime. The stones we had been sitting on were the ruins of a larger building. Around it, there had been high walls surrounding a large courtyard.

Based on the voids in the courtyard's stone pavement, there had probably been gardens. From where I stood, I could see the twisting riverbed below us. The tourists had gotten to it, of course: there was graffiti everywhere, and some enterprising soul had climbed as high as they could and drawn a cartoon penis with googly eyeballs to watch over it all. None of that took away from the old mission's soul.

"This place was beautiful."

Speedy growled about not being able to focus on *an army of the dead!* and climbed down to the ground. He stalked away in the direction of the camera crew, tail fluffed out in anger.

I began to walk around the ruined courtyard, with no clear idea of what I was doing. There was a dead nun here, and she wanted to make contact—no, she had already made contact—but I couldn't see her.

"What am I doing here?" I muttered aloud.

"I don't know."

I nearly fell flat on my face. Tellerman was sitting a few feet away from me, cut off from my line of sight by a broken wall.

"Jesus!" I snarled. "What the *fuck?!*"

He did that thing with his eyebrows that happens whenever someone thinks I've overreacted. I noticed that his shoes and socks were off, and he was messing around with a packet of blister cream.

There was also some blood. Rephrase: a lot of blood. Too much for a single popped blister.

I sighed. "What happened?"

"Walking." Tellerman seemed embarrassed.

"Do you want me to look at it?"

"No need," he sniffed. "I'm the team's paramedic."

Well, that was new information. Fish had been the one treating my roadrunner injury: I hadn't thought about who held that position when an Army soldier wasn't tagging along.

"Suit yourself," I said, even as I flopped down on a nearby rock to watch. It was a *lot* of blood. I realized he had peeled off multiple pairs of socks: his shoes were at least two sizes too large. "Dude."

"Gotta suffer for the camera," he muttered. "We usually don't do this much walking."

"Why didn't you say something?"

He glared at me. "I thought we'd take the Jeep."

I fixed my eyes on Tellerman's, because otherwise they would have rolled clean out of my head and probably dropped onto the ground, gone forever in a single targeted explosion of sarcasm. "If you had just said something—"

"Forget it," he replied, as he looked away first. "These ruins are probably as much as we're going to find, anyhow."

A sense of relief kicked me in the stomach. "Yeah, probably."

"Yeah." His hand moved to his backpack and rested on a particular bulge in the canvas. If I had to guess, it was the end of a poster tube. I wondered what it would take to get a look at that map. "Tomorrow, we'll cut to the west and start there."

My stomach knotted up in rebellion, and then sucker-punched the sense of relief when its back was turned. "Tomorrow?"

"Unless Mare wants to run the drone all night," he replied, somewhat hopefully, as his hand gave the canvas a little squeeze.

"Doubtful." I nodded to the bag. "Is that the famous map?"

Tellerman snapped his hand back as if I had tried to stab him. "Map?"

I leaned back on the rock and smirked.

Lemme tell you about being married to a former spy.

It's…frustrating. And exhausting. They're trained to notice the smallest detail. I'm not talking about restaurant receipts or suspicious texts. No, they notice things like changes in where you put your purse when you come home from school, and what that might mean about how tired you are.

And then they throw out a leading question.

And then you say something about that jackass in your anatomy class, and three tests a week and it's not even finals, and you're just so tired—

Well. Like hiveminds and personal privacy, this is one of those things that Sparky doesn't even realize he's doing. It's part of him, take it or leave it. I don't like it, but I love him, so I took it.

And learned how to use it.

Which is why Tellerman was squirming like a snake on a leash.

"I don't have to see it myself," I said. "But it might help."

He cracked. "Did Keith tell you?"

"Please," I sniffed, and just happened to choose that moment to play with my wedding ring.

He looked around, decided we were alone, and opened the backpack. The poster tube was high-end, a silvered metal with textured plastic endcaps. He popped an endcap and carefully shook a heavy sheet of material into his open hand. Then, he kicked his wadded-up socks aside, and rolled this out across the ground between us.

The map didn't look like much of a pirate's map. To start, there was no "X" on top of a marked spot. No skull and crossbones. It looked like... It looked like an ordinary map.

"What's the backstory?" I asked.

"Made by an amateur historian and cartographer about eighty years ago," he said. "He claimed to have found an ancient city in the hills."

"A city? Like the ones Fish was talking about on the hike?"

Tellerman nodded. "This cartographer was the real deal," he said, as he tapped the center of the map with a finger. This close, the map seemed to have been drawn on paper, and then coated with celluloid. Early lamination? Nice. "He found the city and made this map. Did it over a couple of trips, so he could be sure of his discovery. But when he finally worked up the courage to bring someone else, the city was gone."

"Gone?" I chuckled. "Right."

"Guy was devastated," Tellerman said. "That city was supposed to be his legacy. Didn't handle it too well. He died in the desert a few years later."

"Sounds like a tall tale," I mused, as I poked at the facts. Ghosts (powerful ghosts, that is) can—and I do *not* exaggerate here—

change mortal minds. Something about the chemicals we use to process and store memories. Before I had met Sparky and settled down, Ben had spent years hiding my...uh...youthful shenanigans...from those who would object. He would blank out tiny parts of their short-term memories, so they would forget about the cause of the fire or the explosions or whatever. If enough ghosts were working together? Yeah, a whole city might disappear. But if that's the case, then there'd have to be an entire *civilization* of ghosts in the desert, and at least a few of them would have to be major players to make it work. An application of Occam's Spectral Razor cut straight to the heart of the matter: a lonely guy with decent penmanship made up a lost city for attention.

"Which is why Keith and I went with the pirate story." Tellerman began to roll up the map. "Makes for a better emotional payload for our established audience."

"But you were hoping for a city?" I grinned at him. "Aw, cute. Someone's trying to go legit."

"Can't hunt ghosts forever," he said, as he gently tapped the map back into the case. "If I can prove I'm a pro with an accidental discovery, then we can write our own ticket. Documentaries, biopics—"

"*Shark Week?*"

"A man can dream," he muttered.

"Why not just pack in the ghost shit and chase the dream?"

"They rely on me," he said, nodding towards the rest of the team. They were still out of earshot, busily exploring the ruins, cameras out and panning around the landscape. "I'm their paycheck. I'm not going to ask them to take a leap of faith until I'm sure I can get us there."

"So this is why you wanted me along," I said. "We found the lost library at Rhodes, and you thought lightning might strike twice." He shrugged, and began to dab at his broken blisters. They were...oozy. Quite painfully oozy. "Dude, you can't walk back with those."

"Can and will," he replied. "And Rhodes was part of it."

"Y'know," I said, "you're a lot nicer when you're not on camera."

He grinned. "Nice guys finish last in the ratings."

"Yeah, but I don't want to murder them, either." I watched as he patched up his blisters. He wasn't half-bad at it. "Can we start over? We'll get further if we're not clawing each other's eyes out."

He looked up from the ooze-fest. "You'll help me find the lost city?"

Oh. *Oh!* If Tellerman thought I was helping him, he'd let me steer him away from the haunted regions of the desert. My sense of relief picked itself up off of the floor and rolled up its sleeves for Round Two. "Yeah," I said. "Let's start over."

Chapter Seventeen

The moonlight did strange things to the desert. The colors of the day washed into stark blacks and whites, with long shadows moving across the ground to match the changes in the night sky. I ran, with the moon before me and the sky at my back, one foot after the other across the hard-packed earth.

Speedy rode in a little harness we had rigged up for jogging. It had a basketball net to cradle his butt, and padded straps across my shoulders so he could dig his claws into something other than my flesh. It also let him act as our lookout: the ground was hard but unfamiliar, and I was worried about floundering straight into a patch of sand. Or a cactus. Or a snake.[17]

He was more interested in keeping watch on our tails. "They're getting closer."

"Catching up?"

"Nope." His weight shifted as he squirmed to look behind us. He was holding the super-bright LED jogging light I used when we went running at night. I usually had it clipped to my belt, but even though the moon had begun to set, it was still bright enough to see, so Speedy was using the beam to measure distance.

"Can you see who they are?"

"If you stop? Yeah."

I grunted and kept on running.

(Since whoever was following us was on our group's ATV, it was probably the Increasingly Kreepy Keith. Mare knew where I was going, and nobody else cared enough to stalk me across the desert after I said I was taking advantage of the cooler night air to go jogging, call me if I'm not back in two hours, come look for me if I'm not back in three.)

Seven miles. They had been following us for seven miles.

17 Sometimes I think this world doesn't like us very much.

"When do we worry?" I asked.

"C'mon, kitten, you should already be worried."

"Great. What do they want?"

It was the tenth time I had asked. Or the twentieth. Or the zillionth. Speedy no longer bothered to tell me to shut up.

The trip to the ruined mission was much faster now that it was just me and Speedy.[18] We figured we could get in a quick chat with the resident ghost before the stranger on the ATV made their presence known. If pressed, we could explain the whole thing away as a midnight jog down a familiar path to a familiar landmark and back again.

After half of forever, that whale's back of stones crested the horizon.

"C'mon, hurry up," Speedy said. "I want to get some sleep."

"There's a roadrunner in your bed and I don't even want to know what's happening in mine," I said. "So we're back in the Jeep anyhow. And fuck you if you think I'm gonna risk breaking a leg out here for your convenience."

He stopped talking. After a few moments, I heard a hitching *zaaa-HURK!* as he dozed.[19]

I kept running.

There's a slow heartbeat in a long jog. It's always there, right beneath your feet, and when you find it, that heartbeat carries you along the ground. You can run forever if you catch it. Sometimes I could; usually I can't.

Tonight, it was me and Speedy and the fading arc of the moon, and a heartbeat that both was and wasn't mine.

The dry riverbed shook me out of that rhythm. The stones were loose here: when the annual rainfall evaporated, it left air pockets in the mud. I scrabbled across the largest stones and poked across flat ground, and my feet still poked into hidden holes every couple of feet. I was glad to make it to the other side: I may have had the OACET hookup and a military helicopter

---

18 There's a gorgeous saying from…someplace I can't remember. If you want to go fast, go alone; if you want to go far, go together; if you want to do both, carry the koala. I added that third part.

19 I've been told by veterinarians, zoologists, biologists, and one heavily flummoxed Australian wildlife rehabilitator that koalas don't snore. They usually don't talk, either.

on standby, but a busted ankle in the middle of nowhere is still a busted ankle in the middle of nowhere.

I came up the riverbank and onto what remained of the mission's plaza. This close, the stones of the tower shone like the bones of a huge broken creature. Whiter than bones. In the moonlight, it was a dragon's graveyard.

Eyes were on me. Lots of them. And that itching sensation was back: the closer I got to the center of the ruins, the more I wanted to remove my skin in self-defense. Scuttling sounds came from the edges of the dark as *things* shifted around us.

A figure was seated on the steps of the old mission. A woman, older than me, and playing games on a cell phone. The light from the screen made her face shine blue in the moonlight.

I coughed in that fake howdy-howdy-howdy-there-are-nonthreatening-strangers-here way.

The woman glanced up at me. Her face looked like any female schoolteacher you can remember from your grade school days: soft around the jowls, maybe a little kind, but definitely unwilling to put up with any of your shit.

Also? It wasn't the light from the screen that made her shine blue.

"Aw, hell," I muttered, and jostled the sleeping koala in his harness with my elbow. "Speedy, wake up. Can you see her?"

"Who—" Speedy stretched, put his forepaws on my head, and peered into the night. "I'm guessing that phone's not floating in midair?"

"Nope." I closed my eyes, and did that thing where I stopped trying to feel the presence of ghosts.

"Stop that," said the woman in familiar unaccented English. "It itches."

Marie de Borromeo.

"This whole *place* itches," I replied.

"It doesn't like you," she said, as she flicked off her phone. "It wants to be left alone."

"Listen, I'll be thrilled to give...uh...it what it wants," I said. I closed the distance between us with careful, cautious steps.

The rocks of the old mission were twisty things. "I'm not here because I want to be. Tell me and I'll get—What?!"

The ghost stood and caught my face with her strong blue fingers, her schoolmarm's stare shooting between my eyes and Speedy's face.

I shoved my hands deep into my pockets and grabbed cloth. *We do not,* I reminded myself, *throw the dead nun across the desert.*

De Borromeo dropped my chin and stepped away. "You're Hope Blackwell," she said, eyes wide.

"Yeah. Hi."

"You're Hope Blackwell!"

I had seen this before. Many, many times. The realization that the person you were talking to is famous, and you aren't, and that forced a hard reboot in what you were about to say because apparently you had to talk to famous people using different words. Usually a lot more of them, most of them unnecessary and made of *ummm...yeah...well...* and a few *I know you're really **really** busy but me and some friends are starting this popup restaurant for kale hotdogs...*

First time I'd ever seen it happen in a ghost, though.

"You're Hope Blackwell, and—" De Borromeo stared at Speedy. "—and that's your koala!"

"He's his own koala. Can we speed this up?"

"Don't be rude." Speedy popped me across the back of my skull with his paw.

"What is with you lately—Fine." I turned towards the dead nun. She was wearing the ghost's version of a velour track suit, with pale blue piping down the sides of each leg. There was an unmistakable Florida retiree vibe to the ensemble. "There are some guys following us. I don't know who they are, but let's assume they'll be trouble. Could you please tell me what you need me to do before they get here?"

The nun's mouth opened and closed. "You were on *The Daily Show* last week," she finally managed. "For the Veterans' Mental Health...Health and..."

"The Veterans' Mental Health and Wellness Project. Good cause."[20] I turned to look for the ATV. Whoever was driving it had parked it about a quarter mile away, and was standing in front of the headlights. Unless there was a second person creeping through the mission's stones, we were safe. "Okay, we've got a little time. Hi."

I took a step towards the nun, hand outstretched. She stared at it, unmoving.

Ah, right. De Borromeo had died hundreds of years ago, when ladies didn't do things like shake hands. But right as I was about to pull my hand away, the nun grabbed it in her own.

There was a flash of energy between us, much stronger than when Fish and I had touched for the first time.

"God *damn* it!" I hissed, and yanked away from her, and tried to rub the sting out on my shorts. The contact hadn't hurt in a conventional way. No, this was the kind of hurt that only a sentient cup of extra-strong espresso could slice into your nerve endings.

The nun fell backwards as if I had punched her. "Never take the Lord's name in vain!"

"Sorry, sorry," I said. "Sorry."

"I will not tolerate blasphemy."

"I get that," I said. "I'm sorry. It's not blasphemy. Not really. It's force of habit more than anything."

"Then it's a filthy habit," the nun said, glaring down the length of her nose at me, which was a real trick considering she was a head shorter that I was. "It shows no honor for our Lord and Savior."

I opened my mouth to say that I wasn't really religious, but closed it with a snap. My usual attitude of, *Well, I'm psychic so I've got complicated thoughts about mortality and theology,* probably wouldn't win over the ghost of a dead nun.

---

20 As if I didn't have enough on my plate, my friend Rachel Peng has been on a frea-kin' rampage about mental health problems in veterans. She asked me to get involved, and she's not someone you can say no to. Besides, fame might be a shit cracker topped with shit cucumbers and a side of fresh-made shit, but people pay attention to causes if someone famous supports them. Might as well use what's bad to build some good into this world, right?

"I'll work on it," I promised. "Could you please tell me why you want me to leave the desert? I'm happy to do that—I just need a little more information so I don't make things worse on the way out. I've got a bunch of folks with me who aren't clued in to the whole ghost thing and they might come back without me."

Marie de Borromeo narrowed her eyes. "You're with *Spooky Solutions*. Of course they know about ghosts."

"Please tell me you're fu—" I chomped down on the word before it could escape. Speedy didn't miss it: he shifted on my shoulders, noticing every move I made. "Please tell me you're messing with me. You know about reality television, right?"

"Of course." She looked insulted. "I don't watch much except talk shows and soap operas," she said. "I think I've watched every show since *Guiding Light*, but the real soap operas are more entertaining."

"Real...soap operas..." The conversation sputtered as I tried to find the best way to tell a many-centuries-dead nun about the misnomer that was reality television. "Hang on, okay? We're having a communication problem. How long have you been here?"

The old ghost shook her head. "I don't know," she said. "I'm just...here, now."

"But why?" I asked. "Why do you stay here?"

She closed one hand in a fist, then swept that fist across the center of her chest. It was an unconscious gesture, and one that I hadn't seen before.

Yay.

Did you know body language can go out of style? I didn't, not until I started hanging out with ghosts. We talk with our bodies. Shrugs and grins and eyerolls and all of that good stuff. Some of it is part of being human, but a lot of it is learned, and the learned stuff can drop out of our lexicon just like spoken slang.

The weirdest thing about body language? Everyone expects you to understand it. They'll translate a strange word for you, no problem, but if you don't know fist-clench-sweep? That's *insulting*. No, I don't know why. It's probably got something to do with cultural attitudes. As a species, we are territorial, clannish assholes. Not understanding a word here or there is a slipup of the mind, no big deal, everybody does it. Failure to understand body language is more intimate, I guess. A denial of the person and their tribe.

So, rather than deny whatever culture had claimed a seventeenth-century Spanish noble-cum-missionary (who apparently consumed ginormous amounts of television with little to no discrimination, but she was stuck out here in the desert so who was I to judge?[21]), I changed the subject.

"Where's Hawley?" I asked.

"The pirate?" De Borromeo waved a hand in a *pay him no mind* gesture that I didn't need help translating. "Sealed and bound, beneath the earth, his body gone and his soul chained."

Lack of an effective rhyme scheme aside, the phrase had the cadence of a litany. I repeated it so Speedy could hear the words, then added, "The story I heard is that you fought his ghost."

"Yes." She gave me that patented nun look, the one that reminded me that my brief stint in parochial school still sat on my nightmare spectrum. "As was my duty."

The generic all-American accent was leaving her voice. A deeper, more honest one was beginning to show as she shucked off decades of convoluted storylines and returned to her roots. The edges of her track suit shimmered and blurred into a dress of old hemlines and lace.

"How did that happen?" I asked.

"He came to those I protected," she said. "I did not understand the desert, not at first. It was not my land, and I failed to hear it. The desert hated me for this, and let Hawley stretch his soul from the rocks. It did this so he could challenge me. Me, Hope Blackwell! If I had not come, he would have remained a wisp."

Oh, goody. She was losing her grammatical contractions. That was never a good sign. I pressed a hand to my forehead,

---

21 And no, I wasn't going to ask how she charged her phone; she was literally made of energy. I was somewhat curious about her service plan, though.

and muttered, "Christ."

"Do *not*—"

"I know. *I know!* I'm sorry!" Both hands against my forehead now; something was wet and sticky. The bandage where the roadrunner had bonked me was soaked through in fresh blood. "I'm trying to figure this out! I don't know what a wisp is, or why you're talking about a sentient desert."

"Deserts belong to themselves," de Borromeo said. She stepped into the night air and rose into the sky. The nun floated across the top of the stones, alighting when she needed to push off and change direction. When she did, the hem on her swirling robes pulled up just enough to show off a pair of all-too-real spotless white Keds. "They've pulled themselves together from scraps and tatters. We come in, all brave, thinking we can cut our way into the land, and we take what it can't afford to give."

"You say '*we*,' like you don't belong."

"I do not."

"But you've been here for…"

"This. Is. *My.* **Duty!**"

The stones of the mission shouted her words back at me, echoes on top of echoes. I felt her rage through my skin. It itched, I guess, if itching were fire ants made from tabasco icicles and were crawling through every nerve ending in my body.

"I felt that," Speedy whispered in my ear. His weight shifted as he turned to watch the white sneakers bob across the rocks. "This is when you shut up. Seriously."

I ignored him: those ants needed to stop before I scratched my own flesh from my bones. "What are you doing?!" I yelled. "I ran miles across the desert to talk to you! I'm here! I want to help! So let me fucking help, Goddamnit!"

"Do not blaspheme!"

"They're. *Just.* **Words!**" I put all of my strength into that shout.

The itching stopped.

Everything stopped.

"Welp, we're boned," Speedy said.

"I think you could learn a lesson in humility," the old nun said.

The desert answered her in a low grumble, and the air around her began to thicken.

"Hey, I'm humble!" I shouted, as shapes began to coalesce around her, glowing in that oh-so-familiar iridescent blue hue. "I'm plenty humble! I'm just angry because I'm trying to help this dead woman and she's being a real cu—"

Speedy's forepaws came from behind to slam over my mouth.

De Borromeo rose into the air, high above the bones of the mission. Beneath her, the ghostly blue shapes were emerging from the aether. They weren't human. They weren't anything close to human. Each of them had huge almond-shaped eyes and four limbs, with long, hooked fingers ending in claws. As they pulled themselves from the stones, they turned lanky, their spines and shoulderblades cutting through their thin fur coats.

Monsters, no doubt about it. Monsters that walked on all fours but kept lifting themselves with their hind legs to test the air with their doglike heads.

They only came up to my waist, but there were *so* many! *Too* many! There couldn't have been a hundred of them. No, couldn't have been. It just felt that way as they took form, each of them tumbling over and under themselves, always touching, making little yipping noises to tell each other where they were...

I'd seen videos of hounds behave in that same way. Whatever else these things were, they were a hunting pack.

"...Speedy?" I whispered, as I took a few slow steps away from the monsters. "Can you see them?"

"Yup." His fur brushed against my cheek as he nodded. I felt him settle himself in his harness. "Dunno what they are."

De Borromeo walked into the center of the pack. The ghostly creatures boiled around her legs. Not like loyal dogs do, no. They didn't even look at the old nun. She might have summoned them, but the monsters were on their own clock.

"Your ghosts," she said. "The ones you know. How do they shape themselves, when they go out in the waking world?"

"Pixies," I said. My mouth was really dry. "Small, harmless pixies."

"Why?"

"Keeps the normals from realizing they saw a ghost," Speedy said to the space where, to him, nothing existed but a pair of white Keds floating in thin air. "Don't do this."

De Borromeo ignored him. "Deserts have their own monsters," she said. "And they do not do *pixies*." She said that word with scorn.

I took another look at the pack of beasts milling around her feet. If I squinted, they looked like coyotes with mange. Otherwise known as—

"Chupacabras," I said.

"Today, yes," she said. "Tomorrow, they might choose another beast. But they always choose one of talons and teeth."

"How—" The taste of vomit rose up in my throat. I swallowed twice and tried again. "They seem awfully powerful. Would I know them?"

"No," she said. "These are old souls, and were here before me. A thousand times a thousand souls have died in this desert in the past four centuries, but another hundred thousand times that died before. These are the strong ones. The ones who choose to fight. They borrow their strength from those who will not."

"Um—" The chupacabras came towards me, clawed feet ticking against the rocks. I started to shuffle across the mission's courtyard.

De Borromeo glared at me with eyes of deep blue night. "Run."

"Can we talk about—" was as far as I got before Speedy dug his claws into the padded straps of his harness and shouted: *"MOVE!"*

I moved.

One jump, as far across the stones as my legs could carry us. It put a big gap between me and de Borromeo's horde of blue monsters; I would have turned to try and talk to De Borromeo again, but Speedy yelled: ***"DON'T STOP DON'T STOP!"***

Down the stones, as fast as I could go. Falling when I could. Sliding and jumping when I couldn't fall. Climbing when none of those were safe. Speedy shot profanities like cannon shells.

Beneath this, the unearthly sounds of chupacabras as they began their hunt.

I hit the desert floor. Solid, welcoming ground came up fast and smashed against my hands and knees, or maybe it was the other way around, I couldn't tell, I was moving too fast to be sure. The ground sped up beneath me, and I took off towards the silver line of the moon on the horizon.

"Run, Hope Blackwell," the dead nun called after us. "Run and find your penance."

Chapter Eighteen

And now we've come full circle. Me, running across the Sonoran Desert, a superintelligent koala on my back and a horde of undead chupacabras hot at my heels.

Have I mentioned the ghost of Thomas Paine can go fuck himself?[22]

A bat out of hell couldn't move faster than me. Sadly, I was learning that chupacabras are a darned sight faster than bats, hell-bent or otherwise. There was a full chamber orchestra of panting and snarling behind me, and they were turning up the tempo.

Faster. *Faster!*

My boots hit the ground, puffs of dry earth rising up at each step. The chupacabras drummed across the desert, and I lost the sound of them as my heart began pounding in my ears.

"Speedy?"

He twisted just enough to look behind us, not enough to throw me off of my stride. "Still coming!" he yelled. *"GO!"*

"Stop screaming in my ear!" I yelled back. As I did, I turned my head to see a wave of blue crashing down at my heels, fangs and claws outstretched.

I went.

I could swear I felt their breath against my skin—

A set of claws (or maybe teeth?) touched the back of my leg. I gasped, and Speedy?

He **ROARED!**

---

22 Okay, fine! Never let it be said that I can't learn from experience. So, no, the ghost of Thomas Paine should not go fuck himself, because wishing such a thing on another person would be rude. Instead, let's say I would not be too angry if circumstances align themselves so the ghost of Thomas Paine is forced to undergo a severe audit by the IRS, dating aaaaall the way back to before he fled to France, and held responsible for compounded interest.

(…and then he should go fuck himself.)

Whatever the chupacabras had expected from this mad sprint across the desert? An angry male Queensland koala was not it. Speedy's speaking voice is deep and smooth, but his roar is that of a rubber squeaky toy that's been raised on raw meat and steroids.[23] It's a wild sound, a territorial bellow to warn all challengers that he's from *Australia* and *he eats death for breakfast!*

The chupacabras fell behind.

Speedy watched them for a few minutes. "They're not closing the distance," he said. "Try slowing down."

"Um—"

"Just do it," he snapped. "You can't keep up this pace all the way back to camp."

He was right. My legs and sides were on fire, and my mouth was as dry as the ground. I dropped down to a fast jog for a few steps, then started sprinting again.

"What happened?" I gasped.

"You can slow down," he said. "They're chasing us, but they're not trying to catch us."

I did, happily. Speedy was silent: the chupacabras weren't, but their savage teeth-gnashing chatter didn't get any louder.

"Why aren't they trying to catch us?" I said.

"I'm thinking," he said. "Did the nun say anything to you?"

"Lots." My water bottle bounced against my thigh. Water. So close. "Think I can I stop for a drink?"

A snarl came from the lead chupacabra.

"Don't push it," Speedy said.

I would have nodded, but that took energy. Instead, I just kept going. My body gradually reset itself from sprint mode to jogging mode, which helped with the everything-is-on-*fire!* sensations, but I had no clue where the camp was, or even if I was headed in the right direction. My feet became the low drone of distance running, and I tried to find that elusive sweet spot that opened into a runner's high (Which I can almost never reach anyhow, and I bet can never be done when chupacabras

---

23 It's more of a honk mixed with a donkey's bray, actually, but it sounds as though it's made by an animal ten times his size, so I call it a roar for dignity's sake.

are chasing you. Go figure.). Every couple of minutes, Speedy would tap my head and I'd veer in that direction.

It could have been minutes or hours later that I realized I had lost track of the ATV. "Where's the—"

"At your eight," Speedy said.

A quick glance over my left shoulder and, yeah, there it was. Keeping pace with me as much as the chupacabras.

"I'm getting tired of these guys," I said. I was just getting tired in general, to be honest. Jogging is one thing. Running miles and miles through a desert with a koala on your back and chupacabras at your heels is another.

"Yeah, well," Speedy said, and I felt his weight shift as he turned to look at the monsters behind us. "Suck it up unless you want to test their sweet and generous natures."

I turned towards the ATV.

"Hey!" Speedy shouted. "You're not gonna catch 'em, and camp's the other way! We need to get to other people!"

"They're the closest people around," I said, and tried to put on more speed. The ATV changed course and veered away. "Son of a—"

"They saw our light moving towards them!" Speedy said. "They don't want to get caught!"

"Let's wreck that plan," I said. I fumbled around my belt until I found the jogging lamp, and tried to toggle it off. Instead, I dropped the damned thing.

"Son of a—" I almost stopped to pick it up, but the chupacabras snarled and snapped, and I consigned that jogging light to whatever fate would have it. As we moved beyond its range, the light changed from that familiar warm golden white of LEDs to an unearthly ghostly blue that shot out across the desert in all directions. The edges of the desert were thrown into almost unholy clarity—that chupacabra-cast light was so pure it sparkled where it bumped up against objects. Weird, yes, but definitely enough to avoid running into anything pointy or venomous. "Can you see that?" I asked.

"What, the chupacabra rave party?" he snapped. "Yeah. Yeah,

I can see that!"

"Think they can?" I nodded towards the ATV.

"How the fuck should I know?!"

As Speedy swore, the chupacabras snarled and closed the distance.

"God damn it!" I shouted. There was an immediate answering roar from the pack, and their breath began to hit the back of my calves again. "Okay, *fine!*" I yelled over my shoulder. "I *get* it! I will *work* on it!"

It might have been my imagination, but it seemed as if the pack dropped back. Just a little.

"What's happening?" Speedy asked. "Something about swearing, obviously, but what else?"

"Penance!" I shouted. "That fu—argh! That delightful nun is making us do penance for our sins, and swearing is on the list!"

"Ah! Gotcha!" Speedy turned towards the chupacabras, took a deep breath, and began hurling...blessings.[24]

I don't remember most of them. I do remember the following:

"Praise be to Saint Christopher for bringing you into our lives! We are so fortunate to be run to exhaustion and therefore murdered in cold blood by such illustrious beings!"

"May the year and the day of mourning you will undergo for causing our untimely deaths pass without gathering additional sorrows!"

"The grace of God, gods, and the godliest be upon thee, o monsters who do the bidding of a woman who wants us to attach meaning to the generally arbitrary use of words!"

It was a shouted execution of poetry, flowers, and scorn. Every time I snuck a peek at the chupacabras, they were either eyes-wide at Speedy or had their heads together in growly

24 If you've ever wondered if the pen is truly mightier than the sword, I can lend you a superintelligent koala.

conversation. They had forgotten me entirely; I slowed down to a fast walk, and they did the same.

The ATV was dead ahead. It had stopped when I had dropped my light, and a single figure was standing in its headlights, looking towards the stationary speck of gold as if they thought they could find me in the dark. Which they could not do with the lights on and the motor running, the dumbass.

Sorry. Dumb bunny.

I swung around to the side and—

"Keith," I whispered. There he was in profile. The cameraman had a honking big camera rig draped over his shoulders. He'd hold the viewfinder to his eyes, drop the entire setup down to futz with it, then hold it up again. "What's he doing out here?"

"Looking for you," Speedy said.

I dropped into a hollow in the ground, turned to the horde, and whispered, "*Stop!*"

The chupacabras froze. There was some grumbling among them, but I guess whatever terms de Borromeo had set for our penance had been reached.

My shoulders were suddenly unencumbered by koala. Speedy scuttled up the side of the hollow and perched on the edge. We watched as Keith manhandled his camera. We could hear him talking to himself, but the words got lost in the distance: to me, at least; Speedy's ears flattened against his head.

"What's he saying?" I asked.

"Nothing that needs repeating."

"I'm getting tired of this guy," I said. "He's always lurking in the bushes. Sometimes literally. What's he working on?"

"Thermal camera," Speedy said. "Looks like it's busted."

We watched Keith dick around with his equipment. A smallish chupacabra came up and propped its forepaws on the side of the hollow to watch with us.

Speedy and I glanced at each other, and then at the chupacabra.

"Y'all want to have some fun?" I asked the chupacabra.

The small chupacabra returned to the pack. There was more grumbling, and the pack twisted over itself in blue waves, teeth and claws flashing as they talked among themselves. Finally, the small one turned from the others and nodded at me.

It took us a few minutes to get set up. There were language barriers (apparently only a few of the ghosts were fluent in English—they had slowed down while chasing us so they could translate Speedy's backhanded curses for the others), and one or two of the chupacabras objected to being ridden like bony ponies. And, as Speedy objected to riding on said bony ponies, the plan changed from *Midnight Chupacabra Rodeo!* to *Rattle the Jerk.*

The small one was their leader. She[25] nipped and pushed the others into formation, darting back and forth across the line. Of all of them, she seemed the most comfortable in her skin; her pointed ears moved in the direction of sound, and her tail lashed like she used it for balance instead of decoration. I had the feeling she may have been behind the majority of chupacabra sightings in the region. Hell, maybe she was the sole cause of all chupacabra sightings.

When we were set up and good to go, I took a runner's crouch at one end of the line, the small chupacabra on the other. We looked at each other, and I held up five fingers for the countdown.

Five,
four,
three,
two,
one…

Lemme tell you why ghosts walk around in monstersuits when they're out in public.[26]

It's not because they're more comfortable in skins other than their own; I can't imagine shrinking yourself down to the size of a fat Cornish pixy is much fun, either. It's because they respect the barrier between the living and the dead. Most living

25 At the time, I had no evidence she thought of herself as female, as none of them ever broke character and I made special effort to not go looking for chupacabra beans and franks. Or, alternatively, fish tacos. Still, "she" was plastered against the walls of my mind.

26 The normal reason, anyhow. That minotaur was nothing close to normal.

people can see ghosts. You've probably seen them yourself. It's a sometimes thing—ninety-nine times out of a hundred that ghost will walk right past, and you'll never know it's there. That hundredth time? You're going to think you've seen a leprechaun instead of a dead person. Which is the method behind that madness. Isn't your average drinking buddy more likely to believe you if you tell them you've seen a human ghost instead of a bright blue elephant?

I don't know what makes it so living folks can see ghosts sometimes and other times not, but stress and adrenaline seem to be involved. I *want* to know, though! I *want* to know why I'm a giant freaky oddball and they aren't. But it's not the kind of thing that bends to the scientific method, you know?

Usually.

Now, in this particular situation, we had a man whose livelihood was based on manufacturing ghost sightings for ratings in a subgenre of reality television that's generally considered a joke. Could you pick a safer subject to test the average person's reaction to ghosts?

Me neither.

...go!

The pack surged forward, roaring and howling, and Speedy and I cut left to come at Keith from behind.

The chupacabras swirled around the ATV. They broke over it in waves, brushing against it as they passed.

Keith ignored them.

The horde swept back in a second pass. This time, they hit the ATV hard enough to rock it.

Keith glanced up as the light from the headlights wobbled, took a quick look around, and then dropped his attention back to his camera.

"Um..." I began.

"He lives in California," Speedy said.

"...um...?"

The koala rolled his eyes. "Earthquake zone?"

"Oh. Right."

The small chupacabra swept back towards us, the rest of the horde in her wake.

"Take out the vehicle," Speedy said to her.

"What?!" There's a very good reason I should never ever *ever* do covert work, and it's me. Keith heard me shouting over the noise of the engine; his head popped up and he started scouting the vicinity. He didn't see the horde bearing down on him. Not even when they started dismantling the ATV like animatronic woodchippers.

Turns out that chupacabras are highly efficient at destruction. They zipped across the smooth planes of the ATV, peeling long strips of metal and rubber as they went. I don't know how: they didn't use their mouth or their claws, but as they zoomed past, they took pieces of the machine with them.

Keith had finally noticed that something weird was happening. So, yay for Keith, oblivious except when physical objects began to rip themselves apart before his eyes.

"What the fuck—" he started to say, as the small chupacabra turned to growl at him.

Speedy hopped up on my back and smacked the side of my head. "Go!" he said. "Look scared and play dumb!"

Sometimes it takes me a while to catch on to Speedy's plans, but looking scared and playing dumb?

Nailed it.

I stumbled out of the dark, into the glow of the ATV's remaining working headlight.

"Help!" I shouted. "Something's out here!"

Keith looked relieved to see me. "What's happening?" he asked. "Something destroyed the ATV! Something…I think it's invisible!"

"Keith? Is that you?" Speedy's deep voice was innocent of all possible wrongdoing. Newborn unicorns didn't have a voice that pure.

"Something bumped against my legs!" I cried. "It broke my jogging light, so I came to the nearest…Keith? It is you! What are you doing out here?"

The chupacabras made another pass over the ATV. This time, a tire shredded in their wake.

"What's happening?" I was flapping my hands in panic. "Keith, why are you here? *Are you doing this?!*"

"What? No!" He was still wrestling with the camera. "If I can just get this on...fuck it!" The camera was tossed aside, and Keith kicked pieces of the ATV apart until he found a heavy black case with a glass window. He popped it open and (surprise!) there was another camera. He powered this up and swung it around. "Night vision didn't work, but I've got low-light settings—"

The small chupacabra hit Keith in the stomach. He gasped and dropped the camera, then followed it to the ground. He clawed his way over to me and grabbed my legs.

"Okay, that's enough," I said, as I tried to gently shake him off.

"This is proof!" he gasped. "The supernatural...you saw what just happened!"

"I can't see anything!"

"You're my witness!" Keith's hands were getting a little high on my thighs; Speedy accidentally-on-purpose stuck a claw in the soft skin between Keith's thumb and fingers and *twisted*. The cameraman scrabbled away from the two of us.

"I will never tell anyone about this," I said. "Never!"

"Like hell you won't!"

"Why are you *here?*" I shouted the last word. "Why were you following us?"

Somehow, the question pushed the fear out of Keith. Despite all of the weirdness trying to swallow him, his face went blank.

Yup, we were still in trouble.

Chapter Nineteen

EXT. DESERT, NIGHT. The moon is setting. It is dark. HOPE, KEITH, and KOALA are standing around a wrecked ATV.

Shot of KOALA'S claws in closeup, followed by out-of-focus movement. The camera finally stabilizes on KEITH'S face.

KEITH (angrily): Hey! Put that down!

KEITH tries to kick KOALA. HOPE does judo to KEITH.

HOPE (angrily): Don't you **dare** hurt him!

KOALA (off-camera): Easy, kitten, I'm fine.

HOPE releases KEITH.

KOALA (off-camera): Tell her why you're following us. Filming us too, right?

KEITH (quickly): It's nothing bad!

KOALA (off-camera): Guy makes extra money selling behind-the-scenes footage. Action shots of Oshea and Dina. Probably Tellerman, since he's the frontman of this operation. Niche market for hardcore fans and perverts. This is your big payday—me, an OACET Agent, and Psycho Judo Killer here? You followed us tonight to get some extra footage for the sickos.

KEITH: No! I…we were worried about you going out alone, so we decided I should follow you!

HOPE (angrily): You asshole!

HOPE (quickly, to no one): Sorry, sorry! I'm working on it. But you gotta admit, that's a…a bad thing to do.

KEITH: You've got no proof—

KOALA (off-camera): You really want to double down on this? The head of OACET is her husband. If you've uploaded anything from here to your servers—

KEITH: You can't do that! I'm a private citizen!

HOPE (to KEITH): So we'll go to Tellerman first. Let him know you've gone moonlighting with his shirtless shots. Bet he'll give Mare access to everything you've uploaded. Oh, the twins are gonna kick your butts—

HOPE (quickly, to no one): Hey! Nobody born in this century considers butts a bad word! Get with the millennium!

KEITH (to HOPE): Are you okay?

KOALA (off-camera): We are. You won't be. Not unless you play ball.

HOPE (to KOALA): Ah, it's blackmail! Nice.

KOALA (to HOPE): Good God, you're slow—

KOALA (quickly, to no one): Shut up! I'm not playing that game anymore.

KOALA (to KEITH): Let's get down to business. You're ours now.

HOPE (to KEITH): Your side projects stop. You take down everything you're selling, and you never post anything new again.

KEITH: Okay, fine. Just don't tell them, okay? They'll make sure I'm kicked out of the union.

HOPE: There's a union for ghostbuster reality television?

KOALA (off-camera): Production crews. Try to keep up.

HOPE (to KEITH): And yeah, we're still gonna tell them how big of a creep you are.

The camera jostles as it is placed on its side. The KOALA steps into the shot to stand beside HOPE.

KOALA (to HOPE): No, we won't. Do I have to explain how blackmail works?

HOPE (to KOALA): Morality, remember?

KOALA (to HOPE): Again?

HOPE (to KOALA): Morality's not a one-time thing.

KOALA (to HOPE): How do you humans get anything done?

KEITH (to BOTH): Can I go?

BOTH (to KEITH): **Shut up.**

HOPE (to KOALA): Any reason he can't leave?

KOALA (to HOPE): Nope. He knows he's good and caught.

KOALA (to KEITH): Don't you, bucko?

KEITH nods.

HOPE (to KEITH): Okay, Captain Creepy, take off. I'm gonna call Mare as soon as you're gone, so don't think about ditching us or chewing up some lies.

KEITH'S shoulders slump. He turns to the ATV. The engine grinds, but refuses to start.

HOPE (chuckling): Looks like you're walking back with us, bucko.

KEITH (to HOPE): Who are you waving at?

KOALA: Shut up and start moving, jackass.

KOALA jumps and grabs at his own tail.

KOALA (to no one): All right! We'll work on it, all right? Cut it out!

Chapter Twenty

Yes, we were definitely still in trouble.

On the way back to camp, I had thought that Keith's chicanery would have shifted the balance of the team's working relationship. And it probably would have, too, if it wasn't for the wrecked ATV. Speedy and I learned, too late, that Keith had begun uploading the video to the servers when the chupacabras started to tear the vehicle apart, and by the time we reached camp? Everybody had seen enough camera footage to know the vehicle had been torn apart by invisible *somethings*. By the time Mare (and Fish) had been woken by the excited cheers from outside their shelter, Tellerman was dancing with joy.

"Proof!" he said, as Keith, Speedy, and I walked into camp. "Proof of the supernatural!"

I glanced over my shoulder to glare at the koala.

"Probably fifteen seconds of blur, followed by Keith's confessional," Speedy muttered. "As soon as the adrenaline high wears off, they'll focus on that part of the video."

(To be honest, I wasn't sure if it would take that long; the twins were staring bloody murder at Keith.)

"I think we should just go," I said, pointing at the cameraman. "After what just happened, I don't want to work with him anymore."

"We're not leaving," Tellerman said as he replayed the footage again. Speedy was right; I saw nothing but a dark blurry mess. Tellerman, however, had a professional's eye for spectral flimflam. He pulled Keith aside, and whispered: "This is brilliant! How did you do this?"

Keith was a sharp cookie. He glanced at me, and then said: "Wirework. We staged the whole thing for ratings."

"Liar!" The word found its way out of my mouth.

"So you *will* talk about what happened?" Keith grinned, twisting the knife.

Well, then. I was caught between a rock and a hard place, and if the rock was Keith's side hustle and the hard place was not fessing up to the involvement of the supernatural, I was just going to have to crash face-first into the rock.

I glared at Keith again, and stomped off in the direction of the showers.

The water was hot, and I had to force myself to keep from sitting on the floor, mouth open, sucking down every drop. No, it was a fast in-and-out, with just enough water spent to sluice the suds off.

I wondered where the used water went. Was it recycled? Caught in a basin and lightly filtered so we could reuse it again? Or was the desert below the shower sucking it up, along with the soap bubbles and our enzymes and proteins and shed cells and—

I decided I didn't want to know where the water went.

When I was done and dressed, I opened the exterior door and found Mare waiting for me.

"C'mon," she said, and took me back to our shelter. Fish wasn't there, and neither was the roadrunner; Speedy was stretched out across the foot of her bed, snoring. "He told me what happened.

"I'm sorry," she continued. "You haven't had a full night's sleep since I showed up at your house. You're exhausted—you could have been seriously hurt tonight! And..." Mare gestured towards our shelter, which, while extremely tidy, had the lingering stink of sex in the air. "I've been selfish. I'm really sorry."

"It's fine," I said, as my eyes locked on my bed.

A bed.

A real bed!

"It's not," Mare said. She started to poke me in my kidneys, very lightly, and I moved towards the bed like an obedient sheep. "You were right. If ghosts are just people, that's the scary part…" she sighed, deep enough to cause my own lungs to ache in sympathy, "…because it's really easy to forget how to be a decent human being."

"Mare—"

"You can tell me I'm a good person in the morning," she said. We had reached the bed. I was somehow prone; she was tucking me in beneath a set of clean white sheets. "Right now, you're going to get some sleep.

"And we've only got one day left here, not two," she added, as she placed a large bottle of water on my pillow, just in case. "That ATV was military property. I got Tellerman to agree to cut the trip short, as long as we'll help him with a special project of his tomorrow. We'll still have three full days in Vegas by the pool."

Was I going to argue with the organizational expert? No. No, I was not.

I conked out.

Chapter Twenty-One

It was a city street in broad daylight. Errand day. Grocery shopping (again) because I had married a giant who ate everything that stood still and contained calories. I had plastic bags draped around both arms because I had forgotten the reusable bags (again), and I was wandering up and down the street because I had also forgotten where I had parked (again).

"Oh, I do not want to do this *again*," I snapped.

The nightmare froze in place. The four men stood, leering at me, their knives out. I took the reins of the dream in my hands, and was about to jerk them sideways into a more pleasant place when a woman spoke from behind me.

"Where's this?"

It was Marie de Borromeo's voice. Her flat Midwestern voice, not the one which was nine-tenths anger and accents and lacked any semblance of a contraction. I turned to see the old nun standing there in her velour track suit and white Keds.

"Why are you here?" I snapped. "I thought I had wards or some shit."

She winced at the swear word, but her voice didn't change. "They're down. I think you're overtired."

"And this is helping?" I threw out my arms to take in the frozen nightmare. "No. Lemme change this to a mattress store, and I'll see you in the morning."

"Wait." The nun held up her hands. Yay, she was sticking with body language I could recognize. "Not yet. I'm here to apologize."

"Apology accepted," I said. "I've already added 'Chased by Horde of Chupacabras' to my résumé. We're cool. Good night."

The dead nun simply stared at me.

I...

Look, she was a nun, okay?

"Fine," I said, as I sat on the cracked pavement of the dreamscape. "Talk."

De Borromeo carefully shuffled her way between the men holding the knives, and sat across from me. She kept sneaking glances at a man with a gold tooth. "What happened here?"

"Not this," I said. "I don't want to talk about *this*." I tugged on the dream and pulled it around me like a favorite chilly-day sweater. The landscape twisted and became the penthouse at the Bellagio. I hadn't been there long enough to nail down all of the details, so some of it jiggled around the edges. Like the patterned carpets. The nun blinked at them and looked up at the ceiling instead, which was (in my memory) plain white and less headache-inducing.

I moved myself to the couch so I could sit in the same spot where I had been when Mare and I had had our little heart-to-heart about ghosts. I remembered more about the penthouse from this perspective: the details began to pencil themselves in.

"You're good at this," de Borromeo said.

"Been practicing lucid dreaming since Helen of Sparta hijacked my brain last year," I said, pouring myself a large glass of tequila from a convenient bottle. I poured a second glass for the ghost, and added a few ice cubes to chill it. "I won't let that happen again."

"I don't know who that is."

I didn't say anything, but I pushed the second glass across the table for her.

De Borromeo moved around the dream furniture and sat on a plush loveseat. She balanced herself on the edge of the loveseat, as if testing the validity of upholstery. Then, she fell back into the cushions with a delighted sigh. "Wonderful!"

"You never leave the desert?" I asked.

"*Jorguín* are bound to the land which holds their bones," she replied, as she took a tentative sip of tequila. Apparently it was to her liking; she followed it with several good, long swallows. "Wonderful stuff, this. Yes, I knew when I came to America that I would stay where I died. I loved the Cahuilla and was prepared to guard them for eternity, but..."

"But the Cahuilla moved on," I said.

She closed her eyes. "That is the softest way to describe their fate."

I decided to change the topic from genocide and forced resettlement. "What's a horgan?"

Her eyes opened in surprise. "You and I, Hope Blackwell. We are *jorguín*, like our parents before us, and their parents before them, and on and on, for as long as our blood heeds the call."

"Ah," I said. "Psychics. But you're wrong—my parents weren't...uh...*jorguín*."

De Borromeo's jaw dropped. "Oh," she said. Then, as things clicked: *"Oh!"*

"Yup." I raised my glass in a false toast. "What I don't know might fill books. I've got a few questions for you."

"Oh," she repeated. She looked completely lost and somewhat frantic, as if she had adopted what she thought to be a muddy puppy but a bath had turned it into a giant wharf rat. "I... I cannot answer them. Jorguín can only speak freely to each other."

"Of course you can answer them," I said. The sense of bone-deep exhaustion that had been chasing me for days was getting harder to ignore. But there was a ghost in my dreams (again) and there was no way in hell I was letting myself rest until she was gone. "I mean, you just said I was one, so...?"

"If you are not born to *jorguín*, you are not *jorguín*." That old-timey accent was coming back, and she was sitting a little taller within the puffs of the seat cushions.

"Fine," I said.

(It wasn't fine. Not by a million miles of long shots. However, shouting at de Borromeo until she summoned the horde of chupacabras again? That was... No. I needed some real sleep, and that was more of a priority at the moment than answers or hurt feelings.)

The nun stared at me over her glass of tequila.

"I'm tired," I said. "Really tired, and time is strange in lucid dreams so I might be throwing away the entire night in here with you. Could you please leave?"

De Borromeo set down her glass. "Yes," she said. "But… please. I would like to say I'm sorry for how I acted. You did the courtesy of coming to talk to me, and I was a… I was a *shitty* hostess."

The naughty word twisted in her mouth. I grinned at her; I couldn't help it. She smiled back, almost shyly. Her face crinkled up in well-worn lines, like smiling came easier to her than anything else in the world.

Damn, I think I liked her.

"Apology accepted," I said. "Seriously."

"Thank you."

But she didn't leave.

Oh, right. Business before slumber. "Tomorrow I'll come out, real early, and we can talk over what I need to do to keep those…uh, those *things*…from waking up."

The ghost's mouth opened and closed a few times as she tried to find the right words.

"Oh no," I sighed. "Don't tell me."

She did that clench-fist-cross-body hand gesture again. From context, I guessed it meant, "Yeah, we're dealing with this now," or something similar.

"What are they?" My voice was hollow from exhaustion.

"The angry dead," de Borromeo said. She sounded angry, too. "Those who should have moved on but have let themselves become lost. They're caught between Heaven and Hell, and give an empty land its voice."

"Should you be talking to me about this?" I asked. Not eagerly, no. Certainly not. "I mean, I'm not…*jorguín* or anything. Don't want you to overstep."

"I'm not," she said. "These ideas are my own. I can talk about them as I want."

"Goodie," I sighed. "What happens now?"

"You must put them back to sleep," she said. "I'll do what I can to help."

"The people I'm with are looking for Hawley," I said. "Y'know, that pirate you fought? Is he awake, too? The camera crew's been broadcasting this live. That's got to have given him a nice power boost. I don't really want to fight an evil bloodthirsty pirate ghost."

"No." She sounded firm. "I bound him myself. It would take another force as powerful as a *jorguín* to release him."

I waved at her.

"Perhaps…" The nun looked brutally embarrassed. "Perhaps I should have said that the powerful force would need to know *how* to unbind him."

"Thanks," I muttered. "How do we put the angry dead back to sleep?"

"You fight them, and best them. I shall bind them, as is my purpose."

Of course. "Is there another way? I don't want to fight them."

"What?" She sat up, shocked. "But…you're Hope Blackwell! That's what you do!"

"Did you hear the news? How I was kidnapped?" I said. When de Borromeo nodded, I rolled up my sleeve. The scar on my left arm was too fresh to have burned its way into my subconscious image of myself, so I concentrated until it appeared. "I got attacked twice. Different dudes, both times.

"Both times, they did it to get to my husband through me," I said. "The first time, they wanted me to snap and fight back— they *counted* on it! Me going crazy and beating them down, down, fighting back…until I got myself killed in front of him.

"The second time…" I paused while I ran the glass of tequila along the scar. "The second time was different."

"How?"

I tugged my sleeve back down. The scar stayed; I knew it'd be there for the rest of forever now, even in my dreams. "They just wanted me dead," I replied. "So, maybe don't assume that I want to fight these ghosts, okay? Maybe I'm done with that."

"Then you should leave, right now," de Borromeo said. "As

soon as possible. I'll try and keep the desert quiet until the angry dead fall back to sleep."

"I'm a shi—terrible psychic," I said. I glanced down at the bottle of tequila. The liquid was rocking back and forth, as if the building was caught in a minor earthquake. The edges of the dream were fraying. "Are you sure I'm the one who woke them up?"

"What else could it be?"

What else, indeed. Maybe a viral internet hit which pumped up the name recognition of a dead pirate?

"Leaving might not be the best idea," I said. "Not if it means you're stuck with the angry dead."

"I'll manage." De Borromeo looked incredibly sad.

Wonderful. I'd disappointed a nun.

"And Hawley?" I asked. "Are you completely, positively, one-hundred-percent sure that he's still asleep?"

She couldn't meet my eyes.

"Oh, this is just spectacular," I groaned.

In the bottle, the tequila started to flip around in tiny waves. I heard a distant voice shouting "Kitten! I'm gonna start biting!"

I nearly swore in frustration. Instead, I ordered de Borromeo to leave. "Out," I said, and dissolved the hotel suite around us. We stood in a white featureless space with our feet flat upon nothing. "Hurry. You don't want to get stuck in here. My brain's a dumpster fire."

She opened her mouth, but the white space around us began to crack. De Borromeo vanished as a giant black nose dropped into my awareness.

"Fuck," I muttered, as the gray area around the black nose resolved itself into a koala's face.

"Yeah," Speedy said. "Get up. Fish is missing and Mare's freaking out."

Chapter Twenty-Two

"We were asleep in the Jeep. He said he was going to the bathroom..." Mare was clutching her hair. She had braided it into a thick red rope, and the way she was yanking on it meant it was in danger of being torn from her head. "Hope, it's been twenty minutes, and he wasn't wearing anything, and—"

"Hold up." I put my hands on her shoulders. "Are you sure he didn't go for a walk?"

Her eyes were huge and green. "Yes," she said. "He put on his pants and boots, but nothing else. You know how he doesn't go anywhere in the desert without a compass!"

I didn't, but I'd take her word on it. I glanced at the window; there wasn't any light creeping around the shade yet, so it was still night. God, I was tired! "Have you gone out-of-body?"

OACET Agents could communicate using electromagnetic fields, and this included projecting a digital avatar of themselves into different locations. If Mare wanted to, she could act as her own drone, flying above the camp to search for Fish.

She nodded. "I did, but I started looking only after I knew something was wrong. He was...I didn't see him. I didn't see anything."

I looked at Speedy. He did his rolling-shoulder koala shrug, which I felt more than saw in the dim light. "I was sleeping," he said.

Damn. "Okay..." I said, pressing the backs of my hands against my eyes. "...okay. Okay. Let's wake up the crew and start searching."

Mare glared at me. I peered around her; through the open door of our shelter, I saw flashlights bobbing around.

"She wanted you to sleep as long as possible, dumbass," Speedy snapped.

"God, I'm tired," I muttered.

Speedy and I followed Mare out to the Jeep. When my feet touched the ground, everything tipped sideways. I grabbed at the side of the Jeep and steadied myself before we joined the others.

No one was shouting Fish's name. Not yet. If we got to that point, it meant it was a real crisis. For the time being, we could pretend Mare was overreacting.

"Here!" Dina called. She was standing several hundred feet away from the perimeter of the camp, the beam of her flashlight painting the desert around her. Oshea was the first to reach her. The twins put their heads together, then looked up as Speedy and I reached them.

"Tire tracks," Oshea said, pointing first at the ground, then towards the northwest. "These aren't from one of our vehicles, and they're fresh."

Tellerman stumbled to a stop behind us. "How could you know that?" he asked.

"Different patterns," Dina said. "All of our tires are designed for off-road traction. These treads look smooth. And over here…"

She panned her flashlight to her left. I didn't see anything at first, but Speedy slid to the ground and sprinted over to a spot of scuffed-up dirt. He sniffed at the dusty desert turf like a dog, quick inhales followed by a hard *puff!* on the exhale.

"Blood," he said, pointing one claw towards the ground.

Mare gasped.

"Shut it," he said, still snuffling around. "At worst, it's barely enough blood for a nosebleed."

"But if he's bleeding—"

"I can't tell you anything else," he said. "My sense of smell is nearly as bad as yours, monkeygenes. I can pick up fresh blood on dry dirt and that's it."

"So it might not even be Fish's blood," I said, mostly for Mare's benefit.

"But it might be!" Tellerman was in theater mode. I shut

my eyes and refused to acknowledge the camera that was (undoubtedly) just behind me.

Mare wasn't so forgiving. She pulled herself up to her full height, tossed her hair over her shoulder, and stared straight at the camera. "Turn it off."

Keith gave a nervous giggle—woe is he who confronts a furious Mare through a viewfinder—and tried to scurry out of her way.

(Hell, even I took a couple of steps to the side to clear a wrath-path.)

"Keep rolling," Tellerman said. "Agent Mur—"

Mare turned towards Tellerman so quickly that her hair cracked behind her. "I know I signed a contract," she said. "This is no longer entertainment. Someone might be in danger. I'm calling upon your basic human decency to put the cameras and the drama aside, and focus on finding him."

"Nice," Speedy chuckled wickedly. "Your call, asshole."

Tellerman's attention cut to me.

"Do it," I mouthed.

He gave me a very small nod. "Keith? Shut it down."

Keith recoiled as if Tellerman had slapped him. "Are you serious? This is gold!"

"They're right," Tellerman said. "Fish might be hurt."

Mare stared at him before nodding slowly. "Thank you for confirming your true character, Mr. Tellerman," she said, before scooping up Speedy and moving towards the nearest Jeep.

"Didja get that on film?" I asked Keith.

The two men ignored me. "Where's she going?" Tellerman asked. "I've got the keys."

The Jeep's engine burst into life. "Cyborg," I reminded them. "Even a Jeep has an autostart feature these days."

"Hope, go back to bed. Dina? Oshea?" Mare called. "Can I borrow you for an hour or two?"

The twins ran towards Mare, and hopped into the Jeep. The three of them drove off, slowly, following (what I guessed were) the tire tracks.

Tellerman swore, and sprinted towards the other Jeep. Keith followed.

Me?

I weighed sleep against the need to find Fish. Bed nearly won, but…

I grabbed Speedy, ran after Tellerman and Keith, and swung aboard the Jeep as Tellerman began to chase after Mare's taillights.

Into the desert we went.

Driving north and west.

We kept going. Slowly, because Mare was leading the way, and Mare is anything but an idiot. We probably could have made better time walking. The Jeep rocked back and forth, back and forth, back and forth…

…the man with the gold tooth was back. He leered at me…

I jerked awake and rubbed my face so hard that I felt the roadrunner wound crack open beneath the bandages.

Speedy glanced up at me. "You shoulda stayed at camp," he said quietly.

"I'm just a little tired," I replied. I leaned forward and poked Tellerman, who was driving. "Got any coffee?" Tellerman nodded to Keith, who rummaged through a camera bag and came up with a small bottle of pills. I flipped the bottle around until I could read the label in the dim light. "'Trucker's Darlings?'"

"Better than coffee," Tellerman said.

"Can't," I said, and handed the bottle back to Keith. "Medication reaction."[27]

"What are you on?" he asked.

I glared at him until he turned away, whispering something rude that I was absolutely supposed to hear.

Ahead of us, Mare's Jeep slowed to a stop. In the light from the headlights, I saw her leap to the ground and begin walking forward, with Oshea following. Tellerman stopped our Jeep,

---

27 I stack my amphetamines with caffeine in coffee form only, and never with other prepackaged stimulants. My Adderall dose is as high as my physician will allow, and nobody needs me amped up beyond all natural limits.

and we got out to meet Dina.

"They're gone," she said, shaking her head. "The tire tracks, they're just gone."

"Footprints?" Speedy asked, as he climbed aboard my shoulders. I slid from the Jeep and ran to catch up with Mare.

"Nothing!" Dina called after us.

We reached Mare, where she and Oshea were kneeling by the tracks. Dina was right; the tracks just ended, as if the vehicle that had made them had been lifted straight into the air.

"I've got a bad feeling about this," I said quietly.

"No shit, Sherlock," Speedy said, as he slid down my legs and scampered over to Mare. "Someone laid a false trail."

No way," Oshea said, shaking her head. "I'm not a great tracker, but these are from a vehicle, something much heavier than a person. It would have needed to backtrack along its own trail to hide itself, and we would have seen some sign of that."

Speedy looked up at me. I'd never seen a koala's face say, *Shit, a bunch of ghosts lured us away from camp!* before, but it was a pretty easy expression to grok.

Mare noticed, too. The death grip on her braid went limp with fear.

"C'mon," I said to her. "I've gotta make a private call."

The three of us walked into the desert, far enough away so we were out of earshot. "Ben?" I whispered to Speedy.

"Ben," he agreed.

"Wait, hold on!" Mare was very much unconvinced. "Ben… *Franklin?*"

"We can do this without him, but if you need a cannon and you've got a cannon, you use the cannon," I replied.

Mare nodded, slowly. "Okay," she said. "Will…will the others be able to see him?"

"No," I replied. "Well, probably not. The only one who seems to be even partially psychic is…" I trailed off as something the dead nun had said came back to me. "…oh no."

Speedy sighed. "What?"

"Oh *no!*" I started sprinting towards the Jeeps. "Back to camp!

Back to camp! We've gotta get the drones up to look for Fish, *now!*"

I passed the *Spooky Solutions* gang and hopped into the driver's seat of Mare's Jeep. Dina and Oshea tried to pile in after me; I waved them off and asked them to ride with Tellerman, blaming OACET, national security, possible threats both foreign and domestic, the works. As soon as Mare and Speedy were riding shotgun, I pushed the Jeep towards camp as fast as I dared.

"Hope, please tell me what's happening," Mare said, in an extremely calm voice.

"There's an evil pirate in the desert," I said. "He's been bound and asleep since de Borromeo defeated him, but *Spooky Solutions* has been feeding him a whole bunch of concentrated energy. Enough to wake him up, but not enough to free him. He needs something more powerful than that to let him out…like another psychic who can pick the lock on de Borromeo's cage."

"And they went for Fish instead of you?"

"Wouldn't you? I'm a notoriously violent crazy person!" I snapped. "I know what ghosts are, and that I probably shouldn't poke the dead pirate, and I've got an actual Founding Father as my personal *deus ex machina*. Fish might be underpowered and uninformed compared to me, but I think he can hear ghosts better than I can. I bet they lured him away and are telling him exactly what he needs to do to set Hawley free."

"Why do they want to set him free?" Speedy asked. "Wait— who are 'they,' anyhow?"

"I don't fucking know! I would have gotten more details from the dead nun if you hadn't woken me up!"

Silence in the Jeep. I realized I was shouting, that my friends were maybe a little too quiet.

"What do we do?" Mare finally asked.

"Call Ben," I replied. We were making great time on the return trip to camp; the floodlights surrounding it were already dotting the horizon.

"Okay." Mare was as resigned as rocks. "How?"

"We've already done it," Speedy replied. "If we think about him enough, he shows up."

Mare took a deep breath. "When should he...arrive?"

I glanced into the rearview mirror so I could lock eyes with Speedy.

"Oh," Mare said quietly.

"Yeah," I replied. "He should have been here by now."

I didn't have to add that without a super-powered ghost on our side, we were stomping through thigh-high shit.

Chapter Twenty-Three

We reached camp in a flurry of tires and dust.

"No panicking until we're sure that Fish didn't come back while we were gone," I said. Mare nodded. She was carrying herself like she was made from spun glass, and was on the verge of shattering.

I jumped down from the Jeep and waved over one of the young tech guys. "Did Sergeant Fleishman return?"

"No, ma'am."

"*Fuuuuuck,*" I groaned.

"Hope?" I turned to see Mare. She was holding Speedy against her chest in the same stranglehold she had used in my living room. He was looking a little blue beneath his fur. "What are we going to do?"

"First, gimme," I said, and reached for the koala. He flopped into my arms, and I slung him up to his usual spot on my shoulders. "Next, we should figure out why Ben isn't coming."

"Is he...?" Mare wasn't sure what question to ask. "Why... won't he?"

"I can always reach Ben," I said. "But that doesn't always mean he's available, especially if he thinks we're just on vacation." I was worried—extremely worried!—but ghosts have their own lives.[28] "We should probably get some contingency asskickers, just in case. Mare, put a call out to—" I started to say, but Speedy slapped a paw across my mouth.

"Wait on that," the koala said to Mare. "The three of us? We can pretend this is a vacation, but you get Patrick or anyone else from OACET rushing down here to bail us out, and this'll turn into a media feeding frenzy."

Fuck. He had a point. The only reason my husband hadn't <u>come swooping</u> in to save us during the minotaur incident was

28 Add whatever caveat you want.

because OACET Agents were considered advanced government weaponry and couldn't travel outside of the United States. My husband had spent the entire time we were in Greece working on a legal way to circumvent international law. If he knew we were in trouble, he'd come swooping down here, fast enough to let everyone who follows him around guess that something serious was happening. And if he tried to avoid the crowds and went through the Yuma Proving Grounds or another military base? Holy hell, that'd just mean we had something enormous to hide. Everybody on the planet would be tuning in to *Spooky Solutions* and pouring jet fuel on Hawley's attention-fire.

I moved Speedy's paw away from my mouth. "Can we handle this ourselves?"

"I can't," Mare said quietly. "I'm not an action hero; I'm an organizational specialist. Give me something to organize, and I'll be useful. Until then…"

"Call Mike," I decided. "Tell him to contact Ben and send him out here. Hell, ask Mike if he wants to come fight some ghosts with us."

Mare's shoulders dropped a little in relief. Mike was a friend. A reliable, intelligent, and (most importantly) living friend. "Sure," she replied. "But it'll take hours for him to get here. What'll we do until then?"

"We find Fish before he reaches that pirate," I said. "Mare, make that call. Speedy? Go…go do something smart."

"Jesus wept," the koala sighed, and he climbed down to the ground.

I left them, waved away the folks who had pulled up behind us in Tellerman's Jeep, and walked out into the desert. Behind me, I heard the sound of the drones shooting skyward.

We weren't without resources.

We weren't without allies.

I walked until the dark of the desert claimed me, and then flopped to the ground.

"All right," I whispered to the infinite sky. "C'mon, ghost dreams. Let's do this."

I shut my eyes and waited.

"…any minute now…"

Nope.

"C'mon, brain, I need to talk to a dead nun. Help me out here."

Nothing.

I sat up, and slumped over my knees. "Fuck me," I sighed. I didn't want to run all the way to the ruined mission. Not twice in one night. I sighed, and started tugging my shoes and socks into jogging position.

"Perp!"

I glanced down: Mare's roadrunner had cozied up beside me. It looked up at me, an expectant expression on its face.[29]

"I'm very tired," I said. (I definitely spoke this in my most calm, coherent voice. I did not whine at a bird.) "What?"

The roadrunner ran a few steps to the north, and then turned. "Perp!"

"Are we seriously doing this?"

"Perp!"

"Hey, Speedy!" I shouted, as I staggered to my feet. "I'm following the roadrunner!"

I thought I heard James Earl Jones say *"Like fuck you are!"* but it was way past the normal range of my hearing, and the roadrunner was picking up speed anyhow.

Into the desert we went.

After a mile, I realized I had forgotten to bring water. Whatever. I had my phone on me, so Mare could find me. Or my body. Or…could she find me if the battery ran out? Rumor had it that even when a phone was off, it wasn't *off*, not really, not even if the battery was dead. There was always a little charge left, right?

Right.

After another few miles, I realized I could see the roadrunner. All of the roadrunner, not just a fuzzy blur zooming ahead of

---

29 Not that roadrunners have much of an emotional range, but this one was definitely waiting for something. It might as well have been checking a tiny watch on its tiny wrist.

me and *perping!* at me to catch up. Ahead of us, the huge dark shapes of the mountains began to come into focus.

The sun was rising. I felt as if I had run all night.

"Got a destination in mind?" I shouted.

"Perp!"

"I don't speak roadrunner!"

"Perp!"

All right, then.

Another mile. By now, the sun was up and the cool of the night had ratcheted straight into boiling day. Worse? My legs were asking to speak with the manager, because if they were going to walk all day and run all night in extreme conditions, they should *at least* get a protein bar or something because *this* was *simply inappropriate!*

An owl popped out of the ground and ran alongside me. It had legs as long as its body, and was nearly as fast as the roadrunner. When the roadrunner perped! at it, the owl spread its wings and disappeared into the sky.

"Cool," I giggled. "I'm hallucinating."

The shadow of the mountains hit me a few moments later. The shift between sunbaked gold to dense shade was like a punch in the face. I blinked; I had crashed and fallen face-first into the dirt before skidding to a stop.

The roadrunner's face appeared in front of me. "Perp?"

"I'd like a moment, please."

"Perp."

The bird backed away and began to pace in short lines back and forth across the ground, like a marathon runner who didn't want to let her muscles cool down. I sat up and looked around. The mountains were taller than the ones near the mission....or maybe that was because I was sitting at their base.

I took out my phone. "No signal?" I complained. "Cyborgs, man."

Not Mare's fault, I reminded myself. *She's busy flying drones. She shouldn't spend another iota of her concentration boosting my signal so I can contact her and let her know where I am because I'm in the middle of nowhere and I followed a bird to get here and oh shit I'm really lost in the desert without any food or water and—*

The thumb on my right hand went to my ring finger, and stroked the wide silver band of the ring. It was an ugly thing. The silver was cheap, and the stone at the center looked like a giant chunk of orange resin. In terms of rarity, it was probably the most expensive ring on earth, as Benjamin Franklin's ghost had brought it back from the future.[30] But as long as I wore it, I could contact my husband no matter where I was.

"Perp?"

"Yeah, I'm good," I said, as I stood and dusted myself off. It was a wincy task; I had road rash from that crash landing. "So, what are you anyhow?" I asked the bird. "Possessed? Mystical guardian? I've heard it's a shitty thing to do to call you my spirit animal—"

"Perp!"

"I *said* it was a shitty thing to do," I sighed. "Let's go."

The roadrunner started to move into the mountains. They were shallow hills, and very old. The wind had torn at them for hundreds of thousands of years, so long that the rocks had lost their corners. The roadrunner scurried along a gully which appeared to be carved by a millennium's worth of rain.

Make that a millennium's worth of a *lot* of rain. Hard to believe, but Fish might have been right when he said that one of the most terrifying things about the desert was water.

Up we went.

Once we got out of the foothills, the mountains started to form ledges. And caves. *Biiiiig* looming caves.

The roadrunner scooted into one of these and *perped!*

"Um...no. Sorry."

"Perp!"

I craned my neck back so I could take in the whole of the cave. It was more like a gouge cut into the cliff's face than a cave, and went up twenty feet, easy. Maybe it was more of a <u>cavern than a cave</u>.

30 Yes, I know what I just said.

Still.

"I've got a problem with caves," I told the roadrunner.[31]

"Perp!"

"Look, there was a minotaur."

The roadrunner all but rolled its eyes at me. It turned and ran into the dark center of the cave, and disappeared.

"Ohhh God!" I walked between the dark hollows of the cave's mouth and the edge of the mountain.

From deep within the cavern came a tiny echoing, "perp!"

"Fuck!" I said. I grabbed a rock and used it to etch a large white arrow pointing in the direction of the cave. Y'know. To help them to find my corpse. "Fuck fuck fuck fuck *fuck!*"

"perp!"

"I'm coming!"

The cavern swallowed me.

And the light. Moving from the desert to the shade to the dark was almost as bad as flicking a switch. I was able to see my feet, and the ground beneath them, and little else. At least, for a little while. Then, as my eyes adjusted, I realized the cavern was full of small perfectly round holes which opened to the sky and let in the light.

No, wait. Small perfectly round vents.

"Holy shit," I whispered, as I spun in a slow circle, my mouth open.

I was in the middle of a city. The hollow cavern had been transformed into a series of houses. They were all made from the same dun-colored earth as the walls of the cave itself, with windowsills and doors made from very, *very* old wood. The edges of the buildings were almost satiny-smooth, and the floor of the cavern had been carefully shaped into stairs, slopes, curves…whatever was needed to move people from one level of the city to another.

It wasn't very large. I don't think it would have held more

---

31 This was something I had learned right then and there. To be fair, I didn't have much experience with caves, but the last time I had been in one, Mike and I had dragged a headless corpse through an entire mountain. Plus, minotaur. Look, it was a traumatic experience, okay?!

than five hundred people, tops. But it instantly put me at ease. The city had been shaped by human hands. It couldn't have been easy to build it, not all the way up here.

It had been a community.

It had been loved.

I took a deep breath, and went deeper into the city.

The light was enough to let me find my way. I tried not to touch anything; this place was so old that I was worried my footsteps might cause it to fall in on itself. Some of the vents were enormous; rain and time had caused them to widen, and there were shallow gullies carved by water all over the place. Buildings here and there had collapsed, but most were still standing strong, even after all this time.

I didn't see much in the way of physical possessions. Whoever had built this city had done a good job of clearing it out when they had left. Or maybe time had done it for them. Or maybe the layers of dust everywhere had swallowed anything that wasn't a building. I wasn't much of a tracker, but from what I could tell, the roadrunner and I were the first living creatures to come this way in a long time.

We reached the rear wall of the cavern. It was darker back here. The buildings against this far wall seemed smaller, and not as carefully made. I wondered what counted for prime real estate in the booming cave market: was it at the front of the cave where there was more light and fresh air, or if it was just easier to build there without needing to lug the wood and shit all the way back here?

The roadrunner was scratching around the edges of a pile of fallen rocks.

"Perp?" I asked it.

The bird shot me a nasty look with one beady eye, chose a rock, and sat.

I sighed. "Perp," I agreed, and sat on another rock beside it.

We waited.

And waited.

"So…"

"Perp!"

And waited.[32]

"Mind if I walk around a little?" I asked.

"Perp."

I stood and wandered back into the city.

"I wish I had phone service," I grumbled. Yeah, I was lost and alone and extremely tired, but I also wanted to check Wikipedia and see who built this city. Fish had done his informative TED-talk thing about the Hohokam and how they had built cliff dwellings, but he had said those were mostly to the west of the Salton Sea. According to Fish, most of the surviving Hohokam ruins in this region were smaller trading posts of dubious origin, or had been built by other peoples who had followed in the footsteps of the Hohokam after they had gone missing.

I was also wondering if this was the same city that Tellerman's mapmaker had found a century ago. If not, did that mean there was another city closer to camp? Did that mean there might be clusters of these small cities within the mountains?

I was about to turn a corner and walk back towards the roadrunner when a thought struck me—ancient cities mean dead people.

Lots of them.

"Oh, *shit!*" I shouted aloud.

Which I shouldn't have done, as Fish chose that moment to step around the corner of the building. I had just enough time to process who it was and pull my own punch before his fist slammed into my jaw, and everything went black.

---

32 Ever share an awkward silence with a roadrunner? It's not great. Definitely not great.

Chapter Twenty-Four

It was a city street in broad daylight. Errand day. Grocery shopping (again) because I had married a giant who ate everything that stood still and contained calories. I had plastic bags draped around both arms because I had forgotten the reusable bags (again), and I was wandering up and down the street—

"Oh, come on!" I shouted at the dream. "I'm not doing this *again!*"

This time, the dream kept moving on in spite of me.

Four men emerged from the shadows. They pulled their knives.

"Hope Blackwell!" Marie de Borromeo appeared, semi-stylish in her track suit and white Keds. She stared at the men, at how they were advancing on me…

I tried to stop the dream a second time. No dice. I was either too tired or Fish had done some real damage to my headmeat with that sucker punch. "Crap," I said, as the first man reached out to tap my shoulder in one of those hard *pay attention!* gestures. It hurt, just as it had when it had happened in real life.

Well, shit.

"Are you all right?" De Borromeo asked, as she tried to find a way to move between the four men. They ignored her; they were my memories, and she didn't exist to them.

"Hold on," I told her. I had one last trick to try. Sometimes, if a dream wouldn't let you go, you could split yourself and allow part of yourself to escape. I shut my eyes and imagined myself standing beside the nun, watching the action…

I opened my eyes, half-expecting to see another one of the men pointing his knife at me. Instead, I found myself next to de Borromeo, both of us watching a copy of me get pushed around by four men.

"What's happening?" she asked.

"Just ignore it," I told her, even as my own eyes kept tracking sideways.

"But these men—"

I started walking away. But the dream had the bit in its mouth and was starting to run away with my subconscious: my feet started sliding across the ground, pulling me back towards my double in the center of the four men.

I had to put the brakes on that, fast. So, you know. Own your failures.

"There's a security camera up there," I said, pointing to where a light pole should be. The pole filled itself into the space behind me, a camera lurking about fifteen feet off the ground over a sign that said *SMILE!* "I've seen the footage a dozen times."

The scene rewound itself in time, returning to a couple of minutes before the men jumped me. I walked between them. They weren't paying attention to me-me; they were focused on memory-me, the one with four bags of groceries and a dozen urgent messages on her phone.

"They wanted to send a message," I said, walking past three of the men. I stopped by the fourth. The man with a gold tooth leered at memory-me. He had a prison haircut and a nice new shirt with an Old Navy logo on the chest.

"They thought OACET was fake. Just another way for the government to control its sheeple. They thought I was an actress playing a part. I wasn't real to them—I was a body that could be dumped in a parking lot with a manifesto stuck in her pocket."

The men closed on memory-me.

I tried to step back to watch, but my subconscious was done being passive. There was a pulling sensation and I rejoined my double. It was just *me* now, a single person, and I was paging through texts and worried about the ice cream melting before I could find my car and wondering how I could manage to be in eight places at once that night—

Broad daylight. A busy city street in a safe neighborhood. I never saw them coming.

I nearly bumped into the first man; there was a sudden shape in front of me, so I sidestepped with a meaningless, "Sorry!"

The second shape got my attention when he tried to grab my arm. I twisted and bumped him away with a hip. "My dude," I said. "Don't."

That's when I finally looked up from my phone, and realized I was in trouble.

Four men in different shades of sketchy. They had tried to look nice for my murder, I guess, but slapping new clothes over hard-used bodies doesn't hide much.

The man with the gold tooth took a hunting knife from a leather sheath on his belt. He held it like a disposable comic book villain, the kind of low-level baddie that's used to set the tone for how back-alley thugs are no threat at all to the heroes.

(No, there's no irony there whatsoever. Nor sarcasm. Really.)

"I don't want to do this again," I said. Weird. That wasn't part of my original memory: when it had happened, I had laughed and dropped the bags. Hey, it had been a slow day. "Don't make me do this again!"

He charged, his hunting knife held point-up in his right hand.

I disarmed him and flipped him up and over my shoulder. That had happened in real life. "Don't go near that knife!" I shouted at him as he fell, which hadn't happened. "Don't do it!"

His buddies closed in on me, snatching at my arms, trying to stab me with their own knives. One of them succeeded: my forearm turned bright red. "Your friend is bleeding out!" I shouted, as I turned them around to face the man now lying face-down in the alley. "Call for help! *Call for help!*"

The other three men collapsed, puppets with their strings cut. They dropped to the pavement, face-down, mirroring their friend.

"You dumb assholes," I whispered.

Now that it was over, the nightmare let me go. My body was mine again. The three other men faded away, leaving the man with the gold tooth. He was lying flat on the ground, a pool of blood slowly spreading around him.

De Borromeo came over to me, and put her hands on my shoulders. "What happened?" she asked quietly.

I knelt beside the man and pointed at his left leg. "The security footage shows him grab his knife and try to stand, but he's moving too fast and can't find his own feet. Just dumb luck. Loses his balance and falls with his hand too low. Knife hits the pavement at an angle; he hits the knife.

"Slit his own femoral artery," I said. "Yanked the knife out, made the wound worse. He was nearly dead before I finished knocking around his friends."

The nun was watching me instead of the dying man. "Then his fate is his own fault," she said.

"Maybe. Maybe not," I said. "Maybe I could have saved him, if I hadn't been so busy pounding on his buddies."

The dead man disappeared.

The blood stayed behind.

"His family is suing me, can you believe it?" I asked her, as I sat beside the blood pool. "Civil suit, not criminal. There've been a few hearings, and the case is allowed to proceed because we got a judge who hates OACET. Everyone knows it'll never go anywhere. Everybody also knows that I'll eventually settle, since I'm rich and famous and I've got better things to do with my time.

"This guy was a paycheck to them," I sighed. "If someone else had killed him, they wouldn't even have made a blip in their schedules for his funeral."[33]

The blood vanished from the pavement, as the dream began its cycle again.

"I need to get out of here," I said, as the four men emerged from the alley and began to menace me. "Your roadrunner took me to a lost city, and somebody ambushed me. I've gotta get

33 His name was Mike Atchell. Lived in Monterey, California, for most of his childhood. Shitty childhood, by the way. I can always sympathize with folks who have abusive stepdads. Moved out east to try and start a new life. Broke a couple of hearts, had a couple of kids. Fell in with some assholes. Tried to kill me. Died.

And this entire story would have been exactly the same without this particular footnote, so what does that tell you about the value of a human life?

control—"

De Borromeo said something in an unfamiliar language. The men vanished.

"What did you do?" I asked. I felt…slightly better? As if someone had picked up an arm on a corpse I was dragging around to help me carry the load.

"You don't need to face every fight by yourself," the nun said.

"I don't."

The nun didn't reply. Instead, she knelt in front of me so she could peer into my eyes. "I think you have a head injury."

"Thought so," I sighed.

"Are you one of those *jorguín*…ah…are you able to heal?"

"No!" I had snapped that word at her; she pulled away from me. I took a deep breath. "I know a psychic who's a healer," I explained. "He's dying of cancer. Magic is overrated."

She sniffed. "What we do isn't magic."

"It's close enough," I said. "Even if I had been able to heal the dude who tried to stab me? He'd have died anyhow. That healer I know says that healing an injury is almost always harder on the body than the injury itself. If the injury isn't life-threatening, you can spread out the damage and the patient will recover. But if they're gonna die without your help, you'll still kill them."

The nun's face went flat. "I didn't know that," she said. "It explains many of the problems my family faced when we performed healings."

"Yeah, well," I said. "Mistakes are cool. Mistakes where people get killed, aren't. Now, how do I get out of here? I can't wake myself up."

I had been trying to pull myself out of the dream with no success. A small, nagging fear had grabbed me; what if there was a reason why I couldn't wake up? What if I wasn't just bone-dead tired? What if I had slipped into a coma, or—

Oh, well. One of the only real benefits of being wildly famous is that I'll make one hellishly powerful ghost. Much more powerful than any dead pirate. However, I'm always thrilled to stick a pin in my own death, and consider that my ultimate fallback plan.

In the meantime, I was a prisoner in my own head.

Wasn't the first time. Probably wouldn't be the last. Always got old right away, though.

"I need to get out of here," I said, very quietly. The idea of panicking was extremely appealing, but that would accomplish exactly jack and shit. Instead, I would sit here on the fake pavement and take deep, calming breaths, and imagine what I'd do to Fish when I got out of here. "Somebody knocked me out and I'm just *lying* there—"

De Borromeo vanished. I didn't even have enough time to get mad about being abandoned before she was back. "Your body's safe," she said. "There's a young man checking your vital signs."

"Describe him."

"Young, thin, but very nice legs. He'll be quite a man once he finishes filling out." I raised an eyebrow at the nun, who didn't even bother to blush. "Your generation didn't invent sex."

"That's the same guy who knocked me out," I said. "Is he saying anything?"

"One moment." De Borromeo vanished again, and reappeared just as quickly. "He's saying that a horse is going to kill him."

There was something of a question in her tone, but I ignored it. So Fish had knocked me out, and now he was trying to bring me around? Odds were good that he had done what I had done: he had been shocked to find another person in the middle of the abandoned ruins, and had simply reacted. I had managed to stop myself before I laid him out, but I had different combat training than what the Army gave to their soldiers.

"All right," I said. I was just so tired. If Fish had been an enemy? Well, I had a lot of those. But it looked as if I had been trapped in my head by a stupid, preventable mistake. "Accidents happen."

The four men reformed and stepped out of the shadows again. The man with the gold tooth leered at me.

"This is how it's gonna be, forever," I said. I couldn't even look at them. "Even if I get out of here, they're still gonna be here, in my head. Forever."

"There are many kinds of ghosts," de Borromeo said, as she pressed a hand against my shoulder. "And many kinds of life. Memories are one of these."

"I'm tired of this," I said. Around me, the men charged, their knives at the ready. I didn't move from my spot on the pavement, but they still flew through the air as if I was throwing them around.

"You know what I want?" I asked the nun. I heard myself getting a little too loud, but couldn't seem to stop myself from shouting. The man with the gold tooth crashed into the pavement, and yanked the knife from his thigh. "You know what I've always wanted?"

The nun began to rub my back in slow, soothing circles. "No," she said. "No, I don't."

"To help people." Before us, the man with the gold tooth took his last breath. "You know what I'm good at? No—you know what I'm *great* at?"

"No, Hope Blackwell, I don't."

"The exact fucking opposite." The nun's hand paused; I sighed again. "I know, I know, you hate swearing. It's a habit. I'll work on it."

"I'll let it go," she said. "This time."

I chuckled. It was a harsh, humorless sound.

The four men appeared again. I shut my eyes as tightly as I could against them. No dice—turns out eyelids don't work when you're already stuck behind them.

"Well, now!" de Borromeo said brightly, as her hand fell away. "You may not be a born *jorguín*, but there are no laws which say I can't teach you what I learned after I died."

I picked my head up. "Huh?"

"Come," she said. "I'll show you how to leave your body."

Chapter Twenty-Five

"Now, I was never able to do this when I was alive," she said. "Very few *jorguín* can. It's very difficult to leave behind your own body. It was only after I died that I realized it can be done when you have a ghost to help you."

We were still seated cross-legged on the pavement, but we had turned to face each other. De Borromeo had driven the four men away again, so it was just her, me, and a pernicious bloodstain that refused to disappear.

"I gotta warn you, I don't have the hang of meditation," I said.

"No meditation needed," she said. "Just know that you are tethered to your body. When it is ready to wake up, it'll pull you back to it."

"Tethered," I said. "Okay, cool. Is there any way to break that tether?"

De Borromeo made a face. "Well... Let's say I haven't heard of one. That doesn't mean there isn't a way to break it. But this should be safe for you."

"Should."

"All things have some element of risk," the nun said, raising her hands in mock surrender. "I'd be lying to suggest otherwise."

"Good enough," I said. "What do I do?"

The nun grinned at me, and then tapped me in the center of my forehead, right where the roadrunner had beaned me.

I fell backwards with unbelievable speed. When I stopped falling, I found myself floating outside of my body, looking down at me and Fish. De Borromeo had been right; I was out cold, but not in danger. Fish had put me in the recovery position, and my chest was rising and falling in a regular rhythm. It was, however, one of the weirdest things I had ever seen.[34]

 "Whoa," I whispered.

34 And I am an *expert*.

Fish, who had been sitting beside me with his head in his hands, jolted straight up and started checking my body's vitals again. "Hope?" he said. *"Hope?"*

Right, right, he could hear me. I slapped my hands over my mouth and began to drift away from him—I was not in the mood to do lengthy explanations, definitely not like this, and *definitely* not when I was flying.

Wait, I was flying?

Holy shit, I was *flying!*

Oh wow oh wow *oh wow* **oh wow!**

Okay, how do you fly, exactly? I tried to push off of thin air... nope. My leg just kicked through space. But if I wanted to move to the left...

...okay, *that's* how it's done. I was currently a creature of will, not flesh (look, there's my flesh, right over there on the ground unconscious maybe in a coma *hey stop thinking about it!*), and I could will myself to move around...

Or shoot straight up in the air!

Or *swoop!*

I felt like a koala on his own drone. No. Better than a koala on a drone! This was me, zipping around like...like...

Like me, but *flying!*

I paused at the top of the cavern and looked down. Below, the city seemed much smaller than it had been when I was walking through it. It was less than the size of a city block, maybe seven or eight buildings, total. The dim light and the sense of age made it seem much larger.

"Having fun?" De Borromeo was standing in the air beside me.

"This is great!" I did a little backflip. "Thanks for trying to cheer me up."

The dead nun smiled. "How am I doing?"

"I'm gonna schedule all of my existential crises with you!"

"Come," de Borromeo said. "You haven't seen anything yet." She turned and flew straight through the cavern's ceiling.

Ah. No. No, I was not ready for that. I looked around for

one of those larger vent holes, and followed her out that way instead. Once outside, the sun caught me, and—

"Wow," I whispered.

The desert was a million different colors, blues and yellows, rimmed in purple mountains, and streaked with living green. Everything was glowing, with layers of shimmering light playing across their surfaces. The world had been dipped in golden rainbows.

"It's hard to see with mortal eyes," de Borromeo said in a reverent voice. "Bodies carry too much baggage.

"Did you know, when you're dead, you acquire a few extra senses?" she continued. "I've been told that you can perceive auras when you have left your own body, but all *jorguín* can do this with sufficient training. When you're alive, you need to blend your mind and your body, but when you're dead? There's no need."

I didn't reply—I wanted to! I wanted to ask if she had smellahearing or whatever. I couldn't. The desert was magical. Everywhere I turned was coated in an iridescent glimmer. Even de Borromeo herself was shining; the usual blue hue of ghosts was mixed with... Okay, I don't have a name for those colors.[35] But all of it was lovely and fascinating and full of *life!* Or...I dunno. Energy? Yes, energy. There wasn't a single molecule in the entire desert that wasn't somehow churning with its own power.

And it wasn't just living things, oh no.

I could see the dead.

Okay, admittedly, that's not a new thing for me. But I could see *all* of the dead, from the smallest insects to the cactus plants to the great crashing waves of a vanished ocean and—***omyshit look at that!***

It took a couple of tries before I could find my voice. "Is that a dinosaur?"

"No one is ever truly gone." De Borromeo spoke with the

---

35 I can't even remember what they were. It's as if the space in my head which was able to perceive them ceased to exist once I returned to my body. Oh, right. Spoiler alert: I returned to my body.

same reverence I had heard in church when I was a child. "We each leave our mark upon this world. What you see are echoes of that which came before.

"These echoes of the past are only a small portion of those living creatures which once crossed this desert. These echoes will fade away for you in time—our minds cannot manage what *was* as we manage what *is*. They are only clear to you in this moment because you are new to this way of seeing, and haven't become numb to the wonders of God and His creations."[36]

The Tyrannosaur[37] tipped its head towards the morning sun, and gave a silent roar.

I shut my eyes and drank it in.

After a second or two, I realized I had eyelids, and had closed them.

After another couple of seconds, I realized I didn't need to see. Instead? I could feel the world around me. But I couldn't feel the living. And I couldn't feel that dinosaur, or the memory of the ocean that came before it. I could just feel…

I turned towards the west.

"Ah, it's a shame," de Borromeo said. "You would have made a very good *jorguín*."

"Yeah, yeah," I replied.[38] "What's pulling at me?"

In reply, de Borromeo began to move west. I followed. As we flew, the echoes of the past began to slowly fade away…or, at least fade from my perceptions. If I concentrated, I could bring them back into focus, but there were so many of them and they were all stacked on top of each other and it was so hard to focus on any one of them at the same time and…

36 Two things. Yes, dead nuns really do talk like this, or at least this particular nun does. And no, I wasn't about to have a theological throwdown with the woman who had just given me the gift of the temporal footprint of a dinosaur! Besides, whatever source of creation you wanted to stamp on that moment? It had done glorious work.

37 Did I know for a fact if that particular dinosaur was a Tyrannosaurus rex? Come on, of course I didn't. I still don't. I've intentionally not checked to see if Tyrannosaurs once roamed the Sonoran Desert, because that moment was fucking magical and I don't need scientific names to make it more so. If you absolutely must be specific, I saw a big carnivorous dinosaur which was similar to what I've been told a Tyrannosaur looked like. And if that still isn't enough for you, I hope you're either an armchair paleontologist or you've accepted that your singular purpose is to suck the life out of parties.

38 She had shown me a dinosaur! Of course I was going to cut her a little slack.

There was just too much. De Borromeo was right: it was easier to let them slip back into the past where they belonged.

Instead, I let myself follow the urge to go west.

De Borromeo watched me out of the corner of her eye as we flew.

"What woke up?" I asked her. Whatever was waiting at the end of this flight? It was angry.

"The land," she replied. "The land, and its creatures, human and not, which gave themselves to it. Deserts belong to themselves," she said, repeating what she had said the night before, and then added, "because deserts are made, not born."

"Everything is," I replied. "You catch *Blue Planet*? Takes a zillion years to make a coral reef."

"But they are made from joining together," she said. "A desert is made when things leave."

Ah. Okay. She had shown me the echoes of an ocean. I had forgotten about that because, well, Tyrannosaur. But yeah, an ocean recedes, a couple of mountain ranges pop up to block the rain, and what's left is a little spot in the middle that's forced to fend for itself. Everything living there would either have to migrate or adapt. If I were a desert, I'd be a little protective of everything which chose to stick around, and a little pissed at everything which decided to wander in and set up camp.

Camp... I turned to look over my shoulder. Way, way off in the distance was a little speck of concentrated, busy life. Human life, full of water and—

"Well, nuts," I said.[39] "We brought air conditioners into the desert. That had to pi— Uh. That probably angered the locals."

"Yes, but you also brought attention," she said. "The eyes of the world have turned here."

Oh.

Yeah, I could see how that might enrage an entire...uh... desert. I guess? If it was used to isolation, definitely. Weird to feel empathy for an entire ecosystem, but...I did. I guess?

"Is it..." I had no idea how to phrase the question. I was pretty sure the desert was alive. Then again, it was also dead, and death

39 See? I can learn.

was layered around the living parts so closely that there was no separating the two. Then again (again), maybe life or death wasn't the core of this mess. "Can a desert think?"

"No, but it does have instincts," de Borromeo replied. "A land holds the echoes of what came before, and those which were once here were dominated by their drives. Such deep feelings can leave an impression that's deeper than that which left those echoes." She didn't have to add that the most basic instinct is self-preservation. And maybe there was another reason that she had shown me a giant carnivorous dinosaur. She followed this up by saying, "This is why the desert allowed Hawley to take form once before, so it could challenge me and those I had brought to the desert."

Hoo-boy, we were proper-fucked.[40]

"I really need to talk to Speedy," I muttered. "Wait, no. Mike first, then Speedy."

De Borromeo tapped me on my shoulder, and the two of us slowed. She nodded to the earth below us. There was a hollow formed by three surrounding hills, with more of that iridescent shimmer moving within the hollow.

"This is where I bound him," she said.

"Who?" I asked, before I remembered why I had been dragged into this mess in the first place. "Hawley?"

"Look," the nun said.

I tried to unfocus my eyes. It took a little work, but I finally managed to catch a glimpse of a small boat which had run aground on the desert floor. It was...Well, I guess I thought a pirate ship would be larger. With more skulls. This boat was kinda tiny.

"Wow, it's a schooner," I said. "Is Hawley still there?"

"Yes," she replied. "But the desert will soon free him. There's nothing I can do to stop it."

"Can you reason with it?" I asked her. "There's, like, a bunch of good arguments against freeing a murderous pirate."

"A land doesn't think," she said. "It doesn't reason. It doesn't <u>have the intellect</u>ual sense and free will which God has given to

40 Learning is a process. Shut up.

mankind. It merely reacts." She paused.

"I *think*..." she said, stressing the word, "that freeing Hawley is a reaction. There is so much attention centered on him—if he exists, and whether you will find him if he does. The land itself can't reason. It knows you want Hawley, so it will give him to you, and then you will go away."

"You don't know for sure, though." I was squinting and bobbing up and down in place, as if that would matter at all in terms of focusing on the pirate ship. Sometimes it was clear; sometimes it was a haze of ghostly rainbows. No people-shaped blobs, though.

"No," the nun admitted. "Remember, a desert cannot take action by itself. Those which do its bidding might be shaping its instincts to serve its own purpose."

I blinked as I tried to process that information. If I understood her correctly, the desert had commanded its residents to *Go forth and make them shut up!* and those residents had chosen Hawley as the instrument of their...uh...silencing.

"Someone's got a sense of humor," I muttered. "Or irony, maybe. How do I stop this?"

De Borromeo was very quiet for a moment. Then, she said, "When I fought Hawley, I had to give my life to stop him."

"Not an option," I replied. "Tell me how I can get Benjamin Franklin in here. He's not answering me, so I don't think he can hear me."

"I don't know." She did an odd thing with her hands, and then laughed. "You could leave a video message for him," she said. "With those ghost chaser people."

"Oh my Go—*gosh*, you are a beautiful diva," I said. "I never would have thought of that!"

De Borromeo waved away the compliment. "I hope it works," she said. "If not, you shall have to face Hawley. I will help, of course, but I only had a single life to give to bind him."

"I'm not worried about Hawley," I said. Surprise, surprise, I wasn't. Not really. One homicidal asshole is a lot like another, and at least this one didn't have a bull's head and a rack of horns.

"Especially not if you loan me your chupacabra army."

"I'll ask them," she said. "They are people, not the desert made flesh. They can be reasoned with, but if they decide that the desert is in the right, then they shall not help you."

"Fair enough," I said. "I don't know how to beat geography, though. How do I beat a desert?!"

"Give it something else to focus on," she said. "Something larger and grander than mere human attention."

"Okay," I sighed. "Okay. I have...I have no idea how to do that. Do you have any suggestions?"

"No."

"Okay." I was repeating myself. I didn't know what else to do. Or ask. Wait, no, there was one question that still needed an answer. "Why did your roadrunner bring me to the old city?"

"Roadrunner?" she asked. "I don't have a—"

Chapter Twenty-Six

There was no transition between my conversation with de Borromeo, and Fish slapping my cheeks. Yes, if you want to be specific about it, both of those things were happening at the same time, but I was mentally invested in that conversation.

Also, I have a long history of overreacting when I see a hand flying at my face.

"Hope?" It was hard to hear Fish, given that I had smashed him mouth-first into the ground and had him pinned in that position. "Hope? I didn't mean to hit you. I'm sorry."

"Yeah," I said, as I released him. "I know, I know." My head was pounding. Serious, smashing pain. I released Fish, and curled over my own legs from nausea. Then, I dry-heaved a few times for good measure. Right, right. I was seriously dehydrated, in addition to what was likely a phenomenal concussion.

"Here." Fish was holding out a canteen. "What are you doing out here?"

I took a few slow sips. The water was ambrosia. "Looking for you. You disappeared, and there was blood—"

"Yeah, I saw the blood, too," he said, a little too fast, and glanced down at his leg. He was wearing shorts; I noticed there was a small strip of skin that looked like it had been recently shaved.

"All right," I said, as I watched his face. "Why'd you come out here?"

He started to reply, but caught himself. "Wait," he said. "If you were looking for me, how did you beat me here?"

We stared at each other for a moment.

"Listen, there's a pirate about to break loose," I finally said. "And unless you can tell me how to reason with the landscaping, you and I are the only living psychics around to handle him."

Fish went white. "Psychic?" he sputtered. "I'm not—"

"Stop. Stop right now," I snapped, as I took another drink from his canteen. "I dunno if you can talk to the dead, but you can definitely hear them. And you can hear the past, too, right? Events which left…uh…echoes. You heard the nun screaming in the ruins."

"I… I don't…" A lot of emotions ran across his face. Surprise wasn't one of them.

"So, what is it?" I said, as I pulled my feet under me and tried to stand. "You're from one of the old families? Didn't get the full set of gifts, so they wrote you off and sent you to the Army?"

"I don't know what you're talking about," he said, as he looked away.

"Sure," I replied. I pushed against the wall of the old building, and hoisted myself to my feet. "Whatever. Come on, we've got to get back to camp."

"Hope, you can't walk back. I think you've got a concussion."

"Yeah, well." The wall was wobbling. I didn't have the time to figure out whether it was actually moving or if my head was about to fall off, so I yanked my hand away. If I had anything in my belly, I would barf. "Have you heard from Mare?"

"No. I can't reach her. I can't reach anybody."

"Then we're cut off, so we're walking. Or running." My nerves were beginning to sing. Yeah, it was partially the concussion, but it was also the cyborg thing. Mare could always reach my phone, no matter what, and Fish had one of those super-duty Army phones which had more battery life than a rabbit-shaped corporate mascot. If she hadn't reached out to us, then she couldn't, and that worried the hell out of me.

"You stay here while I go back," he said. "I'll get help."

"The ATV's pooched," I replied. The light was beginning to hurt my eyes. "And the Jeeps won't make it halfway up these mountains. So I'm either getting out on my own power, or we've gotta get a helicopter out here, and a helicopter seems overkill."

At that, my legs decided they were done with my bullshit. I staggered and crashed against the floor. Fish followed me down and tried to break my fall, but gravity and I are old friends and there was nothing he could do.

"Helicopter?" Fish asked.

"Unless you can heal," I muttered into the piles of dust covering the prehistoric street.

He didn't reply, but the silence was so loud it practically screamed.

"You *can!*" I rolled over to face him. Now it was the ground which was wobbling. Completely unreliable infrastructure in these ancient ruins, I swear. "You *can* heal, can't you?"

"...who *are* you?" he said, as cautiously as if I were a suspicious snake he had discovered at the bottom of his empty boot.

"Hope Blackwell. We've been hanging out for the better part of two days, and you've been putting your penis in a good friend of mine. I assume," I added quickly. "I mean, your business is your business, so my apologies if I'm making assumptions about your penis.

"Also, I think I'm getting worse."

"Yeah," he said. "I noticed."

The silence was starting to bubble over. I threw an arm over my head to cut the glare from the light. The part of my brain that had been attending medical school was yelling at the rest of me, but it seemed prudent to ignore it and maybe just go to sleep instead. The light couldn't get me when I was asleep.

"Is this a trap?" he finally asked.

"Probably," I admitted. "I walk into 'em all the damned time. Sorry. Darned time. The nun wants me to stop swearing. She's probably right, so I'm gonna try, at least while I'm at work.

"You cut your leg, didn't you?" I asked. I think I was starting to ramble. "Healed it up. It's cool. I know a great healer. I don't like him, but he's put my husband back together a few times."

"Oh, jeez..." He lifted my head and stuffed his pack under it. "I'm going to deny this ever happened."

"Good. Denial's awesome. You sound like me with Keith and the chupacabras."

"My dad's a healer," he said, ignoring me. No idea why: I'm a delight. "I can do little things. Never tried it on a concussion. I didn't want to risk it while you were unconscious."

"Smithback says that if you can heal the little things, you can heal the big things," I said. My voice sounded really weird. I realized I had forgotten to add most of the consonants, so I tried again. "Since healing's nothing but realigning collections of cells."

"Stop talking," he said, as he put his hands on either side of my head.

At first, nothing happened.

Then, Fish drove the psychic equivalent of red-hot spikes into my eyeballs and started twisting them around until my head turned to jelly.

I had the good sense to black out.

When I woke up, my body felt perfectly normal, and light was no longer a weaponized concept.

"Ow," I muttered, more to protest the absence of pain than any actual complaint.

Fish, who had been slumped against a convenient rock, snapped forward. "Are you okay?"

"Yeah." I sat up and rolled my head around. Everything felt solid. "Kid, you pack a hell of a punch."

"You hit your head on the way down," he replied. He sounded exhausted.

"Come on," I said, as I leapt to my feet.

"Hey!" Fish grabbed at me, but I was already following my footprints back towards where I had left the roadrunner. "You need to rest!"

"No, I *will* need to rest," I said. My consonants were back, along with a rapid clicking noise as my tongue moved back and forth against my teeth. "Adrenaline rush after a healing. Only good for a few minutes, then I crash.

"You're already crashing," I added. "Large jobs take it out of you. Different than small jobs. Oh! I guess I got that wrong. They're not all the same! Sorry!"

Fish was falling behind; I stopped, looped his arm across

my shoulders, and took most of his weight. "So you're not in the family newsletter, I take it?" I babbled, as I dragged him forward. "Or maybe they don't talk about me. I mean, I'd talk about me. That's just my ego, though. Or maybe you're not part of the same family as Mike Reilly? Maybe word hasn't spread. I don't know how the old families work!"

"You've got to slow down," Fish muttered. "I can't keep up—"

"I know *I know* **I know!**" The rocky outcropping where I had left the roadrunner was right ahead of us. The bird was, of course, completely gone. I stopped and allowed Fish to slide to the ground. "The roadrunner led me here."

"Mare's roadrunner?"

"Yup." On impulse, I climbed to the top of the rocks. Nothing was there, not even a little birdy footprint in the dust. But...

There was something cut into the wall behind the rocks. I started to toss them aside, even the large ones, even the ones that weighed a hundred pounds or more. Adrenaline was fuckin' awesome!

"Hey, Fish!" The carvings in the wall were becoming clear. "Petroglyphs! Lots of them!"

The soldier pulled himself up the pile of rocks. "Oh," he said, some enthusiasm returning to his voice. He very carefully reached out and touched a small X-shaped mark. "This is the sign for a roadrunner. Their tracks look the same coming and going."

I grinned at him. "This is pretty cool," I said.

He was a little more cautious. "What's happening?"

"Dunno," I replied. I whipped out my phone and began snapping photos of the petroglyphs. "But Mare's weird-ass roadrunner led me here, and something led you here, and now we're gonna get the hell out of here and check on the others."

Fish ran his fingers along the image of a four-legged creature. It had a snout, two ears, and a long tail. Other than that, it could have been anything. There was a carving of a handprint beside it, followed by a human figure. "Coyote," he said.

"Neat."

"No, Hope, not *a* coyote. This is Coyote, one of the First People. Look, he's standing beside water." Fish was smiling. It was a sweet smile, almost wistful. "This is an amazing find. We've got to bring everybody out here."

"Great." I leapt from the pile of rocks to the cavern floor. "Let's go get 'em."

I was halfway to the entrance before I remembered to go back for Fish. By then, he had managed to climb down and was taking a moment to rest. I pulled him up and started to drag him back towards the entrance.

"How long does the rush last?" he asked.

"Dunno! First time I've been healed!"

"We've got to talk about this," he said.

"Yes, we do!" I was shouting; the kid flinched a little every time I opened my mouth. I found that funny, and began laughing. "I'm the kind of *jorguín* your parents warned you about!"

The entrance was just ahead. There'd be a mountain after that; I was looking forward to getting out of here, feeling the sun on my face, breathing the clean desert air—

And then?

The adrenaline wore off.

I fell. Fish went down with me. The two of us groaned, and slowly pushed ourselves apart so we could lie gasping on our own patch of ground.

After a few minutes, I muttered: "Well, fuck."

"Yeah."

That was all the energy either of us could muster. It took another few minutes before Fish asked: "You're really a psychic, too?"

"Yeah." Another long pause. "I wasn't born to the old families, though."

"Me, neither."

"I thought you said your dad was a healer?"

He sighed. "It's complicated."

Another long pause. This one was slightly awkward; the kid definitely didn't want to talk about his family.

"How long have you known I was one?" he asked.

"Since I first shook your hand." I started to explain about the high-pitched sound, and auras, and how psychics usually find each other in the wild, but that would require more energy than I had. Instead, I went with, "Sound, whistle-thing. Y'know."

"Not really." He paused. "My dad says I'm blind."

"Dude." I tried to laugh. It sounded like someone crushing a dry muffin. "You can hear the dead better than I can!"

"But I can't see 'em."

We fell silent. I think he was all set to doze off, but I didn't want to risk a nap until I was sure I was actually healed. "Thanks for saving my life," I said.

There was the short *sniff!* of a man being woken from a nap. "Hmm? Oh. You would have lived."

"Nah, I would have made a bad decision and gotten myself killed." This was true; I had been all set to run across the desert in the heat of the day, with no supplies and a serious head injury. Common sense had not been anywhere near my thought process.

"I guess," he said.

"Why did you leave last night, anyhow?"

Fish paused, then gave in. "I've been hearing a woman scream."

"Yeah, that's the dead nun," I said, before I caught myself. "Sorry. Go on."

"I got up to use the bathroom," he said. "I heard her screaming again. It was really close to camp, so I decided to see if I could find her. Cut my leg on a piece of metal, then went into the desert."

"When did you pick up your pack?"

"I circled back to camp when I couldn't find her. Grabbed my gear, just in case I got lost, and went back out.

"Didn't you see my note?" he added. "I couldn't find any of you, so I left it on your bed."

I tried to laugh again. This time, it sounded like a small goose filing a complaint. "No. We were out looking for you." I told him about the tire tracks to nowhere, and following the roadrunner. "That bird's not natural."

"Maybe," he said. "I've seen a lot of strange things in the desert."

"Really?" I made a noise somewhere between a groan and a gargle. "Lemme tell you about this woman you've been hearing."

I started talking. It became easier as I went along; I was getting some of my energy back. I told him about de Borromeo, about the chupacabras, about Keith and the ATV. About Speedy, who usually wasn't nearly as polite and restrained,[41] and I was actually kinda worried about him. About the angry desert. When I was finished, the two of us stared up at the motes of dust dancing through the sunbeams.

Eventually, Fish said, "That doesn't make any sense."

"Tell me about it."

"No, I mean..." he paused. Out of the corner of my eye, I saw him make an idle gesture with a hand. Good. He was starting to recover. Three more limbs to go. I tried to move my own arms, and was able to wiggle some fingers, but that was it. "The part about the desert releasing the pirate doesn't make any sense. I mean, it might, but I live on an Army base. We blow things up out there all of the time. If the desert was going to get mad, shouldn't it already be mad at us?"

"Huh. Hadn't thought of that."

"The desert's a tourist destination," he said. "When the rainy season ends, it's beautiful. We get thousands of strangers coming through every year. And people have been looking for Hawley for centuries, right? Why would the desert be angry now?"

Absolutely nothing Fish said was wrong. I pressed my hands against my forehead...oh good, now I could move a little, too. "God! It feels like someone's fucking with us on an epic level," I said. "I need to talk to Speedy."

"Why?"

"Because he's a leading global expert on postgraduate fuckery," I replied.

"Okay." Fish sounded suspicious about the value of a koala's

41 Fish: "Um—" Me: "I know, I know."

input, at least in respect to this particular topic. "Would he know why we were both led away from camp at the same time?"

That single question sent a shock running through my entire body. I sat bolt upright, and shouted, *"Fuck!"*

"What?"

"I got it backwards! They didn't want one of us; they wanted both of us gone! Two psychics in the camp, and both of us are lured away by supernatural whatsits?" My ankles hadn't gotten the message that naptime was over; I tried to stand but wobbled forward, then dragged myself along the ground with my hands. "We've gotta get back there! Our friends are in danger—"

This?

This was the precise moment that Tellerman hoisted himself over the ledge, with Dina and a camera in tow, and shouted: "Hope Blackwell has found something amazing! *Again!*"

Chapter Twenty-Seven

INT. CAVERN, DAY. The cast of SPOOKY SOLUTIONS, *along with MARE and the KOALA, have joined HOPE and FISH inside an ancient city.*

Shot of HOPE'S face. She is leaning against the cavern wall and drinking from a large bottle of water. FISH is beside her. They both have flushed skin and appear to have suffered heatstroke.

FISH: I walked off to get a good look at the stars, and got turned around. Hope found me, and it was too hot to walk back to camp, so we decided to find shelter and then…

FISH waves at the city.

HOPE (coughing): Didn't mean to worry you. Forgot to text. How'd you find us?

TELLERMAN: Well, it's a long sto—

KOALA: Jackass finally showed me the map. I found a couple of likely sites for a lost city, Mare sent a drone over to check them out, and we picked up your trail.

HOPE: We left a trail?

FISH (quietly): I used marking chalk along the way, in case I got…in case we got lost.

HOPE: Son of—

KOALA chuckles.

MARE (off-camera): What is this place?

Camera 2 pans to MARE, who is looking around. She is standing in a pool of light and smiling.

KOALA: Definitely built by a Pueblo tribe. I'd say Hohokam, since there's evidence of irrigation ditches on the way here, but we're too far outside of their accepted historical range.

KEITH (excitedly): Is this worth calling the Smithsonian?

The KOALA sighs and walks away.

HOPE: Is that a yes?

KOALA (off-camera): Yes!

TELLERMAN and KEITH cheer.

TELLERMAN: We need to document everything. C'mon, c'mon. Agent Murphy, are we still live-streaming?

MARE: Yes.

TELLERMAN (gesturing to the crew): Okay, let's check this place out. Stay out of the buildings. They're probably unstable.

Camera 1 shows MARE and KOALA walking with DINA. They are inspecting the exterior of the buildings.

TELLERMAN (off-camera): Hope, did you two find anything?

HOPE (off-camera): There's some petroglyphs way back in the cave. Roadrunners and coyotes and water and shit.

FISH (off-camera): No, not a coyote. Coyote.

KOALA freezes in place, then resumes walking.

KOALA: Show me these petroglyphs.

Camera 2 shows HOPE getting to her feet.

HOPE (tiredly): Coming.

HOPE and KOALA walk to a dark part of the cavern. There is a pile of rocks. The KOALA climbs this. Some whispered crosstalk isn't picked up by the camera.

HOPE (whispering): …roadrunner was just sitting…

KOALA (whispering): …then the screaming woman can't be de Borromeo. You …

HOPE (to camera, pointing at the top of the rocks): The petroglyphs are up here.

Camera 2 shows detail of petroglyphs.

HOPE (to KOALA): Fish said these are supposed to be Coyote?

KOALA: Nope.

HOPE: But he said—

KOALA: Coyote's not a central figure in Hohokam petroglyphs.

HOPE: But you said this might not be Hohokam—

KOALA (rubbing a paw over his face): For fuck's sake, kitten…

Okay. Listen.

KOALA (pointing to petroglyphs): As far as we know, the Hohokam didn't write down creation myths. Those were sacred. Oral tradition only. And if Coyote is standing beside a river? This is a creation myth. These details don't...

KOALA (eyes widening): Oh.

HOPE: Speedy?

KOALA: You said this was hidden behind the rest of the rocks?

HOPE (gesturing): Yeah. Y'know. Roadrunner.

KOALA (hopping down from rocks): Brilliant. Just brilliant.

HOPE (shouting after KOALA): Gonna share that brainstorm with the rest of us?

KOALA flips off HOPE as it walks away.

HOPE (sitting on the rocks): Anybody got anything to eat?

Chapter Twenty-Eight

Tellerman couldn't be happier. He was buzzing around the ancient city like an enormous hummingbird, stopping here and there to shoot new footage and make phone calls. For whatever reason, Speedy had offered to host the program while Tellerman was working. The koala was riding around on Mare's shoulders, pointing at various features of architecture, and explaining why *this* or *that* detail didn't align with our understanding of Hohokam construction.

I found an out-of-the-way spot in the shade on the cavern's exterior ledge, and crashed. Everyone was safe. Or, safe enough. For now. And if I didn't get some sleep, then I'd be utterly useless if (when?) the pirate came to murder us.

For once, I didn't dream at all.

A slight chill grabbed me by my bare legs; I woke with a snort, and saw that the sun had started to go down behind the mountains. Several yards away, Fish was also dozing.

"He's a healer?" Speedy had been napping on my hair.

I yanked my ponytail out from under him. "Howdja know?"

"Your scars are gone."

I turned my left arm so I could look at the long knife wound...or, at least, the place where the knife wound used to be. Nothing. Clean, unblemished skin

"Whoa," I said, and sat up so I could look at the rest of my exposed skin. All of the little scars that had covered my body? Gone. Even the freckles that had popped up after a couple of days under the desert sun had vanished. "Kid's a better healer than Smithback!"

"What? No." Speedy sniffed. "He's worse. Much worse. Smithback can target an injury. This kid had to do the psychic equivalent of carpet-bombing your body."

"Huh." I removed my boots and looked at the soles of my feet. The calluses that I had spent decades building up? Gone. That... wasn't great. Precious, baby-soft skin was a liability on the mat. At least I still seemed to have muscle tone; I'd be furious if I had to start conditioning from scratch again. "No wonder he's exhausted. I guess he had just wiped out everything."

"Bet your appendix is back."

I shuddered. It had burst when I was nine, and I had been in the hospital for a few days while all of the guck got sucked out. I wasn't sure what would happen if it got infected a second time, and I needed to have it removed again—

Never mind. Non-issue: I had married into a clan of cyborgs. Five minutes in my medical records, and for all intents and purposes, my childhood run-in with appendicitis had never happened.

"What happened?" he asked.

"Concussion," I said, and broke down everything that had happened since I had seen him the night before. Including how de Borromeo had shown me the pirate ship in the desert, and the swarm of ghosts circling the ship.

"She says the desert is angry," I finished. "It's waking Hawley to force us to leave."

"Bullshit," Speedy huffed, and curled up to nap again.

I poked him in the butt until he popped his head up, and asked, "Aren't you worried?"

He nodded towards the setting sun. "Not until that goes down," he said. "Where's your ring?"

I blinked. My wedding ring was where it normally was, a thin band of gold riding on the middle finger of my left hand. But the other ring? The special ring that Ben had brought back from the future for me? The one that allowed me to contact my husband, no matter where we were? Gone.

"Guess I took it off before I showered," I said. No. Wait. That didn't seem right. I still wasn't thinking clearly—

"You guess?"

"I usually take it off," I said, even though I thought I

remembered seeing it while I was following the roadrunner. Hadn't I? I mean, I thought I had, but... No. Except when I was bathing, I never took that ring off, and it was designed so it couldn't fall off. Whatever. Brain, dumpster fire, etc. "It's supposed to be waterproof, but I don't risk it if I can help it. I ran out of the camp so fast, I forgot to put it back on."

He snorted. "Go get something to eat, and have Mare bring Ben here. We should make sure we've got at least one cannon ready to fire. No, wait," he corrected himself. "Have Ben bring in at least five or six Founding Fathers. We might need a nuke."

"Five or six?!" I was horrified: the Founding Fathers squabbled like...well...like old men who had extremely high opinions of themselves. More than two of them in the same room created a clash of egos which got in the way of basically everything. "Care to elaborate?"

"Figure it out, kitten," he muttered, as he tucked his eyes beneath a paw. "I need more sleep than you do."

I relented. He was right. Plus, a superintelligent koala was a different kind of big gun, and we needed him fully loaded. I picked him up and tucked him under Fish's arm, and then went to find Mare.

By the way, this is the point in the story where you should start facepalming. While a Founding Father was certainly the ghost equivalent of a cannon, and a bunch of them working together were their own spectral nuclear arsenal, I still didn't understand why we needed that arsenal! Not against, like, annoyed semi-sentient sand and its resident cacti! I was missing the point in a hugely dangerous way.

But I didn't stop to think about that, because my body felt... Good?

I stretched and twisted. All of the small nagging injuries which made up the background noise of my body had gone silent. Old broken bones, cracking joints, a gamey knee that liked to throw twinges of pain for fun...

I didn't like it. I had spent my entire life earning my own body, and now it felt like a toy that had never been out of the box.

And what about the stuff I couldn't see or feel? I had a skeletal system that had been conditioned to withstand a certain level of abuse, and an immune system that had ripened along with the rest of me like a seedy box of wine. Were those like my muscles and had survived Fish's carpet-bombing, or had they been rebooted, too? If so, I was screwed.

Except…I still had creases on the palms of my hands and the soles of my feet, instead of freakishly baby-smooth skin. So maybe I didn't have a completely clean slate, or maybe those creases were cosmetic changes, or maybe—

"Oh, I am going to be *so* pissed if I have a hymen again," I snarled.[42]

Oshea had set up a small serving station just outside of the city. I made my way over, and she set me up with a bowl of high-calorie camp food.

"What's happened?" I asked.

"Tellerman's got a team coming out," she said. "They'll be here tomorrow morning; that's about as fast as they can get here."

"And tonight?"

"Ghost stories in the old city." She winked at me. "We're hoping a pirate will show up."

I started laughing. It was…it was not a sane sound. I made excuses and scooted away, before she could call Dina so the two of them could make soothing noises about padded rooms.

The food tasted wrong. The flavors were familiar, but so overpowering that it was almost inedible. Either Oshea was a shitty cook, or Fish had rebooted my taste buds. I groaned at the thought of having to learn how to eat jalapeños again.

"Hey." Mare appeared with her own bowl of food. She had changed into a pair of shorts and a long-sleeved camp shirt, and was absolutely filthy. She was also grinning.

"Why are you in such a good mood?"

"I've been on the phone with Speedy's contacts at the Smithsonian all day," she replied, as she dug in to her rice and beans with a titanium spork. "They're freaking out, in a good

---

42 I shall not tell a lie. And you shall not know what transpired in the vicinity of my goodie box.

way. I've been their eyes and ears, and they've had me crawling around the ruins."

"Good public relations for OACET?" I guessed.

Mare nodded. "*Spooky Solutions* has been streaming, and the Smithsonian is sitting in on the feed. We're up to something like fifteen million visitors. It's like discovering and exploring the *Titanic* in real time.

"With, you know, ghosts," she added. "Only not real ones."

"Oh, right," I said with a sigh. "I'm gonna need you to make a call. We need to bring in some ghosts of our own."

Mare's face went blank. The traitorous part of my brain that tracked emotions felt her vanish, as if the shock had knocked her out.

"It'll be okay," I promised her. "Ben is a great guy, and a better friend."

"Hope!" Tellerman, standing in the center of the city, was waving at me. "C'mere!"

"Call Sparky," I said to her, as quietly as I could. "Make sure he sends Ben and all the powerful Founding Fathers he can contact. Even George—he'll know who I mean. We're gonna need backup, and we're gonna need it as soon as the sun sets."

"Hope!" Tellerman was walking towards us.

Mare's face was still completely blank. I gave her shoulder a quick squeeze, and went to talk to Tellerman so she could call my husband in peace. As soon as I got within arm's reach, he gave me a hug.

"Thanks," he said into my hair. "I knew you could do it."

"Give Fish the credit," I said, as I wormed my way out of his arms. "He found this place. We were just looking for a place to get out of the sun, and there it was."

"Sure," he said, grinning at me. "Can I interview you?"

"It's not really a great time for—"

"Dina!" Tellerman waved to the camerawoman. "Get over here. I want to do a live interview with Hope Blackwell."

I glanced over my shoulder. Mare hadn't moved, but the sun was still up. We still had some time. And when Ben and the other Founding Fathers arrived, we'd all be as safe as houses. There weren't more powerful ghosts anywhere in the United States. If it came to a throwdown between them and an irrational ecosystem, the smart money was on the Founding Fathers.

I put on my usual camera smile, and took the viewers at home through a heart-wrenching story of getting lost in the desert, heatstroke, and an accidental find made by an intrepid Army soldier. That soldier? He had saved my life and discovered an ancient city at the same time. What a guy![43]

Fish showed up, his eyes slow from sleep, with a koala on his shoulders. Then, Mare arrived. They spoke to Tellerman, the three of them telling their own versions of my story. Yeah, it'd hold up in the court of public opinion.

I wandered off, and found myself at the cavern's entrance in time to see the sun begin to drop behind the horizon.

"Showtime," I whispered.

"What do you mean?" Mare had joined me, with Speedy in her arms. I glanced over my shoulder to see Fish still chatting with Tellerman.

"The desert. Angry...thing." I realized our backup hadn't arrived. "Wait. Where the fuck is Ben?"

"Ben?" Mare asked.

Speedy's ears laid flat back against the sides of his head. "Shit."

"You didn't call my husband and ask him to send Ben?"

"What?" Mare's eyebrows knit themselves together. "No!"

"Mare, you didn't call—" This was seriously bad news. I took a breath to pull myself together. "Mare," I whispered, "I asked you to call my husband. What happened?"

"No, you didn't!" She was shaking her head frantically. "I mean, you asked me to make a call, and then you—"

Somewhere nearby, a coyote howled.

Mare's face went blank again. This time, she slumped forward, as if she had forgotten how to stand. I barely caught her before she reached the ground.

"*Shit!*" Speedy leapt from her limp arms. "She didn't get the

43 At the time, I figured if I could give Fish the credit, at least some good would have come of this.

call out!"

In the background, Tellerman was shouting about how the feed had just gone dead. I barely heard him; I was checking Mare's pupils. "She seems okay!" I slapped her lightly across her cheeks; no response. But her breathing and pulse were normal; she seemed catatonic, or at least in very deep shock. "What happened?"

"Ghosts," Speedy said, as he looked out towards the deep pools of night and shadow that were swallowing the mountains. "Make that one very powerful ghost."

"How would a desert know that it needed to shut Mare down?"

"What?" Speedy glanced up at me. "Oh, for fuck's sake, kitten, why would a desert want to screw with us? How *could* it? Try and keep up.

"Coyote is coming."

Chapter Twenty-Nine

"I'm gonna need more details," I hissed, as I carefully laid Mare on her side in the recovery position. "Spill. Fast. Tellerman will be over here soon."

"Yeah, okay, how about the short version? Say you're an infamous trickster who's minding your own business, when a team of ghost hunters invades your territory. They've got two psychics with them, and are broadcasting live to the rest of the world. What a gift, right? You play with them, let a little drama happen, maybe give them a hidden city to get the traffic up… And then? The feed suddenly stops. When the search parties arrive, all that's left of *Spooky Solutions* are their cameras. The found footage documentary-slash-horror film will be fantastic."

At that moment, I could have drop-kicked the little shit straight into the open maw of the Sonoran Desert. "You figured all of this out when the roadrunner showed up! That's why you've been so…so…so *nice!*"

"I've been *quiet,*" he corrected, as he gestured for me to put him on my shoulders. I obliged; he used me as a vantage point to peer out of the cavern into the gathering twilight. "Otherwise, I would have tied Tellerman's dick to his shoelaces by now. If you're going up against a ghost with Coyote's reputation, you don't want to tip your hand too early."

I stood, flexing my fingers. My knuckles didn't crack; that was wrong. Usually, everything cracked. "You coulda gotten us out of here days ago!"

"This is my Superbowl, kitten," he said. He bumped me with his head, cat-like; the little shit was *happy!* "If I thought we wouldn't survive, I'da pulled the plug."

"And Mare?" I gestured helplessly at our friend, lying motionless upon the rocks.

"Kitten, *think*," he laughed. "It'd be easier to simply kill her than to put her into deep shock. This is just a game to Coyote. Remember Fish's story? He likes humans, because he likes what they do for him. Right now, he wants to play with us. As long as we keep him amused, we'll survive. She'll be fine."

"But…" I was gesturing helplessly towards Mare, towards the cavern, towards all of it.

"Well, *maaaaybe* Coyote's ahead on points right now," he admitted. "We coulda shut him out with Ben and the other Founding Fathers. Now, we'll just have to play hard on defense."

"I'm gonna murder you!"

"Then you're fucked!" he said cheerily.

There was another howl from down below. It sounded suspiciously like agreement.

"Coyote likes to play with psychics," Speedy said in a low voice. "It's more interesting for him. Normal humans are boring—psychics know what's happening, and can put up a better fight."

"You think he killed Marie de Borromeo?"

"I think de Borromeo expected to see a demon, so that's what he gave her—the ghost of a pirate that happened to look like a Cahuilla demon."

"Ah." Now I got it. "And since we expect to see a pirate, we're getting a pirate."

"Not just one pirate," he replied. "The nun says she bound Hawley, right? Sounds like it's taking a bunch of ghosts working together to unbind him."

I swallowed a curse. I thought I had sensed an army on the move, but it might have been a prison riot.

"Think he's loose?" I asked.

"By now? Yeah." Speedy began to climb down; I knelt, and he hopped to the ground. "Better get down there, kitten."

"You asshole." I pressed both hands against my eyes, as if I could wish myself back to the Bellagio. "I can't fight a god!"

"Ghost," he corrected me, as he curled up next to Mare. "They're called the First People for a reason. He's ancient, and he's got a lot of power behind him, but he's still just a person."

"What if you're wrong?"

"Then I'm gonna have to completely rework my understanding of the universe." He shooed me away with a paw. "Go on, kitten. Buy me some time. Go do what you do best while we wake up Mare."

The coyote howl rose again. This time, it was joined by another, and then another.

I went inside the cavern. Fish watched me with worried eyes. He had managed to keep Tellerman and the rest of the team away from us, and they were all staring at me. They might not know exactly what was happening, but the little hairs on their arms and the backs of their necks were standing at attention. Something was wrong, and they knew it.

"I need a knife," I said to Dina. "Best one you've got."

"Hope…" Fish came over and pulled me aside. "Can you see what's outside?"

I shrugged. "Nope," I replied. "Pirates, I assume. Well, probably pirates with a bunch of murdering cowboy sociopaths, to bring their numbers up. Can't imagine too many pirates died in the desert. Oh. Gold prospectors, too, I bet. Miners? Yeah, we passed those mines on the way—"

"You can't go down there!" He looked as though he wanted to shake me.

"Yeah, I can," I sighed. "Or they'll come up here."

"But—"

I held up a hand. "Does anybody's phone work? Or your radio?"

He shook his head.

"Go to Mare," I said. "Wake her up. She's our only link to the outside world."

Dina arrived with two knives: the first was a bread knife, while the second was a decent tactical knife with a six-inch fixed blade. I went for the tactical; she pulled it out of my reach before I could take it.

"What's happening?" she asked.

I didn't reply.

After a moment, she flipped the knife around and placed it, hilt-first, into my palm. "I want this back," she said.

"Keep your boss in the back of the cavern," I replied.

I turned and walked out of the city. Speedy flipped me off as I passed him; I returned the gesture. When I reached the sloping ledge which led down into the gathering darkness, I paused, took a deep breath…

…and jumped.

Lemme tell you about Speedy.

He's an asshole. He's the biggest, ripest bag of used diarrhea diapers you'll ever meet.

But he loves me.

If he's sending me out there to buy time? He either thinks we're already dead (which he doesn't, or he'd have packed us up into the convertible the second that roadrunner arrived), or he knows I'm not going to get killed in the process. Hurt? Well, we've got a healer, and I'm no stranger to weird-ass injuries.

But he's not sending me to die.

My feet hit the path which led to the cavern, and I started running. The ground was torn up in spots, level in others. Once, this path had probably been a nice, smooth road, the kind that allowed donkeys or burros or whatever the Hohokam had used to haul carts up and down a mountain. Did they have burros back then? Or…or carts?

What happened to the Hohokam, anyhow?

Did Coyote really eat them all up? And if so, where were their ghosts? Did they—

I stopped my downward slide, and looked back up at the ledge above me.

"You asshole!" I shouted.

From high above came the deep sonorous voice of a talking koala. "Took you long enough!"

I had just remembered the brainstorm I had right before Fish punched me in the face.

That all cities are filled with ghosts.

Even ancient cities.

And I had just realized that those ghosts in chupacabra form which predated Marie de Borromeo? They had to come from somewhere.

There were a few large, flat rocks at the base of the mountains. I picked the one with the most surface area, and jumped. The ground shot up to meet me; I landed, and cursed. "God damn it!"

"What did I tell you about swearing?" De Borromeo was there.

"The kid with great legs undid twenty-five years of physical conditioning," I growled, as I hopped in place to try and push the unfamiliar stinging sensations out of my feet. "If I live through this, I'm gonna have to get vaccinated for everything again."

"Ah." The nun looked out over the desert, to where shapes were forming within the twilight. Shapes that shone in ghostly blues, and had the edges of skulls and bones where their flesh should be. "Are you ready?"

I flipped the tactical knife around. Whatever Fish had done hadn't blunted my reflexes; the blade spun in my hand.

"Good," de Borromeo replied. She had chosen to appear in old-fashioned robes, and carrying an extremely heavy walking stick. "Watch me, and I shall teach you how to fight the dead."

"I already know," I said, as the ghostly shapes came closer. Oh. Oh, yes. That was definitely a small army of skeletons marching towards us at supernatural speeds. Fan-fuck-all-*tastic*. "Hit them hard enough so they can't escape the pain."

"Oh, really?" She chuckled. "Watch and learn, Hope Blackwell."

The nun leapt into the air. And kept *going!*

The speed of that single bound took her straight over the heads of the spectral skeletons. She hung there, a middle-aged lady in an old Spanish nun's outfit, and then fell into the center of the army.

The silence was absolute.

The explosion which followed was blinding.

The silent flash of blue light lashed out from where de Borromeo had landed. It swallowed the skeletons whole, reducing them down to motes of blue light. Some of these motes tried to reform, but couldn't quite congeal into skeletons again; others spiraled up into the evening sky, disappearing like old embers.

Not all of the skeletons had been swept up into de Borromeo's attack. About two dozen of them had been outside of the blast radius. I looked for the nun within the cloud of blue dust, and saw her swinging that oversized stick like a scythe. When the stick cracked against a skeleton, the bones collapsed in upon themselves in a flurry of swirling specks of sparkling blue.

The skeletons tried to fight back. They really did. Against a mortal, they would have been deadly.

Against de Borromeo, they were hilariously inept.

They'd swing their weapons at her, swords and knives and whatnot, and utterly fail to connect. She'd anticipate their movements and sidestep, then lash out with that stick. Sometimes, they'd trip and fall to escape it; usually, they'd puff away into the twilight as specks of glowing blue dust. De Borromeo toyed with some of them: they'd tag her harmlessly with their weapons, and she'd spin sideways to parry. Then, when their swords and pickaxes and whatnot had swung wide, she'd reach out with a hand, give it a little twist, and—

"Daaaaaaaang," I whispered, as skeletons flew backwards across the dry earth, and then broke apart into blue light.

I'm familiar with a lot of fighting styles. Not this one. It was... It was ancient. It hadn't been processed through the history of *stuff*. It predated modern inventions, like metalworking and riding on horseback.

It was beautiful. It was primal. It made me ache to learn it.

It wasn't, like, the Platonic ideal of martial arts or anything. There's a reason that even the most traditional forms of martial arts evolve over time. Just from watching, I knew I could kick de Borromeo's ass with zero effort. But this was something which had survived from a different age. It was as pure as the echo of that dinosaur, and just as rare.

However, I *definitely* needed to learn that little twist of the hand that blew a skeleton clean across the desert. Considering the circumstances, that seemed an especially useful technique.

"Huff."

I tore my attention from de Borromeo laying waste to the battlefield. Beside me—no, make that around me, all around me, *holy crap I had let them sneak up on me!*—were a whole bunch of chupacabras. Dozens more than the other night.

Wait, was that just last night?

God, I was still so tired.

The little chupacabra appeared, cutting through the rest of the pack to reach me.

"We cool?" I asked.

She made that huffing noise again, and shook herself like a war horse warming up for a charge.

I blinked; for a moment, she seemed to be a young woman. Eighteen-ish, with dark hair and skin, in an outfit that had a *Clan of the Cave Bears* aesthetic. Then, as fast as mistakes, she was nothing but a chupacabra again.

"Were you...*are* you Hohokam?" I asked her.

She gave me a monster's great toothy smile and skipped sideways, with all four clawed feet leaving the ground. Whatever she had been, it was clear that she had enjoyed life (Afterlife?) in a devilishly quick chupacabra costume.

"Big question: are you guys with us, or the pirates?"

The little chupacabra pointed her nose at the pirates, and a deep growl shook her entire body. I wasn't sure if I'd get an answer to the Hohokam question, but she was clear on the topic of pirates.

"Anyone speak English?" I asked the pack. "I'd like to speak to...someone. Y'know. About the skeletons."

The chupacabras smiled at me.

"Are you fu—messing with me?"

There was some whispered snaggletoothery, and then every

single member of the pack nodded.

"Of course you are." I stared down at de Borromeo. She had eliminated the last of the skeletons, and was walking towards us, very slowly. If I didn't know better, I'd have said she was exhausted. "So, if you're here to help, why aren't you helping?"

As one, the pack turned, noses pointed towards the desert. In the distance, miles away, a bright blue glow touched the edge of the horizon.

"Oh." I sighed, and sat on the rock.

We were caught up in basic battle tactics, at least as far as battle was defined during the Sticks-and-Stones Age. Send a bunch of cheap foot soldiers to draw out the enemy's best fighters, and if you get lucky, they'll blow their wad. Then you send in *your* best fighters, and… I dunno. You get to collect a couple of heads and a maybe a crown or whatever. I wondered if de Borromeo knew what was coming. Or maybe she did, and she was faking exhaustion to draw them in again. Or maybe…

De Borromeo began to climb up my rock. I leaned forward and gave her a hand up. As we touched, I felt her emotions: she was so tired that I nearly passed out in sympathy.

"Dude," I groaned, as I pulled her up. She was heavier than any ghost had a right to be; whatever she had done had drained her to the point where she forgot she no longer had mass.

"I think I'm out of practice," she gasped, as she dropped to sit on the ground beside me.

"When was the last time you did that?"

"Half a century ago?" She allowed herself to slump. "Perhaps a small bit more. We—*whew!*—we were due."

"Wait. What do you mean, 'due?'"

"This is a restless land," she said. "It rouses itself whenever a *jorguín* wanders into its wild places."

I turned towards that knife edge glowing along the edge of the horizon. "Speedy was right," I muttered. "Someone's playing games with you."

"Eh?"

"Have you ever met Coyote?"

A snarl came from the small chupacabra. All eyes of the pack were suddenly on me, shining, although only half of them lashed their tails in anger.

De Borromeo slapped her hand over my mouth. "Each of us holds some things sacred," she said, speaking slowly and *very* carefully. "They chased you across the desert to defend my beliefs. What do you think they would do to you in defense of their own?"

I nodded. The nun released me.

"I'm sorry," I said to the monsters. "I'm sorry if I've done something wrong. I have no idea what's happening here."

"No one understands their own gods," de Borromeo said solemnly. "Let alone anyone else's. Gods exist beyond the limits of our minds. All we can do is show them respect."

I turned to watch the blue light. It didn't seem to be coming any closer, but every bit of sunshine was finally gone, and that blue light was definitely glowing brighter.

"Respect…" The word rumbled around my mind like thunder.

No, wait—was that actual thunder? I turned to take in the whole of the sky.

No. Not a cloud to be seen.

"Well," de Borromeo said, as she gathered her skirts around herself and stood. "I think we should go and see what that light is, don't you?"

"No."

She stared at me, bemused. "The land calls to us, Hope Blackwell. We must go and end this."

"I don't think it's the land that's calling us," I replied. "And I think that light's a trap. They're trying to lure us out, so they can get behind us and kill the people in the cave."

De Borromeo squinted at me, as if her vision was suddenly on the fritz. "The *desert*," she said, with a little too much emphasis, "does not think. It cannot plan. It's using ghosts as its tools, Hope Blackwell, and cave walls don't matter to *ghosts*."

"Yeah," I said. "Unless this is all just…uh, someone's god… toying with us." The nun looked offended to the point of open rebellion, but before she could respond, I added: "What happens if we wait here?"

De Borromeo caught herself, and took a deep breath. "Is there anyone you hold dear to your heart back at your desert camp?"

I thought about the kids who were guarding the vehicles and the equipment. "Uh…I don't want them hurt, but I wouldn't say—"

"Well," she said, her temper still flashing around her. "If this is just a game, then they should be safe, yes? It will not matter if you refuse to confront the enemy."

Oh, great. Not only was she losing contractions again, but I was gambling with an additional set of human lives. Speedy was almost never wrong, but when he was wrong, he was **wrong**. Someone was fucking with us, but was that someone a pissed-off desert? Or one of the First People? Or something else, something…*other*, something none of us had considered?

"I really want a shower and a nap," I muttered to myself. "This might make sense after a shower and a nap."

De Borromeo pulled herself tall. "I am going into the desert," she said. "You can choose to fight with me, or not."

"I can't leave my friends," I said. "And I don't think you should go."

"I did not think you were a coward."

I shrugged.

De Borromeo glared at me, and then stepped over the side of the rock. The chupacabras flowed around me as they followed her.

I sighed again. "Yup."

"Huff."

I glanced down; the little chupacabra was still standing beside me.

"I'm sorry," I said. "She's letting herself be manipulated. I don't think she's that great at tactical planning."

The chupacabra nodded, but didn't move to catch up with the rest of the pack.

"You gonna stick around?" When she nodded again, I asked,

"Can you go human? I don't like just thinking of you as a monster."

She flickered in place. There was that brief glimpse of a young woman again, and then nothing. Nothing at all.

"Chupa...girl?" I waved at the space where I had last seen her. My hand brushed against something solid. It felt like a bare leg. I yanked my hand back. "Oh! Sorry."

The chupacabra reappeared. "Huff!"

"Great." I had run into this in Greece, when I had met an extremely powerful ghost I should have been able to see, if power alone had been a factor. "It's the Helen of Sparta problem all over again."

"Mruph?"

"I'll tell you about my theories on culture and ghosts on the way," I said, as I flipped the combat knife over and over, until my hand learned its weight. "There's a pirate lurking around here somewhere, and I want to find him before he finds us."

Chapter Thirty

"...but don't call her Helen of Troy," I warned. "Long story short, our brains can't process too much difference at once." I glanced over at the chupacabra. She was hopping from rock to rock to keep pace with me, her clawed feet utterly soundless. "So if you were, like, a suburban housewife from Connecticut, I'd be able to see you as you are. But my brain is having a problem dealing with a girl from a culture that's totally alien to mine. Somehow it's easier to process you as a monster."

"Wow." I realized what I had just said, and shook my head, disgusted at myself and several billion other people. "Does that just sum up all of humanity or what?"

The girl in chupacabra form huffed in agreement.

"I bet I wouldn't be able to see de Borromeo if she hadn't watched a zillion hours of television," I added. "And I'll probably be able to see you in human form soon. I just gotta pound on my brain until it's a little more flexible."

We reached the base of the mountain. The rocks ended, and the hard-packed earth shot out all around us. I flopped onto the ground, sitting cross-legged. Beneath me, the detritus embedded within the dirt poked my butt and thighs.

The chupacabra tilted her head and made a curious chirping noise.

"I've gotta do a..." I waved towards the world at large. "...psychic...thing. Unless you know where Hawley is?"

The chupacabra sat.

"Yeah, me neither." I shut my eyes, and tried to listen to anything and everything. The air. The sky. The wind kicking up in the distance, bringing with it the smell of something wet and—

Nothing.

No…

Wait!

I kneewalked around to face the west, back the way we had come. Something was… Something was coming…

Something was coming at us from behind the mountain range.

"Oh boy," I muttered. "Speedy was wrong, and now we're *extra*-fucked."

"Chirp?"

"He thought Coyote would play by the rules—" I stopped talking, fast, as a low growl started, deep within the chupacabra's throat. The girl in the monster costume stared at me, eyes glowing blue. I had the impression that if the undead color palate allowed for it, they'd be bright red, maybe flashing with yellow sparks.

I held up my hands. "Apologies," I said. "Wasn't thinking. But we gotta get moving."

I was up and running towards the ledge which led to the cavern's entrance before she could answer. A few moments later, the path in front of us lit up in blue as she caught up to me.

"Thanks," I said. As we climbed the ruins of the old road, I tried to explain. "So, Speedy—the koala you met last night— thinks that…um…" I paused to choose words that wouldn't end with a set of claws in my jugular. "…a certain First Person might be playing a game with us." The girl stayed silent. I took this as a good sign, and pressed on. "And since this is a game, there are rules.

"But now, it looks like there aren't any rules" I said, as I leapt forward and seized a rock. The new skin on my fingers complained; I squashed the urge to curse Fish out for saving my life by wrecking my body. "De Borromeo was right, I was wrong, and the pirate-cowboy-skeleton things are simply gonna walk through the back wall and murder us all."

The girl coughed. When I kept going, she coughed again, an intentional *"A-hem!"*

I turned toward her. She was standing on a rock, scratching

something into its surface with a claw. I peeked over to see that she had written, in very tidy letters: "TUNNEL."

"Whoa." My head snapped between that word and the cavern's mouth, just above us. "Really?"

She nodded.

"I suppose that's not cheating." I began to climb again. "That's clever. That's really clever. I'da never guessed that the cavern has a back entrance." The road leveled out, and we started to run. "So this is really…him? The…First Person?"

She sighed.

"It's complicated?"

I glanced over my shoulder to see her nodding.

"Yeah," I said, as I sighed in sympathy. "Always is."

The old road ended; we skidded to a stop in the cavern's mouth. The humans were assembled there, lit by the hellacious cold white light of LED camping lanterns: Tellerman and Keith, Dina and Oshea, Fish and a still-unconscious Mare, lying in the same place I had left her—

"Where's Speedy?" I asked Fish.

"Here!" The koala's deep voice came from the back of the cavern. "Heard you talking! Get over here and bring more light!"

I ran past the humans, grabbing a spare lantern on the way. Speedy was standing beside the pile of rocks.

"Genius," he said. "Sheer genius."

"The back entrance is behind the rocks?"

"Nowhere else it could be," he said. "I already went through the buildings. Who's your friend?"

It took me a moment to realize he was talking about the girl-monster. "I don't know her name," I admitted. "She's the one who led the pack when they were chasing us."

"I remember. You," he said, pointing to me. "Move the rocks."

"You kidding?" I climbed up the rocks, put a foot against the rock on the top of the pile, and pushed with all of my strength. It barely moved, then settled back into place. "Last time I moved them, I was hopped up on healing juice."

"Then get hopped up on self-preservation." He turned to the girl. "What's your name?"

"Can you understand her?" I asked, as I threw my entire weight against the top layer of rocks. They shifted, and one *neeeeearly* toppled off the pile.

"Since I can read? Yeah."

"Aw, hell," I grumbled. I hadn't thought to ask her to write out her name.

The chupacabra scratched a claw across the rock. I had to rub my eyes to make sure I was reading her answer correctly.

"Goldie Hawn?" I read aloud. *"Goldie Hawn?!"*

"Note the flower," Speedy said, as he pointed his own claw at a little doodle she had added at the end of the name. He said something in an exotic language, and the girl-monster's eyes went wide as she tried to say something. Her words came out as a long snarl.

The sound of running feet beat Fish to the rock pile. The kid skidded to a halt, and looked around. "Sorry," he said, embarrassed. "Never mind. I thought I heard a strange woman."

As he turned to leave, Speedy snapped: "Stop!" He pointed at the girl-monster. "You! Talk." To Fish: "You! Tell me exactly what you hear!" To me: "Move those rocks, or we're screwed!"

I swore under my breath as I kept throwing myself against the rocks. They gradually began to shift; some of them were a couple hundred pounds, and I couldn't do much of anything with them until Dina appeared and added her considerable muscle power to mine.

"What's happening?" Dina whispered, as the two of us watched Speedy use Fish as a dimensional psychic translator.

"I don't even know where to start," I whispered back. "Do you believe in ghosts?"

She glanced over her shoulder, at where the girl-monster had etched "Goldie Hawn" into the stone floor. Like the rest of the *Spooky Solutions* crew, she had walked the streets of the city a dozen times or more: she knew that the writing was new, and that there was no way that Speedy or I could have done that, not without firing up a power tool or two. Plus, y'know, Goldie Hawn was still writing things out for clarity, and Dina couldn't help but notice that letters were magically appearing in the bare ground. "I didn't."

"How about literate chupacabras?"

Dina glared at me as if I had grown a second head. Which had four extra eyeballs and maybe also a mullet.

"I'm not sure what's going on, either," I semi-lied, as I went to my old reliable fallback for weirdness "Maybe OACET and the Army are working together in a field exercise."

"Really?" Dina's relief was so overwhelming that it was almost a physical assault; I had to shut my eyes and concentrate on the beating of my own heart until it passed. Dina couldn't help it, I reminded myself. Everyone grasped for normal, even if today's version of normal was a supercomputer shoved into our thinkmeats.

"I think something went wrong," I said, as I pointed towards Mare. "She was our connection to the outside world. I don't know if we can end the exercise until she's awake."

"Shouldn't they know?"

"It's the government," I said, as we finally managed to nudge a big rock off the pile. "They don't know anything."

The rock bashed against the floor. Behind it, the dark mouth of a hole loomed at us.

"Hey, Speedy!" I shouted. "We've got some hole action over here!"

"That's what your mom said!" he shouted, as he turned back to Fish and Goldie Hawn.

I didn't think we could move more rocks; the rest of them were easily five hundred pounds, maybe more. I could fit through the hole, if I got wiggly. Dina had broader shoulders and might get stuck. I handed her the combat knife. "Watch my back," I said.

"The koala can make it," she said.

"You don't ask an arboreal prey species to be the first one to dive into a tunnel," I replied.

Fish peered over my shoulder. "You sure you want to stick your head in there?" he asked.

"Yeah, I know," I said. I didn't want to run face-first into a ghost pirate's cutlass, but we needed to know what was in that hole. Plus, Goldie Hawn didn't seem too concerned. "I'll keep an eye out for the slasher movie villains."

"Actually, I was going to warn you about the wildlife."

"More roadrunners?" My forehead was still a mess of bandages. I probably didn't need them at this point, because of the healing bomb and whatnot, but that bird kept attacking me, so a little padding was a blessing.

"I was gonna say owls," he said. "They're about a hundred times more dangerous than roadrunners."

"That's absolutely terrifying," I said. "Gimme a light."

Dina handed me a tiny LED jogging light, a smaller version of the one I had lost in the desert. It popped off its magnetic lanyard with a click, and burst into life. I gently lobbed it into the hole, and chucked a few decent-sized rocks after it.

The rocks made an echoing noise, but nothing came zooming towards us with pointy talons extended. Or, y'know, shining spectral swords of doom.

"All right," I said, and knelt beside the opening. "Cross your fingers and hope I keep my eyeballs."

I slithered through the opening. Once I got past the bottleneck of the entrance, I found myself in a short tunnel that was tight, but not frighteningly so. I pulled myself along with my hands and elbows, chasing the light of my tiny lantern. The light changed at the end, following a sharp drop into...

...the cave?

...no...

There was less light than I had expected; my body was blocking the hole, and the tiny lantern couldn't compensate. I picked up the lantern and shone its thin beam around.

The walls of the cave were rock, but they were nearly sheer. No, this wasn't a cave. This wasn't anything like a cave at all. And there was something decidedly square and manufactured about that opening in the far wall—

"Fuck fuck *fuck!*" I tried to back out of the hole, but I was panicking and instead of staying down my body's fight-or-flight mechanisms were telling me to *stand* and *run* and maybe *murder*. "Speedy! Minotaur! *Minotaur!*"

A set of claws dropped onto my bare calves. "Calm your tits, kitten," Speedy rumbled in his deep voice. "Or you're gonna experience some aggressive acupuncture."

I took a deep breath, lowered myself flat, and squirmed backwards.

"What's wrong? What happened?" Dina helped me to my feet and pressed a canteen into my hands.

I drank gratefully. Fifteen seconds of pure terror was dehydrating.

"It's not a cave," I said when I could breathe again. The panic wasn't gone: I barely noticed that Keith had appeared, camera in hand.

Speedy rolled his eyes, snatched up the camp lantern, and walked into the hole before I could stop him. His head popped out again a moment later.

"Congratulations," he said to me. "You found a second part of the city. Probably storage, and an escape route if they were attacked."

"Okay," I said. My heart was pounding hard enough that I could feel it in my knees. "Okay."

"You knew that when you went in there," he said, shaking his head at me.

I flipped him off and trudged away.

Okay.

Okay, apparently I had developed a mild phobia of minotaurs. Unfortunately, the ghost pirate was still coming, so I needed to put that first fear aside and focus on developing a second one.

Right.

Pirate, Hope. Focus on the *pirate*.

I dropped to the ground and slumped forward, hugging my knees.

I didn't want to be here.

I wanted Mare to be awake, and safe.

I wanted the two of us to be back at the Bellagio—or better yet, back home in Washington.

I wanted things to make *sense!*

My fingers were running up and down my left arm, searching for a scar that was no longer there, but I could barely feel—

Oh. Shock. I was in mild shock. Everything was catching up with me, and—

I turned and drove my fist straight into one of the rocks.

"Gnaaaah!" I gasped, as the skin on my knuckles split open.

Fun doctor fact: you can't snap out of shock. What you can do is add a new symptom for your body to manage, and it tends to prioritize physical injury above mental injury. Which makes sense, evolutionarily speaking, as it's darned hard to process psychological trauma if the tiger has already eaten you. Pain is a hell of a motivator. So I wasn't fixing my brain, just postponing the breakdown. Plus, gross weeping holes ruining my brand-new skin.

I lurched to my feet, pounding my bloody knuckles into my palm to keep the pain going

"Knife," I said to Dina.

She slapped the combat knife into my hand. "Are you okay?" she asked. "Why were you screaming about a minotaur?"

"Bad dreams as a kid." It was an autopilot answer. "Where's the light?"

Dina pointed towards the black mouth of the tunnel. There was a tiny spark in its center, nearly swallowed by the dark.

I hopped up the rocks, shoved the combat knife through the belt loops on the back of my shorts, and dove headfirst into the tunnel.

Into the dark.

A little wiggling, and I was through.

The LED jogging light was lying in the center of the tunnel where I had left it. I took a deep breath, and picked it up. The light spilled from between my fingers, glinting off the blood on my hand.

"Ghosts are just people," I whispered, as I shut my eyes. "There's no such thing as monsters."

Which was only half a lie, and only because that first sentence devoured the second and spat out its bones.

"Perp?"

There was movement to go along with the sound. The roadrunner zoomed up to me and inspected my ankles.

"I was wondering where you ran off to," I said, and then I grabbed it by the neck.

Roadrunners are fast. Like, *fast*-fast. Much faster than any human. But no human is stupid enough to grab a roadrunner by the neck, because while the beak is a deadly weapon, those talons are little buzz saws. I, however, was using pain as a coping strategy, and I had decided the talons would be a big assist. The roadrunner never saw me coming.

It screeched and tried to wiggle loose, mostly by shoving those talons into my skin for leverage.

"Knock it off," I told it.

The roadrunner's feet slowed, then stopped. It left two talons stuck in my palm.

"I'm guessing you're Team Coyote?"

The roadrunner blinked.

"Got a message for your boss. You ready?"

"...perp."

I leaned in as close as I could, and whispered: "The kid and I are shit psychics. Neither of us have any training. If your boss wants entertainment, have him wake up the redhead with the long hair. Then the *real* game'll start."

I knelt and gently released the roadrunner. Its talons were still embedded in my hand; we spent a few awkward moments trying to detach them. Once we did, the roadrunner scampered to a safe distance and began to complain at me.

"Consider it payback for beaning me in the head," I said.

The bird rolled its eyes, and disappeared.

Not 'ran off,' mind. Actually literally vanished.

That shook me. Most ghosts could teleport inanimate objects. Only the truly powerful ones could teleport a living creature, and there were always consequences. Ben did it with Speedy all the time, because Speedy wasn't able to talk while he recovered, and omy*god* sometimes you just needed a *break!*[44]

I squeezed my injured hand until blood splattered against the dry earth, and focused on how much it hurt.

"Huff?"

Goldie Hawn poked her head through the tunnel's entrance.

"Hey," I said. "You get everything sorted out?"

"Yeah," came a deep muffled voice from behind her. Goldie Hawn's lips curled over her fangs in surprise as Speedy shoved against her butt. "She's not Hohokam."

"Really?" I realized I had already written Goldie Hawn's backstory in my mind. And that was…well, that was a pretty shitty thing to do.

Speedy finished pushing Goldie Hawn into the tunnel. "She predates the Hohokam by at least ten thousand years."

If I had been drinking, I would have done the most marvelous spit take. *"Really?!"*

Goldie Hawn made a sound that could only be a chupacabra's version of a chuckle.

"Yup," Speedy said, as he put his paws on my legs for a lift. "She's Clovis. One of the first cultures in North America to develop after the last Ice Age."

"Nice to meet you," I said to her.

"She's going to teach me her language," he said, shaking in delight, then added: "If we live through this."

"Ah." I turned towards the darkness in front of us, and began walking. It was easier to see when Goldie Hawn was there; she threw off more light than any other ghost I'd met.

"Goldie, why are you helping us?" I asked. "Not that I mind! I'm just curious."

"That's getting close to sacred ground," Speedy said, as Goldie Hawn nodded. The blue glow she cast bobbed up and down in time with her head. "From what I can tell, she's seen this

44 I'm aware this is a jerk thing to do, thanks.

scenario play out a lot over the millennia. She thinks it's cruel."

"I agree," I said to her. "Thanks. And you're fluent in English?"

Speedy laughed and swayed on my shoulders. He was almost woozy from joy. "She's fluent in *everything!*"

Oh, joy. The super-genius linguist has found his prehistoric ghost of a dream girl. I could make a billion dollars on their odd-couple screenplay.

"Does she know how to fight Hawley and the rest of his crew?" I asked.

"She says that's your job."

I made a fist with my injured hand, and squeezed until I felt a fresh trickle of blood. "Why. Why me?"

"Psychics are nature's way of maintaining the balance between the worlds of the living and the dead."

I shook my head. "That sounds like what de Borromeo said. But I don't know how to do that!"

"You kidding?" Speedy laughed and rubbed his head against mine, like a happy cat. "Kitten, the only thing you know how to do is beat some ass!"

Quick as I had grabbed the roadrunner, I reached up and seized Speedy by his scruff. I just wanted to *shake him* and **shake him** until—

I dropped him on the floor.

"Hey!" He took a swipe at my ankles with his claws. "What's your problem?"

"Go back to Mare," I said. "I'll hold the tunnel."

He shouted after me, but I couldn't seem to hear him. There was a scrap of light ahead; the tunnel came out on the other side of the mountain, and the night sky was waiting. I kept walking towards that small scrap of open air.

Goldie Hawn came with me.

Through the tunnel, towards that little piece of sky.

Goldie Hawn poked her head out first, then gestured for me to follow. We came out of the mountain above a small valley. There was a ledge beneath our feet, but if there had ever been a path to this rear entrance, time and erosion had carried it away.

The air felt…wet?

I took a deep breath. Yes, the air was definitely wet. Everything seemed to be waiting, as if the entire world was about to explode.

I peeked over the side of the ledge.

Below?

Ghosts.

They had gathered by the foot of the mountain. There weren't as many in this group as there had been in the one which had attacked de Borromeo. I counted twenty, maybe twenty-five, all of them waiting for that same unknown signal. They wore the illusion of their old clothing over their blue bones and what they had chosen to keep of their raw, broken flesh.

Hawley was there.

He was unmistakable. Taller than the others and dangerously thin. A sword with a slight curve to it, and a raggedy coat which floated around him. He was the center of the action; the other ghosts, pirates and cowboys and whatnot, kept looking to him for direction. He had that same quality of power which I had seen a hundred times in politicians, as if Heaven itself had blessed him with the ability to lead.[45]

"How did his crew mutiny against *him?*" I wondered aloud.

Goldie Hawn growled something, which sounded very much like: "Starvation drove them to it."

I wheeled around. "I understood you!" I said, delighted. "Human you!"

Her ears perked up, and she gave me a wide toothy grin.

The ghosts at the base of the mountain heard me, and roared.

I shut my eyes. "Oh, shit."

Snarl-growl: "Whoops."

I leaned over to see the ghosts bounding up the mountain in huge ground-eating strides. Up, up, each leap taking them straight up, up to where we were sitting—

I yanked out the combat knife. The belt loops shredded as it slid into my hand.

Up, up…

We could see their tattered flesh. The rust on their weapons.

45 Total lie, definitely, but they made it work for them.

The bones poking out through the holes in their shoes. These ghosts had gone to great lengths to make themselves as terrifying as possible, and hot damn, it was working.

I stood and stretched out my toes in my boots. I couldn't feel my own feet. They might as well be nothing but bones, too, for all that I could tell.

"I think I'm having a breakdown," I said to Goldie Hawn. "Right now? Like, right now this second? I'm having a massive breakdown. These ghosts? They aren't even really a thing. They're just the *latest* thing. And the only reason I've got all of these bullshit things to manage is because I'm *me*."

I stood and turned to face the ghosts.

"Well, I can't fuckin' stop being *me*."

And then they were over the edge of the ledge, and the battle was on.

Chapter Thirty-One

Time stops.

The dead feel pain.

They can't help it. It's muscle memory; they remember they had muscles, so they remember that a knife sliding through those muscles hurts like hell. It's temporary pain, gone as soon as they remember they're dead. But it slows them down, and I move through the ghosts, putting that combat knife through a dozen different ribcages.

Gravity is my friend. Those ghosts might have all but flown up the side of the mountain, but when I throw them off of it, they plunge towards the ground. That's what their memories think will happen, and they can't break away from those memories long enough to remember they can walk on air.

I grab an arm; its owner is shocked into forgetting that its true body had rotted to pieces several centuries ago. I want to cause as much pain as possible; I break the elbow, and then rip the arm from its socket. The ghost screams, and I hurl both the ghost and its arm over the edge of the mountain.

They keep coming, pouring onto the narrow ledge as fast as they can. They stink of the grave; I notice that some of them are wearing actual clothing, not just illusions they've crafted as costumes.

I wonder how long they've been in this world as ghosts, and if any of them regret the decision to stay.

Goldie Hawn fights beside me. In the heart of the battle, I see her as she truly is; a young woman, her eyes shining with power. She keeps the swords and weapons from my body, moving in the wild steps of the same ancient martial art that de Borromeo had used on the pirates.

I begin to match her technique.

Low, sweeping thrusts to break their ankles. Upwards strikes which end with a knife to their unbeating hearts.

That twist of a hand which de Borromeo used to blow the pirates across the desert.

And (*holy shit*) it **works!**

Not at first. The first couple of times, I nearly lose my hand as I leave it hanging in midair. Goldie Hawn is there to pull me aside, to knock the swords and daggers and hatchets away. The ghosts keep coming.

But I work at it. It's a peculiar twisting movement with a finger gesture which is rather like flipping the bird, so I start to shout: *"Fuck off!"* instead of the usual martial arts *kiai*, and the ghosts are blown from the mountain.

How am I doing it? I can't tell. I'm definitely not doing it right. De Borromeo glowed like lightning and *pushed*, and her pirates disintegrated. Mine stay in one piece, unless I put in the effort to tear them apart with my bare hands. There's just not enough of me and there's too many of them, and then—

They're gone.

As cautiously as I can, I peer over the edge. Spectral projectiles fly at my face.

Time starts again as I fall backwards.

"Shit!" I slammed against the rocky wall of the mountain, all but wrung dry. That quick glance had shown the ghosts regrouping, none the worse for wear.

I looked at Goldie Hawn. At least she was still a woman; my brain had finally been knocked out of monster mode.

"I can't do what de Borromeo does," I gasped. "That thing where she turns them to dust? Yeah, no. That's not in my toolkit. All I can do is slow them down.

"Hi, by the way. You're human."

"Hello," she said, smiling. Her true voice was as smooth as running water. "Can you keep going?"

"For a while, but eventually one of 'em will get lucky and I'll get dead." I was tired. My entire body was shaking. Nothing made sense except the fight...especially the part where I knew that no fight lasted forever, and I wouldn't survive this one. I was outnumbered and outclassed on a truly supernatural scale.

"Retreat?" she asked.

I nodded. Goldie Hawn helped me to my feet. We fell back, out of the night and into the mountain.

If she hadn't been dragging me along, I would have missed it. Instead, I nearly cracked my head on the pile of rocks which lined both sides of the opening. I dodged, and saw something we had missed on our way outside.

"Wait," I said. "Look!"

We stopped. The rocks were much like the pile that Dina and I had moved inside the old city, with heavy boulders at the base. Except these? Some ancient engineer had put both stacks of stones on slopes, and had angled them towards the opening.

"Go," I gestured towards the far pile. Goldie Hawn moved to press her back against the stones. I did the same to mine.

"On three!" I shouted. "One, two…"

A ghost in an old Stetson hat and a long rotting duster came through the entrance. It spotted me, and its mouth opened in a skeletal roar.

"Three!"

Goldie Hawn pushed. Her rocks moved easily and tumbled across the entrance. The cowboy cried out as the rocks pulverized the memory of his body.

Mine—

"C'mon," I snarled, as I threw my weight against the rocks. "C'mon!"

There was a grinding noise as the rocks slid over each other, slowly…too slowly…

The dead cowboy had remembered it was already dead. It pulled itself from under Goldie Hawn's rocks and turned towards me, its mouth open wide enough to swallow me in a single bite. Behind it were a knot of ghosts, howling for blood, fighting to get through what was left of the opening.

"*C'mon!*" I shouted, as the rocks finally tumbled over themselves. They crashed against the rocks from Goldie Hawn's pile, stacking themselves high, blocking out the other ghosts. Even the cowboy got caught in them a second time. It gave me just enough time to shuffle over to our tiny landslide and shout, "Now, *stay the hell out of my mountain!*"

"Come." Goldie Hawn slipped her arm beneath mine. "They'll be able to move those rocks. We have to get your friends out of here."

"Yeah." I wanted to collapse on the ground and sleep for a year. Five years. A nice round decade. Instead, we retraced our steps through the mountain.

The glow that Goldie Hawn threw off as a chupacabra was muted when she was in human form. I had to strain to see through the gloom. The tunnel looked extremely labyrinthy... Nope. Breakdown Brain was having none of that. Instead of dwelling on past monsters, I heard myself say, "You can walk through walls, right?"

Goldie Hawn nodded. Her hair moved against my bare cheek. "Yes."

"Or jump from one location to another?"

"Yes."

I looked back over my shoulder. There were no ghosts behind us. Not yet. "So what's going to keep them from walking through those rocks? Or jumping straight into the tunnel?"

"Tonight, barriers cannot be penetrated; they must be moved, and they cannot be moved by supernatural strength. They must be moved for the same reason they had to use the tunnel in the first place, as there are rules in effect," she replied. "Your animal friend was right about that. Otherwise, this wouldn't be a game."

"Game." I started to laugh. "Right. Best game ever. So much fun."

Goldie Hawn began to laugh along with me. "Oh," she sighed. "I hope you live through this."

"Me, too," I cackled. "You don't want me hanging around your desert for the rest of eternity!"

She howled while laughing, chortling like a hyena. I joined in, even though it hurt to breathe.

"Hope?" Fish's voice came from just ahead. "Do you need help?"

"Probably!"

Goldie Hawn began to howl again.

The harsh white glow of LEDs appeared, followed by the mouth of the tunnel. I went through first, pulling myself along the tunnel with my elbows. I squeezed through the little hole at the end, and came out in the main cavern.

"Jeeze!" Fish took in my battle damage with wide eyes. "What happened to you?"

"Ghosts don't bleed. These ghosts are hella-dusty tho'. Great sense of theater, all things considered," I groaned, as he helped me crawl down the stones to the floor of the cavern. "They're coming. We've gotta seal this entrance."

Fish shouted for help. Tellerman and the others came running, and, very slowly, the rock pile was rebuilt.

Not well, though. We didn't have the raw power or the equipment to lift the biggest stones. I saw the small hundred-pounders go back up, and shivered. If Dana and I could move them, then two dozen dead men would have no problem.

Goldie Hawn had watched all of this in silence. When she was sure that we had done all that we could, she nodded to me. "You'll be safe for a little while," she said. "I must go and check on my friends."

"Gotcha." My heart sank a little. She had saved my life more times than I could count in that one battle. "I hope they're okay."

"I'll return when I can," she replied.

"Thanks for all you've done."

She smiled at me, and slipped into her chupacabra form. She danced a few quick steps, as if happy to be back on four legs again, and turned to leave.

"Hey!" I whispered. When she turned back, I held up my right hand so I could wiggle my fingers at her. "One thing. If you see a ring anywhere out there, could you bring it back to me?"

Goldie Hawn nodded, and then ran towards the cavern's entrance until she was nothing but a speck of blue against the night…and gone.

I was having suspicious thoughts about my missing ring. I had taken a couple of hard hits to the head today, but I was pretty sure I remembered seeing it while I was chasing the roadrunner. That ring couldn't fall off.[46] Someone had removed it. Which means that someone had known what it did, and that removing it would keep me from using it.

It wasn't looking good for de Borromeo's angry desert theory.

And then, the part I was dreading happened: Tellerman came over and sat beside me.

"I need to know what's going on," he said.

"No, you don't." I pressed my face into my knees. "And you wouldn't believe me if I told you."

"Try me."

"No." I knew I had to get up and move around, or I'd stiffen up and be useless, but nothing seemed to work. Ah, shock.

"Hope—"

"I can't tell you anything," I said. "Need-to-know, only."

"You look like death warmed over," he began, and cut off only when I began to laugh. If I had sounded on edge when I was laughing along with Goldie Hawn, now I was a full-bore maniac.

"Hope," he said. "We're scared. You've got to help us."

A bright flash of brilliant light swept over us, followed by a crash which shook the entire cavern. We all turned towards the rear tunnel; the stones we had piled against the opening were still standing. The front entrance? No, nothing. What—

The flash and the noise shook the cavern again. This time, water began to sprinkle through the ventilation holes in the roof.

"A thunderstorm," Tellerman said, as he gave a relieved chuckle. He shook the tension from his body, and slumped over his knees. "Just a thunderstorm."

A thunderstorm. That explained why I had caught the scent

46 Because Science Reasons.

of water when Goldie Hawn and I were outside. We were far enough away from the vents that we'd stay dry, but it was yet another complication we didn't need.

Well, it was a complication they didn't need. I found myself utterly unimpressed by the rain. I wondered if the ghosts would mind if I stayed right here and sat out the storm.

Tellerman turned to me. "Hope?" he said. "C'mon. If this is really an Army exercise, you can tell me. I know how this kind of thing works."

"Go away," I whispered. It hurt to speak. My voice had broken on that last bout of insane laughter.

"What'd she say?" Keith came over, camera on his shoulder. He wasn't looking at me, just the screen in front of him.

"Not now," Tellerman told him.

"Yeah, not now," I said. Or maybe I just thought I said it. In either case, Keith knelt beside us, and swung his camera around.

That great shiny glass eyeball stared right at me.

I balled up my fist and smashed it straight into the camera.

I knew it was wrong. I knew there was no coming back from it. You don't *hit, you don't hurt, you don't **break!***

I also knew I didn't care.

The lens shattered, and the camera popped out of Keith's hands to smash him in the face. I didn't hear the sound of his nose breaking, but he howled with pain and dropped the ruined camera.

Dina and Oshea came running, and there was a *lot* of shouting. Oshea slid between me and Tellerman; Dina grabbed Keith by the shoulders and hauled him away from me.

Unnecessary. I didn't want to hurt Tellerman. Or even Keith. All I cared about was that goddamned camera, and it was finally dead. I decided to kick it for good measure, and it spun across the cavern floor in circles, spewing a very satisfying amount of glass.

"Oh, hell." Speedy was in my lap, checking my eyes with a flashlight. "Kitten? Don't do this."

It seemed like an excellent time to lay down on the cavern

floor, and maybe rest for a while.

"Is she okay?" Dina asked Speedy.

"Obviously not!" he snapped. "She's—"

Whatever he was about to say? It got stuck in his throat, as those phenomenal ears of his swiveled in the direction of the rock pile.

The rocks were beginning to move.

Chapter Thirty-Two

INT. CAVERN, NIGHT

The camera is stationary. There is picture, but the lens is damaged and the image is indistinct. Voices and shapes of Spooky Solutions team can be heard, along with those of KOALA and FISH. Two prone shapes that are not interacting with the others are HOPE and MARE.

KEITH (crosstalk): I think—I think that bitch broke my—

OSHEA (crosstalk): Can you blame her? You shoved—

DINA (crosstalk): —told you to stop, and you—

KEITH (crosstalk): —not gonna apologize for doing my job.

Sound of thunder in the background.

TELLERMAN: Keith, put it away. Just for a while, okay? Something happened to her when she was in that tunnel.

DINA: Is it the same thing that happened to Mare?

TELLERMAN: I don't know.

HOPE kicks the camera away from her. The image spins. Some of the broken glass is removed and the picture improves.

KOALA: Gimme a flashlight.

KOALA shines a flashlight in HOPE's eyes.

KOALA (to HOPE): Kitten? Don't do this.

HOPE lies on the ground.

DINA (to KOALA): Is she okay?

KOALA (to DINA): Obviously not! She's—

KOALA falls silent.

KOALA (quietly): Okay, everybody, get moving. Third building on the left is the most structurally sound. Let's go.

TELLERMAN: What's happening?

KOALA points towards the rock pile. The smallest rock slides off and falls to the ground.

KOALA (quietly): Pick up your stuff and move. **Fast.**

Movement as KEITH picks up the camera. The humans and KOALA move from the back of the cavern into a building. HOPE and MARE are carried. A large piece of old wood is propped against the opening to serve as a door.

KOALA (whispering): Turn off the lights.

The scene goes to extreme low light. The major source of illumination is lightning coming from overhead. A secondary source is a camping lantern left in the cavern.

There is a sound of large rocks falling, followed by a low strange-sounding howl.

FISH (whispering): Oh my god.

KOALA (whispering): Shut it.

FISH (whispering): But—

KOALA (whispering): I know. I hear him, too. Panicking won't solve shit.

TELLERMAN (to KOALA): What's happening?

KOALA: C'mon, fuckos, how many times do I have to say this is none of your business? You're not helping. Just let it play out.

TELLERMAN (to KOALA): Hey, you—

HOPE (to TELLERMAN, quietly): Don't touch him.

TELLERMAN (pausing): …

TELLERMAN (to KOALA): …sorry.

The howling noise is heard again.

KOALA (to FISH, whispering): …her.

FISH (loudly): What? No!

FISH (to KOALA, whispering): …last time…she was psychotic.

KOALA (to FISH, whispering): …better get your ass in…need her up and moving.

The howling noise is heard again. This time, it is much louder. Everyone falls silent.

A scratching sound comes from the makeshift door. Then, the door is torn away by an unseen force.

HOPE (leaping forward, knife drawn): **Motherfucker!**

Chapter Thirty-Three

Let's back up about ninety seconds, right before it all went pear-shaped.

I had given up. I'd like to say that I was lying in a ball on the ground because I was weighing options, figuring out the best course of action, and all that snazz. Nope. As soon as those rocks began to move, Shock-Me decided it was over and we were done.

It was actually comforting. If I had known how de Borromeo had sacrificed herself to defeat Hawley, I might have dug up enough energy to try it. Since I didn't, and since we were all going to die anyhow, it was nice to lie back and watch everyone else freak out for a change.

I wished Hawley would stop howling, though.

I knew it was him. How? I don't know—I suppose the barriers I had slapped up around my brain had finally fallen down. I knew that he was alone, that he had left his minions outside, and that he was the only one who had enough strength to enter the mountain. Goldie Hawn and I had managed to do that much, at least.

The howl moved up and down four different octaves at once. Eerie? Yes. Annoying? Definitely.

Speedy prodded me onto my feet. Tellerman and Dina each took one of my arms and carried me between them. Fish cradled Mare against his chest as if she was a delicate flower. We shuffled from the back of the cavern into the ancient city. The building Speedy had picked had an old piece of wood stacked against the opening where a door should be. We moved this, slipped inside, and tugged it shut behind us.

I hadn't given much thought to the interior of the buildings. All I could think was that there were eight of us, and the single room was extremely tight.

Speedy pushed me over to the corner of the room, next to Fish and Mare. I slumped down and used her lap as a pillow.

"Hope?" Fish was close to begging. "C'mon. You've got to do something."

I thought about reminding him that I *had* done something—hell, I'd done *everything!*—but spending my last few minutes in a shouting match was meaningless. Besides, we'd all be dead soon, and then I'd probably have to fight Hawley anyhow. Might as well enjoy the peace while I could.

Speedy seized the hand I had bashed open on the rock, and held it out to Fish. "Fix her."

"What?" Fish drew away from us. "No! You shoulda seen her last time—she was psychotic."

"Can you fight these ghosts?" Speedy hissed. "Because if you can, you better get your ass in gear, since you've already forced her to do the heavy lifting. And if you can't? Then we need her up and moving."

"She'll crash again," Fish said, but he took my hand anyway. His skin was cold, as if he was already readying himself for the grave.

"A lot can happen in fifteen minutes," Speedy said. "We both know what happens if she's still lying here when Hawley finds us."

Fish nodded, and shut his eyes.

This time, the pain was minimal. Honestly, it was more intrusive than painful; I could feel the tiny creeping sensations of cells showing, growing, stretching…

That eerie howling stopped.

Mike always says that psychics dealt with the living and the dead. Nothing inanimate. Nothing that didn't contain that intangible flicker of stardust which made us…*more.* But as Fish forced my cells to hurry on their natural path, I thought I could feel…*more.* The desert was (*blue mist began to move into the room*) starting to change, starting to drink (*a ghostly chuckle*) in the rain, and the rain (*long blue fingers, long blue bony fingers, long blue bony fingers scratching at the makeshift door*) was calling the land awake.

Hawley tore the door away and swept into the room in a maelstrom of ruined blue.

Oshea screamed.

Hawley went straight for her, those long blue fingers reaching for her throat—

I was there to meet him.

I drove the combat knife straight into the hollows of his rib cage, right where his heart should be. I pulled the knife out, and then drove it in again and again.

I think I was howling.

A flash of surprise moved across Hawley's empty eye sockets. In that moment, I saw him as he truly was, a man not much older than myself, wracked by a genetic disorder and the better part of a lifetime spent at sea.

Did I feel pity? I can't remember. Probably not. At that moment, I was nothing but adrenaline-fueled rage.

Hawley fell backwards, out of the room and into the city. I kept after him, attacking with the knife, with my hands, with my feet, driving him back, back—

Hawley seized the knife.

He had waited until I had stuck it between his ribs again, and then clapped his bony hands across my own, trapping the knife—and me—against him.

He opened his mouth as wide as he could, all teeth, all stench, all death, and leaned in as if he wanted to swallow me whole.

Pro tip: never, ever trap the hands of someone who's sunk several decades into practicing judo.

I spun sideways and went straight into a modified *Tai otoshi*…a body drop. I spun, stuck a leg out, and sent the ghost over my hip and straight into the ground, head-first. There was an incredibly satisfying *crunch!* as the back of his bare skull cracked against the ground.

Hawley groaned.

My hands were free: I reclaimed the knife, but instead of

more stabbing, I decided to start stomping Hawley's face into the dirt instead. Some distant part of my mind noted that since the face(ish) part of his head was pointing up, that would take a little additional effort.

Well, might as well get started. Not like he had much actual facematter to work with, anyhow.

"Kitten."

stomp

stomp

stomp

"Kitten!"

stomp

stomp

stomp

"Kitten!"

I stopped, blinked a few times, and realized Speedy was standing beside the puddle of Hawley's ghost.

"Kitten, you gotta move."

The words swooped around my brain, bats looking for a place to roost.

"C'mon." He put his head against my legs and shoved. "Move."

Hawley groaned.

"Move!" Speedy shouted, swiping at me with his claws, and I finally understood. I grabbed him around his pudgy stomach, tucked him under my arm, and began to run.

I glanced over my shoulder. Behind us, Hawley began to drag himself across the ground. Slowly at first, one hand after the other, as if he were in agonizing pain. Then, he started to shake the pain off, his skull began to round itself out, his hands began to move faster and faster...

He stopped, and turned towards the open doorway of the building which sheltered our friends.

I screeched to a halt. "Hey!"

Hawley chuckled, his body flowing back into its original unstomped form. He moved towards the others, clawed fingers reaching out—

Oh, *shit.*

How do you get a pirate's attention?

On my best day, my headspace is populated with rabid bees. On a day when I needed to find a way to keep a zombie pirate away from my friends? Those bees did advanced zombie pirate calculus. The answer was inevitable, really: there's only one surefire way to get a dead pirate's attention.

"Hey!" I shouted again. "I know where your ship is!"

That got his attention.

Hawley whipped towards me in a cloud of blue, his mouth hanging open in a skull's silent scream.

"And I know where your treasure is, too!"

The pirate charged.

"Go *go go!*" Speedy shouted.

I was already gone.

Speedy and I raced through the city.

I made the mistake of looking over my shoulder again. Whatever rules were in effect, Hawley had decided they no longer applied to him. Not when his treasure was threatened. He was flying towards us at an inhuman speed, roaring, ready to tear us to pieces with those claw-like fingers.

I was still holding Speedy like a football, with his head pointed behind us and his butt leading the way. His little tail began to twitch in earnest. "C'mon, kitten!" he shouted, as Hawley reached for his eyes. "Pick it up!"

We crossed from the cavern into the night as the storm broke open. The light rain turned blinding; we were soaked to the skin within seconds. It slowed me down; the old road was in terrible shape, and we were on a cliff. One misplaced foot would result in a short, slippery scream.

Hawley didn't have to deal with anything as mundane as feet. He kept coming, still howling, still stretching out those claws of his towards Speedy's face...

A streak of blue darted across the rocks and plowed straight into Hawley.

Speedy began to laugh.

Another blue streak flashed across the rocks, followed by another, and then another. Too many to count. Too fast to make out any details.

"What's happening?" I shouted through the rain.

"Reinforcements!" he cried.

I slowed down long enough to find a safe place to descend a washed-out section of road. Hawley was screaming beneath the pack of chupacabras.

"Damn," I said, impressed, as the chupacabras started to pick him apart. Today was the first time I had seen ghosts fighting against ghosts,[47] and they were definitely doing damage to each other.

"Keep running," Speedy snapped. "They can't hold him for long."

He was right. Hawley had taken a page from de Borromeo's playbook, and was lashing out left and right with his long hooked fingers. When these jabbed into a chupacabra, the poor ghost dissolved into blue motes of dust.

"We gotta help them," I said.

"Don't stop." A familiar honeyed voice came from beside me. "They are buying you time."

I turned to see Goldie Hawn in her human form, holding onto the cliff face beside me. "Is he...what's he doing to them?"

"It takes a great deal of energy to manifest in this world," she said, as she held out her hand to help me over a spot where the road was flooding. "He is dispelling this energy. They are unharmed, but it will take time for them to recover."

Speedy wriggled out from beneath my arm and climbed up to my shoulders. He draped himself over my head and turned his arms into a furry hat brim to keep the rain off of my face. "Where do we go?" he asked her.

"To de Borromeo," Goldie Hawn replied, and pointed in the direction of the pirate ship. "She will bind him within his prison again, but you must bring him to her. She has lost much of her

---

47 At least, the first time I had ever seen ghosts fighting for keeps. The Founding Fathers settle a lot of disagreements with an old-fashioned punching match, and then they go out for a drink.

own strength tonight."

"Right," I said. Above us, Hawley had his fingers deep in the chest of a large chupacabra. The poor soul screamed once before it was torn apart in a cloud of dust motes. "What about Hawley's crew?"

Goldie Hawn looked me straight in the eyes. "Be smarter and faster than they are."

There was nothing else to say, so I took a deep breath, and leapt into the storm.

Down the mountain, wet from rain, my feet sliding out beneath me so I slid halfway down on my ass.

Down to where the desert floor began, water starting to puddle and creep, the ground still too dry to soak it up.

Towards the ruins of the old caravel, lost beneath the earth.

Speedy hunkered down as best he could. I wasn't wearing his jogging harness, and I was keenly aware of his claws digging into my shoulders. It didn't hurt.

Nothing hurt.

Was I still in shock? Maybe. But we had reached the point where the adrenaline rush from Fish's miniature healing job had burned itself out, and I didn't feel any different. No crash, no burn. No feeling.

No, wait. I wasn't numb. Not anymore.

For athletes, there's a zone called a runner's high, where emotions smooth themselves out and pain becomes an afterthought. I had never found it before—I've run marathons and the ol' bee-brain keeps buzzing the entire time. In spite of the rain, despite the ghosts, I felt...

What *did* I feel?

I felt the desert around me. It had come fully awake as it welcomed the rain. The water moved into the cracks within its broken earth, into its nooks and crannies, beginning to fill the soil with enough moisture to sustain it for another year, for another *decade*, maybe, for the seeds lying dormant within the ground to come alive, for the plants to drink and drink and drink until each individual cell of their bodies was full to bursting.

I felt the sky above me, and somehow just *knew* this storm was a wild creature caught in a trap. It didn't belong here; it was supposed to be five hundred miles to the west. It had been lured here. The desert hadn't earned it!

The storm wept. It wanted to punish this greedy, thirsty land.

I felt like crying, too.

What else did I feel?

For once, I *didn't* feel the eyes of the world on me. It was me and Speedy, and nobody else. Maybe a ghost or two knew where we were.

Maybe Coyote.

No one else.

It was exhilarating, to be here, to be alone. Finally. Finally! *Privacy!*

But…

But we had no backup; we had no safety net; we had no one and nothing to help us.

Maybe privacy was a tradeoff. Maybe the bigger the problems, the more you needed help to solve them. And all of my current problems were layered on top of each other, where a pirate and a desert and a trickster god were tangled up together, and it was up to me and a koala to find a way to pull it all apart.

Be careful what you wish for, I thought, and began to laugh. Just a little, at first, a small chuckle which soon built to a wide, warm laugh which stretched out through the cold rains. It was all just so *funny!*

What else did I feel?

There was an angry storm all around us, and a thirst-starved desert beneath us. The one was nourishing the other. It wasn't fair, but what was fair for a storm, or for a desert? They might be full of life and death, but neither of them could reason. The storm raged its denial of the natural order, while the desert took advantage of the opportunity.

Me?

I was a human being. I wasn't trapped. I wasn't stuck in one place.

I lived. I learned. I could change.

I felt *free*.

The brief flashes of lightning came faster now, one right after the other. I thought about asking Speedy what would happen if the lightning touched down near enough to electrify the puddles, then decided against it. There was nothing I could do to change *that*, except get out of the water as fast as I could. The water was up to my ankles, but the ground was finally beginning to soften up. It'd become mud soon enough, and that'd bring with it a new set of problems. For now, it was firm enough.

"You okay?" Speedy's voice was a slow undercurrent beneath the storm.

I mulled over what he had asked, long enough for him to repeat himself. "Yeah," I replied.

"You sure?"

"No. It's a process."

That's when the first of Hawley's zombie-looking minions swung up from his hiding place behind a large boulder. I recognized him from the fight on the mountain; he had branded himself with the memories of an axe and a long knife, both razor-sharp. He never got close enough to use them: I did that little hand twist with the *"Fuck off!"* command, and he soared across the desert.

"You're getting good at that," Speedy muttered. "Keep an eye out. There'll be more of them."

He was right...and also wrong. I had expected to be attacked by the two dozen ghosts from the mountain, maybe accompanied by a bunch of those who had been in that first direct assault on de Borromeo. Instead, maybe a handful of ghosts popped up, their weapons at the ready, and never more than one at a time. These were easy to throw aside, and they didn't come back once they were gone.

Speedy stood tall, and used my hair as his handholds to move around.

Rain began to fall in my eyes again. "What are you doing?" I asked.

"Something's wrong," he said. "There should be more of those guys. And where's Hawley? He coulda caught up to us by now, easy."

I slowed but couldn't stop; the mud was starting to suck at my feet. "Think we should go back to the city?"

"No," he said, veeeery cautiously, as if he wasn't sure.

"Speedy—"

"I know it's a gamble!" he snapped. "But I'm almost positive that Hawley's already waiting for us by his ship."

"What?" I began to pick up speed again. By now, the water was cascading towards the low places, and I was fighting to keep my footing. "Why?"

"Because he's a fucking pirate, kitten."

"More details."

Speedy sighed. "Because he's a fucking pirate who's just received a massive power-up from reality television. He's going to try to do something with that power."

That made sense. Even if Hawley hadn't gotten his hands on a boatload of pearls, there might have been some treasure in his ship. You couldn't take it with you, after all.

And then it was just one more hill between us and the ship. A single little hill, up and over. It'd be nothing if the ground was dry; between the rain and the mud, I had to fight my way up to the top on my hands and knees.

De Borromeo was waiting at the top. She was lying flat against the hill, as low as she could get and still peer over the top.

"Hey," I said, as I flailed my way towards her. The rain was going cold; the mud was beginning to suck the warmth out of me. "Glad you're all right." When she didn't reply, I added, "…you *are* all right, right?"

"I am well," she replied, her attention fixed on something on the other side of the hill. "For the moment."

"What do you…" I trailed off as I finally reached her, and could see what was on the other side of the hill. "Oh."

Down in the hollow where Hawley's ship had been entombed?

Ghosts. Lots of them. *All* of them, at least all of the ones who had made it through the night intact. Hawley was at their center. Their attention was on the water gathering within the center of the hollow.

"We're too late," de Borromeo said. "He seeks to escape the desert and return to the sea."

"Ooooo-kay," I said, as I squinted through the curtain of pouring rain. "Can we do anything?"

De Borromeo shook her head. "This is now beyond our ability to stop. We can only bear witness."

"Ominous," I muttered, as Speedy and I settled ourselves in the mud beside her.

There was a ghostly shimmer beneath the water. It was larger than any other ghost I'd seen, and had an unnatural shape. It stayed just out of sight, its form blending at the point where the desert floor met the water.

Hawley appeared to be furious. He would seize any ghost foolish enough to get within arm's reach, and plunge them into the water. Those unfortunate ghosts would scream as they dissolved into blue motes, which were in turn swallowed by the blue shape beneath the water. The rest of the ghosts joined hands and focused every bit of their spare power at that shape.

It wasn't enough, so Hawley began to call down lightning.

He walked into the center of the hollow, where the water was deepest and glowed the brightest. He shouted and raged at the storm, and as he did this, he stretched his too-long arms up, up, up towards the churning sky.

Lightning struck him, casting him in an aura of blue so bright that I had to turn away. When my vision cleared, I saw Hawley with his arms deep in the water, cramming one-point-twenty-one gigawatts of energy into the ghost which lay trapped beneath the water.

Slowly...*so* slowly!...a woman made from a hundred different hues of blue began to emerge. It was a ghost; that was clear enough. But it was also lifeless, as if it had been carved from stone...or wood. More of the woman broke free, and—

Hang on, she had a tail?

Then, before I could figure out where Hawley got his hands on a mermaid, there was a great rush of blue as the rest of the ghost pulled itself from its tomb within the desert.

Hawley's ship—the spirit of Hawley's ship—floated upon the rising water.

Speedy shook his head and sighed. "Bingo."

Chapter Thirty-Four

"That's a thing you don't see every day," my mouth said on its own.

"I haven't seen that in four hundred years." De Borromeo's mouth was operating independently of her good sense, too.

"I guess…" I had no idea how to process the concept of a literal ghost ship, let alone the concept of how to fight one, so I let my mouth have total control. "I guess those old sailors were right about ships having souls."

That was either the absolute right or absolute wrong thing to say, as de Borromeo snapped out of her stupor. "Only human beings have souls, Hope Blackwell!" she whispered angrily. "God did not waste His precious gifts upon animals, vegetables, or such things as *ships*."

I snuck a quick side-eye at Speedy. As he didn't appear ready to rise up and stab the nun, I guessed he was still unable to see or hear her. "Let's table theology for the moment," I said, and pointed at the ship. "What do we do about *that?!*"

"I don't know," de Borromeo admitted.

"Speedy?"

"Thinking," he said. His attention was fixed on Hawley. The pirate captain had climbed aboard the ghostly ship, and was encouraging his crew to board. None of them appeared especially interested in being the first one to join Hawley.

"They mutinied against him once," I said.

Speedy nodded. "Yeah, but I'm not watching them," he replied. "Watch the ship."

The ship kept trying to rise into the air. It didn't get very far. After a couple of inches, it shuddered and dropped back into the water.

"How do you fight a ghost?" Speedy asked. When de

Borromeo opened her mouth to answer, he snapped, "Not you. Hope."

"Wait, you can see her?"

"Of course not," he snarled. "She's not a juiced-up monster. Kitten, tell me how you fight ghosts."

"You hit them as hard as you can," I replied.

"Why?"

"Because they remember pain."

"Exactly. Ghosts can be anything, go anywhere, but it takes an act of will. It's easier to put on a chupacabra costume than forget you can't feel pain." He nodded towards the ship. "That thing's got no mind of its own. It's a boat. It goes where the water goes."

"That's good," I said. Hawley was whipping the boat with a lash made from a thickly braided string of blue. The boat shuddered, and lifted itself from the water again. It made it a little further before it splashed down with a slow groan. "Gonna make it hard to sail that thing all the way to the Pacific Ocean," I said, grinning.

"Child, do you think this is over?" De Borromeo turned the full force of her nun glare on me. "Hawley is too strong for me to put back in his tomb. He will feed the strength of those who are lost in the desert to his ship until it bends to his will."

Ah. *That* was a problem. Hawley's boat might never be able to fly, but he probably thought it was a matter of inadequate fuel. Wholesale murdertimes would soon commence in the Sonoran Desert.

I shook my head. Water sloughed off and went flying, but it didn't make a difference. Everything was cold and wet and nasty, and I was slowly sinking in mud. If we hadn't been lying on top of a small hill, Speedy and I might have been in danger of being swept off of our feet, or worse. I glanced up at the storm, which showed no signs of breaking; around us, there were signs that this was about to turn into a spectacular hundred-year flood. The situation wasn't going to improve.

"All right," I said. "What do we do?"

De Borromeo turned her eyes towards the sky. "We pray."

"Hold that thought," I said, as I pulled Speedy from the mud with a *schloorp*-ing sound, and hauled the two of us through the mud on all fours. Once we were out of smiting range from the nun, I plopped him on a flat rock. "Any ideas?"

"That boat," he said, jabbing a claw towards the ghostly ship. "It's a hell of a liability. If Hawley was thinking clearly, he'd see that. It's gonna drain all of his power until he gives up on it."

I nodded. Habitual thought: ghosts feel pain because they think they must. Hawley has his ship again, because he thinks he should. If we took the ship from him... Well. Hawley looked the same as always (horrible, drooping skin hanging in ruins from his face with bits of bone sticking through, yuck and double yuck), but there were waves of exhaustion coming from him. He had poured most of the energy he had gotten from *Spooky Solutions* into his ship. Take out the ship, seriously cripple the Big Bad. Then, de Borromeo could plant him back in the dirt.

I grinned. "I've always wanted a good swashbuckling on a pirate ship."

"Talk to your husband about that," Speedy said, as his gaze darted over the boat. "How do we get up there?"

"No idea."

"Can you jump it?"

I didn't need to eyeball the distance from the top of the small hill to the ship in the bottom of the hollow. "*Hell* no! Not even if I hadn't burned myself out on this day-long marathon."

It was true: over the past twenty-four hours, all I had done was run. I was really feeling it, too. There wasn't much left in the tank. It wouldn't have been so bad if I had just been running, but I'd been running in extreme heat, followed by slogging through monsoon season. In the middle, there had been not one, but two, shocks to my system which had literally changed my physical makeup. I was going to crash—probably very soon—and nothing other than rest and calories would be able to get me up again.

In fact, this mud? This extremely cold mud I was lying in right now? It was *astonishingly comfortable*.

Ah, yes, the desert's version of hypothermia. At least I wasn't far enough gone to not recognize the symptoms.

"C'mon," I said, as I shook myself. Speedy dragged himself up to my shoulders, and I squelched our way back to de Borromeo. She appeared to be deep in prayer; I wasn't sure how to proceed.

Even if he could see her, Speedy has zero hangups. "How do we get aboard that pirate ship?" he snapped.

De Borromeo didn't open her eyes. "Pray, small animal."

I wasn't going to translate that. "She doesn't know, either."

"Yeah, well—" Speedy paused, and then snapped: "Get down!"

I fell face-first into the mud, with Speedy burrowing beside me like a chubby big-eared otter. De Borromeo vanished. For a moment, I thought Speedy was punking me. Then, wind. Strong enough to cut through the rain, strong enough for me to feel it through the thick layer of mud caked across my body. But not moving fast. Just *strong*, as if it had been displaced by an enormous moving—

I turned my head to see Hawley's ship rising out of the hollow. Hawley was standing on the prow,[48] his arms held aloft as if he was moving the ship by his will alone. Which, y'know, was most likely the case.

"How'd he convince the ship it wasn't a ship?" I asked.

Speedy ignored the question, and pointed towards the underside of the ship where a series of ropes were slowly waving in the wind. Some of them resembled ladders. These were dangling juuuust overhead...

"Right," I said, and tucked Speedy under my arm in a football carry.

"Um, kitten—"

"You got us into this," I reminded him. "There's no way in hell you're sitting this one out."

"Fine." He squirmed out of my grip and climbed up to my shoulders, and then locked his paws around my neck. "Go."

48 I'm pretty sure this is the word used to describe the pointy part at the front of a boat.

I went.

There was a rope not too far from us. Thick, twisty rope, made from the memory of plants. As the ship passed over our heads, I grabbed that rope and gave it a little tug. When it stayed firm in my hands, I started to haul us up, hand over hand.

"Keep us under the boat," Speedy whispered.

I would have told him that *yes*, I was trying to do that *exact thing*, thank you *so much!* but it was too much effort. Instead, I kept climbing.

If you've ever had to climb a rope, chances are it was tied to a gymnasium ceiling. That's never been a problem for me. Used to do it all the time at martial arts camps. Hell, once I did it on a dare, and spent an entire night clinging to the rafters after the rope broke.[49]

Never climbed one that whipped around in a blackout rainstorm while I climbed, tho'.

Hands on the rope, hold, step-lock with the feet, stand, move hands up, hold, lift knees, step-lock... Over and over again, as quickly as I could, I hauled us up the rope. My arms and legs were sore, and my hands with their brand-new callous-free skin? Screaming. And every couple of minutes, the boat crashed down in the desert, and we were all stuck in the mud again until Hawley whipped his ship back up into the storm.

"On your nine," Speedy whispered.

I glanced to my left. There were a second set of ropes, of the ladder-like variety. I tucked my legs tight, and used my weight to build us a little extra momentum. After a few decent swings, we were close enough to make the switch.

Up.

We reached the side of the boat, and then there was the added stability of the (not really) wood against my feet as I climbed. I searched for a porthole or a window or something, a way to get inside without charging the pirates head-on... Nope. No luck.

49 The pantysnitches who dared me to climb up there? They *fled*. And they didn't call for help. So when my arms got tired, I had the brilliant idea to tie myself to the rafters using my clothes. The next morning, they had to get me down with an inflatable bounce castle. By the way, this happened at a parochial school. What I'm saying is, I have a long history of climbing ropes and scandalizing nuns, sometimes simultaneously.

"We're gonna have to climb all the way up to the deck," I whispered.

Speedy grunted. "That's a great way to walk straight into an ambush."

I started giggling. "Hey," I snickered. "Hey, you remember your history?"

"Volumes more of it than you do," he replied. "You thinking Blackbeard?"

"Yeah, but we don't have any fire."

He reached out and swiped a pawful of mud from where it had stuck to the side of the boat. "We'll work with what we've got."

Picture it.

The Sonoran Desert.

Night.

The kind of hundred-year storm you saw maybe once in your lifetime, and only a few times since you died.

You're a ghost. You were a pirate—in your mind, maybe you still are a pirate, which makes you a pirate even during what should be your eternal retirement. And your boss is something of a shouty dick who's threatening to feed you to his boat. You're already having a crappy night, so when the swamp monster climbs over the side of your ship, roaring profanities in multiple languages?

You decide you are *done*.

As we leapt over the railing, Speedy held onto my head with his back claws and let fly with his strongest squeaky-toy bellow, waving his forearms and wiggling his ears. Out of the twenty pirates left? Four of them straight-up jumped over the side, right then and there.

Hawley didn't budge. He stood there, standing tall on the prow,[50] arms extended and unmoving, a statue as unmoving as the mermaid on the...prow.[51]

Fine, whatever. I charged the nearest pirate. No, I'm wrong: I charged the nearest cowboy—my old buddy in the beat-up

50 Same question.
51 Okay, maybe I should look up the definition of that word.

Stetson. When I got within throwing distance, I took out his legs and hurled him at the deck as hard as I could.

Then, something extremely strange happened: Stetson expected to hit the deck, but *the deck wasn't expecting to be hit!* Stetson's face met the deck…and got stuck there, his skin smashed into the wood, blurring into the same featureless blue energy. Small tendrils of blue reached up from the deck and began to peel Stetson's body apart, very carefully, as if ripping off snack-sized pieces made him all the more delicious.

Stetson began to scream. It was muffled, and I couldn't make out any words, but his hands clawed at the wood decking around him. His frantic scrabbling slowed, and then stopped, and he started to sink into the deck as the ship began to digest him.

"Well, that's utterly horrible," I muttered to myself, even as I grabbed another ghost and slammed him into the tall wooden mast. The mast shuddered, but this time the ship seemed to welcome the meal; the ghost couldn't even muster the energy to scream before the ship absorbed the ghost into itself.

Speedy paused in his multilinguistic bellow-barrage long enough to growl, "You're feeding it."

"Gimme another option!" I snapped. The odds were still against us, even though another couple of ghosts had seen what had befallen their pals, and had jumped ship. The remaining ghosts were decidedly terrified; the freakish mud-monster had weaponized their transportation.

Except we weren't much of a mud-monster. Not anymore. The rain kept pounding down, and Speedy and I were losing our camouflage. We were quickly transforming from a creature out of legend to a filthy woman with a talking koala standing on her head. I was worried until I realized that the pirates couldn't seem to process this, either: we might have lost the element of surprise, but we had definitely gained the element of weird.

Besides, the boat had finally learned that ghosts were easy pickings. Any ghost unfortunate enough to be touching the ship was slowly, sneakily, drawn down into the spectral mass of the ship itself. By the time the ghost had realized that the ship had started to suck at their energy, their feet had already been dissolved to their ankles. The ghosts were panicking—a couple of them remembered they could sacrifice their own feet without any true harm coming to them, and they would fly away from the ship in a flash of blue. Most were caught in the trap of their own minds, and they went down, down, into the hungry gullet of the ship, screaming.

I lunged at one of the remaining ghosts; he tripped and fell against the deck, and even that small contact was enough to awaken the ship's appetite. The boat sucked at his hands and feet, drawing him down, down, dissolving him into nothing but an echoing scream.

"We're coming for *yoooou!*" Speedy howled, reaching out for those last few ghosts, his claws fully extended and his mouth open to show his fierce eucalyptus chompers.

Those ghosts fell into bedlam. Absolute panicked bedlam. They soared up and away to escape the ship, as fast as they could, crashing into each other, casting each other down towards the ship as they went. It wasn't like that old joke about being faster than your buddy to escape the bear, tho': when a carnivorous ship was coming for you, it could eat the slowest ghost and the fastest ghost at the same damned time.

It was terrifying to watch. So terrifying that I almost didn't notice the slow tugging at my boots—

I leapt straight up in the air, fast enough to get a shout from Speedy. The ship, unable to digest leather, wagged a dozen long tendrils at me as if to tell me to settle down and become edible.

"Knock it off!" I snapped, hopping back and forth on my feet so those tendrils couldn't latch on and feed. After a moment, the tendrils sulked back into the body of the ship, as if they were disobedient puppies I had smacked with a rolled-up newspaper.

Speedy tapped me on my shoulder. "Kitten," he said. "Problem."

Hawley was still standing on the prow,[52] still deep in his statue

52   Prow: (noun) the forepart of a ship or boat; bow.

impression. He was watching us, a grin plastered across his face that had nothing to do with how his lower jaw broke straight through his skin.

I took a fast inventory of the ship. All of the remaining ghosts were gone; they had either fled or been eaten. "Whatcha thinkin', Smiles?" I shouted at Hawley. "You and your monster boat here are the only ones left!"

"Don't taunt the pirate," Speedy muttered.

"Let me have a little fun," I retorted.

"Fun?" The koala eased himself down from my head to his perch on my shoulders. "Look at him."

I didn't know what Speedy meant. Not until I put aside the idea that Hawley was a pirate.

No. He *had been* a pirate. Now he was a ghost, and we had managed to cheat our way through a successful whupping of his minions.

So why was he just…

…standing…

…there…

"Oh, shit," I whispered, as I finally saw past his illusion. It was minor. Extremely minor. Probably because Hawley didn't want to spend the energy to make it last past a couple of strong blinks. But he had no feet. His legs ended just above his ankles, the rest of him blending into the deck of the ship. Unlike the others, tho…

"Oh, shit," I said again.

Hawley wasn't being slowly digested.

He was already part of the ship.

Chapter Thirty-Five

"Can you see that?" I asked Speedy. "The real Hawley?"

"Don't have to," he said, as he pointed at Hawley. "Dumb-ass boat couldn't so much as float six inches above the water, and all of a sudden it's soaring and gobbling up the undead on its own? This boat found itself a human brain."

"Okay, this keeps getting more and more horrifying." I spun to look for an escape route. Hawley was getting better at controlling the ship; behind him, ropes were zipping back and forth within the rain, touching items all across the deck. *Hands.* Hawley had gotten himself a hundred new hands, and was familiarizing himself with how they worked.

One of those ropes cracked itself like a whip in midair.

"Time to go," I said, and sprinted for the side of the boat.

Ropes darted towards us, casting off the rain with a sibilant *hiss!* They went for my legs, my arms; I jumped and dodged, and Speedy snapped at the ropes as they came. If Hawley had possessed the ship—oh God, this meant ghosts could possess other ghosts, or maybe they could just possess the memory of objects, or—*focus, Hope!* If Hawley had possessed the ship for five minutes longer, we'd have been toast. Instead, he was still figuring out how his new body worked, and it slowed him down.[53]

We moved, we dodged. We survived. We reached the rail, and I jumped into the dark, and—*oh God we were so high up! Wait, no, that's just a reflection*—hit the water. There was a moment of panic as the water closed over my head, and I felt Speedy's

---

53 I sympathized, sort of. My own body still felt like I was sliding around in a mitten made from newborn skin. At least it was my own newborn skin, and I didn't eat other people to keep it. Honestly, I was really worried about those other ghosts. I was sure that some of Goldie Hawn's people had been caught up in the hungry chaos. And was I going to judge whether or not an evil cowboy should spend the rest of forever as boat food? No. No, I was not.

paws slip away.

"Speedy!" I found I could stand; the water was waist-high. But it was moving quickly, and he was so small—*"Speedy!"*

"Hope!" His faint cry came from the west. I tried to run, and my legs shot out from under me from the force of the water. There was a low point in the terrain somewhere nearby, and the water was rushing to fill it.

"Hope! Here!" Speedy again, his voice much louder.

The water carried me into something solid and extremely sharp. I gasped as a whole lot of pain seared its way straight through my baby-soft skin, and flailed around until I found my footing. A flash of lightning, and there was Speedy standing above me; he had found a pile of rocks and had pulled himself to safety. He scrambled down the rocks and sank his teeth in the collar of my shirt, and between the two of us, I managed to reach a spot just above the water line.

"You okay?" I gasped.

"Yeah, you?"

I shook my head. That sharp whatever-it-was had bruised a couple of ribs. "No more running," I said. "I'm done."

"Then you better start swimming," he snapped, and pointed over my shoulder. *"Now!"*

I tried to turn; pain flared low in my ribs and roared up my side, but I managed to catch a glimpse of a huge blue blob flying straight at us.

I grabbed Speedy by the scruff of his neck, and dove.

I couldn't shut my eyes. If I did, I was a little bit scared I wouldn't be able to open them again. Instead, I pressed my back against the sharp, solid whatever-it-was and held Speedy tight against my chest, as the blue belly of Ship-Hawley touched down just above us. It cut through both the water and the top of the whatever-it-was as cleanly as cutting butter with a hot knife, and then lifted up and away again.

We bobbed to the surface, gasping, and pulled ourselves from the water as the boat began to turn.

"He's searching for us," I panted. There was nowhere to hide.

We were lying on the edge of a football-field-sized patch of land which was mostly rock, and there were more rocks all around us, square rocks, carefully positioned rocks, and that pointy whatever-it-was had been the broken corner of an old building— "Wait." I sat up, and looked around. Nearly everything lower than the stones we were lying on was covered by water, but there was something familiar about the place. "Where are we?"

"De Borromeo's mission." Speedy nodded at the highest point on the pile. There was a flash of lightning, illuminating a familiar drawing of a cartoon dick with eyeballs.

"C'mon," I said. We dragged ourselves as far from the water as we could, trying to tuck ourselves within the space between the rocks. Speedy found a little bolthole and darted inside, but immediately darted out again, his wet fur sticking straight up on his hackles.

"Snakes!" he said, and began licking his front paws.

"Did it getcha?"

"Came close." He shot another glance at the boat. Ship-Hawley was slowly moving in a zig-zag pattern as it tried to locate us in the water. "We can't stay here. This place is crawling with creatures trying to ride out the storm."

"There's nowhere else to go!" I gestured at the lake around us. By now, it was probably deeper than my waist, and there were places where it was moving fast enough to throw up waves. If I wasn't beaten to hell and back, I might be able to wade us over to the mountains. In the shape I was in, there wasn't a chance. And the water was still rising. In about fifteen minutes, we'd be out of shelter.

"I know," he said. "But we're not beaten until we're dead."

"This isn't a game!"

"Sure it is," he said, as he began to poke around the rocks again. He found one that was twice the size of his body, and started sniffing around its edges. "It's just a game in which we can die. C'mere, kitten, this rock is loose. Help me slide it out—I think there's something behind it."

I grumbled, because koalas have never "helped" move anything, *ever*, but the rock shot straight out of its nook as if it had been greased. There was a large white object behind it. I shoved one foot in the hole and kicked around my boot. When nothing crunched down or stabbed me full of venom, I reached in with my bare hands. Hard bumpy plastic met my fingertips.

"It's a cooler," I said, dragging it out into the rain. I popped the lid, and found a bunch of junk. An old phone, a pair of white Keds— "Hey, this is de Borromeo's stuff."

Speedy snatched up the phone and tapped on its screen before he tossed it back in the cooler. "It's got power. No service. Where did she go, anyhow?"

"I think she's still praying. Or maybe she went to rally the chupacabras." There wasn't much in the cooler. The Keds had taken up most of the real estate. The rest was various bits of tourist junk, including a familiar baseball-sized dome with a metal clip on the reverse. "Look! My jogging light."

"Gimme." Speedy snatched it out of my hands before I could turn it on. He flipped the cooler over and used it as a cover to hide the light, then flicked the switch. The bright yellow light snapped on, as strong as ever. He turned it off, and tossed it between his paws, considering. "What else was in there?"

"Some headphones, and, like, six titanium sporks." I picked up the Keds. "If we're getting MacGyver, the shoelaces are in good shape."

"Yeah, gimme those laces," he said, and began turning over smaller rocks. "And get me the biggest rock you can throw."

"Whatcha thinkin'?"

"This is waterproof, right?" He held up the jogging light. When I nodded, he twitched his ears in the direction of Ship-Hawley, which was at the far arc of a sweep. "We need to buy ourselves some time. If he sees this under the water, he'll think something's down there."

"And then he'll dive down and check it out, and know we're close enough to turn on a lightbulb and tie it to a rock!"

"No, he won't," Speedy said. I found a shoebox-sized stone

and pushed it towards him. As soon as I did, I regretted not choosing a smaller stone; throwing it might be the last thing I did before I fell down. Too late; he had already lashed the jogging light around it. "He's a ghost out of time who doesn't know what a lightbulb is. He'll think he's found magic. Besides, he won't go in the water. Not unless he severs his connection with the boat and dives in himself. He's a sailor; he won't be able to imagine a scenario in which a boat can go under the water. He'll just cruise around in place for a while, and we can use that time to think of a way out of here."

In the distance, Ship-Hawley was beginning its pass. Lightning broke the sky behind the boat, a streak of white which burned its way through the storm. I could just barely make out Hawley on the prow, mouth open in that silent laugh.

"Turn it on, and throw it to the south," Speedy said. "That's where the courtyard is. It'll be shallow enough to cast the most light."

"No," I said, very quietly, but thunder ate up the word.

"What?"

I grabbed the stone with its dome light, and shuffled towards the east side of the clearing. Behind me, Speedy fluffed in irritation. "I said south, dumbass!"

"That's not where the riverbed is," I replied.

"What? The riverbed? Why?!"

"Face facts, Speedy. Unless you're keeping a spare helicopter in your ass, we're not getting out of this alive." I reached the edge of the water, and waded out as far as I could. It wasn't very far; my legs were shaking so badly, I was barely able to walk. "But if we don't do something, Hawley's gonna sail out to the Pacific Ocean. People will *die*, and then he'll *eat* them!"

Ship-Hawley was cruising towards us, slowly, scanning the waters. When he saw something in the water that was human-sized, ropes shot down and tore it into pieces.

It took me a couple of tries, but I finally got the words out. "De Borromeo gave her life to bind him, right?"

I turned to look at Speedy. It took a moment, but he nodded.

"I don't know how to do that," I said. "But I can at least try that hand-twist move she showed me, and put everything I've got into it."

"Kitten—"

"I'm good at one thing," I said, as I turned on the jogging light. "Might as well go out doing it, right?

"Besides," I added. "If this doesn't work, we can always come back as ghosts and kick his ass."

I turned and spun, hurling the bright, beaming rock like a shotput. It arced though the air, and then dropped into the water.

"Stay here," I said to Speedy. I had already begun to swim out towards the light when I heard frantic paddling behind me, followed by sharp claws digging into my shoulders.

"Buddy—"

"Shut up," he said.

I hung in the water. There wasn't much of a current here, and I could keep afloat without too much effort. But it was very cold, and nothing hurt anymore, not my legs or even my bruised ribs. My doctor brain said those two facts were scary-related; my regular brain was finding it hard to care.

At least it'd be over soon: Ship-Hawley had spotted the light, and was speeding towards us.

I dipped under the water as low as I could, so only my eyes and nose were clear. Speedy shifted his grip, and his big nose popped up beside me, nostrils flaring.

I chuckled. His mouth was closed. Small blessings and all that.

My legs bumped against something solid. When it didn't bite me or roll away, I decided it was the far wall of the mission's garden courtyard. I slid my feet around until I found a solid place to stand, and knelt so the water would carry my weight. Another small blessing.

Then, the pirate and his ship were there, and everything else ceased to matter.

Chapter Thirty-Six

The ship had raced to reach the light, but it stopped well short, drifting in the air a goodly distance away. Ship-Hawley circled the spot warily several times, passing over Speedy and me in the process. Each time it did, I wondered if those ropes would shoot down and snatch us up, and that'd be the end of it.

They didn't.

Ship-Hawley moved with all of the caution in the world, as if he knew the light was a trap but he couldn't quite figure out how. He was a cat with dangerous prey, and he knew it was playing dead.

But nothing happened.

It felt like forever, watching Ship-Hawley work up the courage to investigate the light at the bottom of the water. Eventually, a single bright blue rope uncurled, broke the surface of the water, and shot back up.

"This is embarrassing," I muttered.

Speedy's whiskers brushed against my cheek. "Can you hurry up? The water's freezing, and I hear great things about Hell."

"No." Overhead, more ropes were descending as Ship-Hawley began to prod the depths. I was hoping the water was deep enough. I was hoping he wouldn't realize he could change the lengths of those ropes. I was hoping Speedy was right, and Ship-Hawley had no idea what a lightbulb was, and that a time-lost pirate wouldn't be able to resist an unexplained golden glow.

I was hoping.

The jogging light was pretty far down, and it was so small. I had been worried that it'd be swallowed up by distance and debris, but it was still shining, still a bright yellow beacon that Hawley couldn't ignore.

I held my breath as Ship-Hawley reeled in its ropes.

Finally, the ship landed on the water.

Speedy's whiskers buzzed again, as he asked, "Now?"

"Shhh."

The ropes went down, moving through the water as Hawley tried to locate the source of the light. I held my breath until they returned to the surface, empty.

There was a long, long pause.

"Now?"

"Still waiting," I replied as quietly as I could. "It's not just Hawley that's stuck in that ship."

After a moment, he nodded. "You think you can get the other ghosts out of it?"

"I know I'm at least gonna try."

And then? At the line where the railing met the sky, Hawley appeared. Hawley the pirate—no, Hawley the person, a scrawny stretched-thin man with a raggedy beard. He had done away with illusion when he had separated himself from his ship.

And he was *tired*.

Oh, God, I could *feel* his exhaustion! He was barely holding on. All of the power he had gathered to himself had gone straight into the ship, and when he had broken from it, he had left all of that power behind. There was almost nothing left to him, just this...

Just...

This.

He stepped from the boat and fell into the water.

Speedy waited until Hawley had disappeared beneath the water before he asked, "Now?"

I didn't bother to answer. Instead, I shut my eyes and took in the whole of the world—at least, the world within my grasp. That giant puddle of water all around us. Beneath it was the desert. Soon, probably within the week, it'd be covered in autumn flowers. And then winter, when it would be dry as a bone. The snakes and lizards and other living things that had been driven out by the storm would return, if they could, and they'd eat the bodies of those that couldn't.

It had happened before.

It would happen again.

The desert was life, built on death, built on life, forever and ever. Amen.

"I saw a dinosaur," I said, smiling, and I opened my eyes to see Hawley rising from the water, the golden jogging light cradled in his hands and a blissful expression on his face. The pirate had found his treasure.

"Hey, Hawley!" I shouted as I stood.

He looked up, blinking in surprise. He recognized me, and his face began to fall apart as he gathered his illusions around him. Skin and muscle tissue receded from his bones—

I was having none of that. I took a breath, extended my right hand, and shouted:

"GO TO HELL!"

Hawley had just enough time to scream in rage before De Borromeo's tricky little hand gesture blew him into motes of bright blue dust.

I felt a little twinge around my ring finger before my legs stopped working, and everything went black.

I'm not sure how long I was unconscious. It was pretty great. Nothing hurt, there was nothing to do, no ghosts to banish, no government conspiracies to solve, no classes to attend, nothing.

And then a set of koala teeth crunched straight through the juicy meats of my upper arm.

"C'mon, kitten, wake up. It's five feet. You can crawl five fucking feet!"

I cracked an eyelid. I was lying on my back. Speedy was standing in shallow water, shouting at me, slapping me across the face with a paw and not even trying to pull his claws.

"C'mon!" he shouted again, when he saw I was awake. "I got you this far! Put in the work and get out of the water!"

I tried to look around, but my body wasn't listening to me anymore. All that I could see was a bunch of stones, plus a little doodle of a dick. Somehow, Speedy had dragged me back to the ruins of the mission.

There wasn't much left of it. We were as high up as we could go, and the water was still rising. And there was nothing I could do about it. My body was done. I had gone as far as I could go. It took all of the energy I had left to lick my lips, and say, "Get out of here."

Speedy met my eyes. "Fuck you."

"Go," I said. "At least try. Sparky needs you. If we both... y'know..."

"You think he'd ever forgive me if I left you?" Speedy forced himself between my arms, as if it were bedtime and we were both preparing for sleep.

"Love ya, kitten," he said in a soft voice. I could barely hear him above the sound of the rain.

"Back at ya, asshole," I whispered.

Thunder rolled. There was a strange sound within it, like a small *pop!*

I knew that sound. I couldn't place it, but—

Speedy began to laugh.

"Shut up," I told him. I barely had enough energy to die properly. The delay, plus his laughing, was somewhat irritating.

"Kitten, look!" he shouted, as he squirmed out of my arms. "Hail, hail, the gang's all here!"

Wait, what?

I shifted my head, veeeeery slightly. I was...dry? Yes. Dry. For the first time since the storm had broken, I was warm and dry!

We appeared to be behind an invisible shield of some kind. The water rose around it: we could see the small detritus of the desert pummeling the shield, before it bounced off and vanished into the distance. I shifted my head the other direction, veeeeery slightly, and then a little more, so I could take it all in. The shield appeared to be a perfect half-sphere; the water flowed around us, over us, and away, with nothing seeping beneath the line where it joined against the ground.

Someone had put us in a bubble!

We were saved? No. Impossible. This was a temporary reprieve to get our hopes up. Once we thought we were safe, Coyote or the sentient desert or whatever was planning to yank this shield away. A final decorative piece of shit frosting on the doomcake.

But the shield stayed put. Even while the water rose around it, high enough to drown what little was left of the mission, it stayed put.

We were…alive?

I didn't understand. Not until I heard a familiar voice say, "Dearest?"

Ah. Now I understood.

I rolled my eyes around until I could see an older man, all in blues, looking dapper in a pair of spectacles, and an embroidered waistcoat and matching pants. His hair was unbound, and floated around his head in a wispy crown.

I smiled up at my best friend. "Hey, Ben."

Benjamin Franklin, the water parting around his shield as if it were a ship's prow,[54] returned my smile. "Hello, Dearest," he said. "Do you need a hand?"

"Yeah," I replied.

He lifted me up, as easily as if I were a child. Speedy climbed Ben's pants leg, and nestled himself on my stomach. This close, I could sense Ben's raw power. Few other ghosts in America had the kind of name recognition that Ben enjoyed. Could he change the course of this flood? I didn't know. It wasn't important. Not when he could pull a Moses and part the waters around us.

He stepped into the air, and we left the water below.

"What happened to you?" Ben asked, as he walked across the sky. The rain avoided us; we were still surrounded by that bubble. "Why didn't you call me?"

"Tried," I muttered. "Coyote."

"Oh? Coyote the trickster?" There was something slightly dangerous lurking within Ben's voice.

Speedy caught it, too. "Friend of yours?"

54 Tah-dah!

"We've met."

"Did he tell you to come save us?" I murmured.

Ben chuckled. I didn't understand why, but it didn't matter. Not when I felt warm and dry, and safe.

He flew us back to the hidden city. I wouldn't have been able to find it again, never in a million years. There was water everywhere, swallowing up all possible landmarks. Here, there, were spikes of rocks, or the crowns of the tallest cactus. Nothing else. Only rain, only water.

Once we reached the city, I realized why Ben had been able to find us.

Mare was awake.

What's more, Mare was *organizing*.

She stood on the ledge, drenched by the rain, and surrounded by a dozen ghosts, all of whom pulsed with deep, powerful energy. Founding Fathers. And each and every one of those persnickety bastards was jumping when Mare said frog.

"You!" She pointed to a ghost I recognized—John Adams. "There's a cluster of pirates about a half-klick to the west. We need them back here!" Once she was done with Adams, she moved to another Founding Father, and sent him off on another task.

"They're rounding up the evil ghosts?" I asked.

"A friend of yours said it would be easier to manage them if they're all in one place," Ben said. "I believe she said her name is de Borromeo?

"A formidable woman," he added, beneath his breath.

"Please do not hit on the nun," I sighed.

"She was an earthly woman first, dearest. In her time, the clergy was a retreat for women who wished to—"

Somehow, I found the strength to slide to the ground and stumble away from the lecture. Ben laughed, and resumed talking about the limited opportunities available to women in the Whatever Centuries as he followed after Speedy. They fell into their usual habit of verbal sword fighting, with Speedy snapping off swears and Ben parrying them right back at him.

I didn't mind.

Safe.

We were safe.

I picked a dry spot just past the edge of the rain, and was planning to sleep right there for the next fifteen zillion years when Mare spotted me. She rushed into the cavern. "Hope!" she shouted, waving. I managed to stay upright as she slammed her arms around me. "I'm so glad you're okay!"

"Me, too," I gasped. I returned her hug, mostly for stability. "Where're Fish and the others?"

"He's kept them in the cave," she said. "When I woke up, I called Pat. These guys showed up almost as soon as I told him what was happening."

"How did Fish wake you up?"

"He didn't." She shook her head. "I just woke up."

As she moved, her hair slid to the side. And there, on my right hand…

"Whoa," I whispered. My special unobtanium ring was back where it belonged.

"What?"

"I'll explain later," I said. "So…how are you? With the…you knows?"

Mare released me, and tossed a couple of handfuls of wet hair over her shoulder. She glanced over at the remaining Founding Fathers. They had greeted Ben as the beloved brother who had begun an argument last Thanksgiving, and they were determined to finish it tonight. "You were right," she whispered. "They're just people."

She turned to leave, raising her voice ever-so-slightly to insist that *gentlemen* there was *work* to be done and we should all perhaps *concentrate on **that!***

"Good hands," I assured myself. "They're in good hands."

I shuffled a few more steps into the cavern. I was aware (almost) that the Spooky Solutions crew was still hiding in the back of the cave, and they were calling to me. But the ground was dry, and that was all I needed.

I collapsed face-first in the dirt.
Then? At long last?
Everything stopped.

Chapter Thirty-Seven

There were no dreams.

I had expected de Borromeo to make an appearance. Maybe Goldie Hawn, or even Hawley. None of them showed up.

The first time I woke up, Oshea crammed food and fresh water into me. Nothing made sense, so I let her, and then went back to sleep.

The second time I woke up, I had to pee like never before in my entire life. My nose led me to a little latrine area not far from the cavern door. When I was finished, I peeked outside; the ghosts were gone, and so was the storm. The water reflected the light of the half-moon, and everything was silver and blue and black, and beautiful. I ate another helping of camp food, and went back to my pile of blankets to get more sleep.

The third time I woke up, my husband was staring down at me.

"Hi, Sparky," I said.

He picked me up and engulfed me in a bear hug.

"Don't crush me," I gasped. "It was a really crappy night."

"We heard." A crotchety voice, like death warmed over, and (sadly) quite familiar. I turned to see Fish standing with two men. The first was tall and stocky, with thinning red hair and freckles. The second man looked like Patrick Stewart dipped in pickling brine; he was the one who had spoken.

Mike Reilly and Richard Smithback.

I knew why Mike was here: I had spent the last few days leaving him weird-ass voice messages about finding another psychic. And Smithback…well, Smithback was our healer, and I had a lump in my stomach when I realized why *he* was here.

My husband released me. I reached out and brushed his dark blond hair back from his face.

"Speedy told us everything," he said.

"Including how this might have been his fault?"

He shut his eyes for a moment, then amended: "Speedy told us almost everything."

"Don't be too pissed at him," I warned. "I'm still not sure what started it all."

"Figure it out later," Smithback said. "Give me your hand."

"Nooo," I whined.

"Yes," Mike said, grinning.

"I don't want another adrenaline crash," I pouted, as I dropped my hand into Smithback's waiting palm.

"Stop bitching. You're further from death than I am," he said, and pushed me back onto the pile of blankets. I let him: Smithback had no problem playing the terminal cancer card, and there's no good defense against that. "Fleishman, come here. Put your hands on her bare legs. Now, pay attention to how I do—"

I stopped listening, and rested my head against my husband's chest as they put me back together. I almost drifted off to sleep; compared to Fish's clumsy hammer-slam healing, Smithback's healing technique was surgically precise. He even put my calluses back, and tweaked a formerly bad knee so it stopped feeling so exactingly perfect. After they were done, I walked around the cavern for about five minutes, with Sparky's arm around my waist to keep me from zooming straight off the cliff face. Right before I was about to crash, the Army rescue helicopter returned.

"They dropped the three of us off, and took everyone else back on the first trip," Sparky explained, as he helped me wrestle with the safety harness. "They're all at Yuma Proving Grounds."

"I was gonna call you, but we didn't want to start the usual media feeding frenzy."

"Don't worry about that," he chuckled. "The storm and the sudden signal loss gave us a perfect excuse to make sure you were safe. We came down with a team from the Smithsonian."

"Tellerman's gonna get a nice documentary out of this," I said.

He didn't answer me. Instead, he swung his legs around me to use me as his chair, and gestured for the team on the helicopter to start the winch. There was some fussing—apparently hauling up two bodies when one wasn't secure was a no-no—so Sparky did some cyborg magic and started the winch himself.

As we rose above the mountains, he tipped the harness towards him, and we kissed. He tasted of worry and sweat, with a hint of peppermint.

I broke away and rested my forehead against his. "Next time, we're going on vacation together. Somewhere with taxi service. You have no idea how many miles I've put on me in the last few days."

He chuckled. "And Speedy isn't coming."

By then, we were close enough to the helicopter to hear a deep voice shout down, *"Like fuck I'm not!"*

We didn't go straight home. No, I still had three days left in my vacation, and by this point I thought I had earned some aggressive self-indulgence. So, back to the Bellagio we went. By the time we reached the hotel, I was feeling somewhat like myself. Sparky hustled me up to the penthouse, and stuck me in the tub to rest. When I got drowsy, Speedy hopped in the tub and swam laps to keep me awake. Ben hung out on the couch in the main room with Mike and Smithback, and I smiled as the sound of crappy daytime television took over the suite.

Then the others began to show up.

First? Fish arrived. Mare had gotten him on loan from the Army for a few more days. Something about discovering a major archaeological site, and the need to debrief him, although her version of "debriefing" was probably more literal than the Army expected. The two of them vanished into her room and only came out for ice.

Since the *Spooky Solutions* team was stuck sitting on their hands until the Smithsonian cleared the site, they were back in Las Vegas, too. They came by at least a couple of times a day. They wanted…

I don't know what they wanted.

I think Dina wanted answers that she could understand. She kept asking questions which scratched at the edges of what we had gone through. However, Oshea always came with her, and Oshea wanted *nothing* explained. Of the two of them, I think Oshea understood the most, and it scared the hell out of her. She knew how to manage her sister, so every time the conversation swung towards the supernatural, she dialed it down to normal. We did a lot of shopping, hit a few excellent restaurants, and even caught an evening performance of Cirque du Soleil.

Keith came by once. Just once. He tried to talk about the ATV and the chase through the ancient city. Speedy and I sat across from him at the kitchen island, and did nothing but drink straight whiskey and tell the raunchiest jokes we knew until he got frustrated and left.

Then there was Tellerman.

He came alone. When my husband, Mike, or Smithback were in the room, they joked about the intricacies and hypocrisies of government work. But when they weren't there, he would sit down and stare at me, waiting.

He broke me down one time. "I wish I could tell you," I said.

"Do you?"

"No."

He smiled a little. "Was it really the Army?"

I sighed. We were sitting on the rooftop balcony, taking in the evening air before the rest of the crew showed up for dinner. Speedy was asleep in Tellerman's lap, and I was finally able to get through a whole hour without sucking down a whole pizza. If Tellerman knew how to take no for an answer, it would have been pleasant. "I'm not allowed to talk about it."

There was a small *tink!* of ice chips as he sipped his drink. After a moment, he said, "I've got a lot of it on tape."

"Yeah, well."

"I'm not threatening to blackmail you."

I laughed aloud at that. "Okay."

"I'm warning you that I'll probably put out one final *Spooky Solutions* about this trip."

I kept laughing. Speedy and Mare had already gone through the footage. Anything that even hinted at proof of the supernatural had been accidentally taped over during a server backup. Oops! The conspiracy theory nutjobs would cry foul on OACET, but the conspiracy theory nutjobs always cried foul on OACET, so we weren't worried.

As I said—small blessings.

Tellerman paused. It was a weighty pause: it had the small whistling sound of a distant bomb closing in on its target, so I stopped laughing and let him drop it. "Keith found a tape from that night of the storm in one of his cameras," he said. "It never got uploaded to the servers."

Yup, there it was. "I thought you wanted to go legit."

"I also want to make money," he replied. "I'm not blackmailing you, honest. I'm just warning you that we've already got bids from the Discovery Channel. I'm holding out for HBO, Showtime, one of the premium channels. But it'll be out there."

"Unless?"

He tipped his glass roughly in the direction of the Sonoran Desert.

"You want to know that badly?" I asked him. "You'd sacrifice a truckload of money and publicity for *that?*"

"I think…" he paused to find the right words. "I think there's more to life than what we've come to expect.

"I didn't go into ghost hunting by accident," he added. "I want to *know.*"

I got up to refresh our drinks. "No," I said, and ruffled his hair as I passed him. "No, you don't."

"Hey, now—" He moved Speedy from his lap to my empty chair, and then stood to follow me. Wait, no; make that he *tried* to stand, but toppled over with a sharp scream, his hands pressed against his crotch, and his legs curled up as high as he could bring them.

Speedy hopped down from my chair and walked off to our bedroom, his head and tail held high.

The next day, Sparky and I left Las Vegas in a rental Land

Rover,[55] with Mare and our friends following us in an extremely comfy Cadillac SUV. We were heading for Yuma, where we'd drop off Fish. From there, we'd catch a military flight back to D.C., where we'd have to convince the Army to take control of a thousand square acres of the Sonoran Desert. Then, we'd have to convince them to put up fences and No Trespassing signs posted at key locations, and the paper trail—if you knew where to look for it—would suggest that OACET was involved in every step of the process. After that, I would have to take a trip out there every six weeks for the first six months, and make sure I was in the public record when I did. Photographs, interviews, the works.

Since that protected land was a good fifty miles from de Borromeo's mission, we felt pretty confident that the inevitable crackpot conspiracy theories (and their corresponding nutjobs) that would spring up after Tellerman's documentary would be completely wrong. Hawley would stay lost, at least until the next psychic stumbled down from the Smithsonian's new tourist destination into de Borromeo's territory.

So, like, next Thursday, probably.

Which is why Sparky and I turned off the main road before we got to Yuma, and drove west down an old maintenance road which dead-ended in the middle of nowhere...and at the edge of an enormous lake which stretched as far out as we could see. It wasn't anywhere near de Borromeo's mission, but since that part of the desert was still under eight feet of water, this was about as close as we could get.

I took a shopping bag out of the back of the Land Rover, and went to the edge of the lake. I wasn't sure how to make contact with de Borromeo or Goldie Hawn, but I couldn't leave without making the effort to say goodbye. Sparky stood nearby, not saying much.

---

55 The kids we had left at the *Spooky Solutions* camp had the good sense to get out of the rain. They had abandoned one Jeep in the desert with the keys in the ignition in case we came back, and had driven the other one back to where we had left the vehicles. The three of them took the Mustang, the Jeep, and the van straight to the high ground for shelter, and had weathered out the storm in an IHOP. I gave them very generous tips in thanks for keeping my car insurance premium from breaking the stratosphere.

"Perp."

I took a deep breath. I didn't want to look down. I *wouldn't* look down!

I looked down.

The roadrunner was standing beside me, leaving its small X-shaped tracks all over the rain-beaten earth. "Perp."

"Go perp yourself," I told it. "I'm here to say goodbye to the ghosts who didn't try to murder me."

The roadrunner made a rude noise and stepped away.

I ignored it.

I half-expected that de Borromeo wouldn't show up, and I'd have to come back out to the mission again after the floodwaters had receded. But after a few minutes of studiously ignoring the roadrunner, I saw the nun gliding towards us over the surface of the lake.

"You see her?" I asked Sparky.

"No," he said. "Would you like me to go out-of-body?"

"Nah," I said, as I patted him on his butt. "We'll keep it short. Besides, I think she's a fan of ours."

"Ah," he said, and walked away, following the edge of the lake to give us some privacy.

De Borromeo arrived, stepping from the surface of the lake to the shore with grace. She didn't hesitate; she walked straight over to me and embraced me.

"Thank you," she whispered. "Thank you so much."

"Least I could do. Sort of," I replied. "Since it was my fault for coming here."

She let me go, but kept hold of my hands in hers. "How were you to know?" she said. "You did more than I could have asked of you. Hawley is bound in his tomb, and desert is sleeping once more."

"Yeah, about that," I replied. "Are you entirely sure the desert was to blame for this? Because there's this roadrunner—" I paused to look for the bird. It was, of course, nowhere to be found.

De Borromeo's smile fell. "I was sure of a great many things before you arrived," she said. "Now, I am not so certain. If I am right, the desert was given a great flood, and that occupied its attentions more than our fumbling mistakes.

"But," she said, as she turned to greet the lake with her arms outstretched, "no matter the cause, we are dealing with forces greater than ourselves, and those never offer any easy answers."

I chuckled. "Seems like a bit of an easy out for you."

"That, too."

I laughed in earnest as I held out the shopping bag. "Here."

"Oh?" The nun took it, and peered inside. She let out an exclamation of delight as she took out a new phone and a pair of Keds.

"There's some tequila in there, too," I said. "No ice, though."

"Yes, well, perhaps I can find my own ice." De Borromeo paused, and then said in a great rush, "I feel I am due for a vacation!"

"Yes!" I clapped her on the back. "Yes, you are. Where are you going?"

"I haven't decided," she replied. "I need to find some *jorguín* from this time and ask their advice. There is still the problem of the boat."

I winced. "Oh, no. What's happened?"

The nun waved in the direction of the Sonoran Desert. "It's still sailing. I hoped it would break apart, but—"

"All those poor ghosts," I said. "They're stuck in there forever?"

"Not forever. But today, the ship is still too strong to manage," she said, as she did that fist-clench-sweep gesture.

I nodded. Yeah, we were dealing with this now.

"Go on your vacation," I told her. "I'll come back in a couple of weeks. By then, the boat might be weak enough to pull apart. Have you seen anyone from the chupacabra pack?"

"No." De Borromeo's mouth was set in resignation. "I hope they have gone to take time for themselves to heal."

We exchanged goodbyes and good wishes, and the nun told me that my husband's legs were much nicer than the other young man's. Before she left, she kissed me on both cheeks and said, "I meant it when I said you would have made an excellent *jorguín.*"

"Maybe," I replied. "But for now, I figure I'll just be me."

De Borromeo smiled, picked up the shopping bag, and slowly faded away into the afternoon sunlight.

"Is she gone?" Sparky asked, as I walked over to him.

"Yeah. She says that Goldie Hawn and the others are missing. I promised I'd come back soon to help her wrangle the ship. If they haven't come back by then, we'll search for them."

He groaned. "If she drags you into another pirate battle—"

"Don't be too hard on her," I said. "She also says you have great legs."

"Nuns never lie," he said, and sidestepped as I tried to goose him. We spent a few minutes stomping around in the lake and splashing each other before we headed back to the Land Rover.

"Did you get what you needed?" he asked, as he stripped out of his shoes and socks to dry.

"I guess," I replied, as I slid behind the wheel. "I'll probably never get answers to the really big questions, but, y'know, who does? We have to deal with things as they come, and adapt as best we can."

He grinned at me, a sweet sunshine smile which made me especially glad that I hadn't drowned in the desert a few days before.

"One thing I still don't understand," I said, as I threw the vehicle into reverse and started to put it through a three-point turn. "There were some guys at the Bellagio our first night there. Real bruiser-types. They followed us all over the casino, but after that they disappeared."

"Ah," my husband said. "You see—"

"I knew it!" I jabbed a finger into his chest. "Do you know how many problems you caused? What did you do, call the manager of the Bellagio and ask for him to put some undercover security on me?"

"You'd just been assaulted!" he said. "Twice!"

I was ready to snipe at him, but then I saw the roadrunner. I had all but forgotten about the bird until I caught a glimpse of it in the rearview mirror as I was turning. It disappeared over a small rise in the land. I watched the edge of the hill on the other side, waiting for it to reappear.

It never did.

Instead, a coyote—the first one I had seen all week—darted across the ground. It turned its head towards me and a giant toothy smile engulfed the entire mirror for all of a heartbeat, and then it took off running.

"Well," I said. "Well."

Notes

As always, this book wouldn't have been possible without the love and support of my husband, Brown.

My thanks goes to the beta readers who were so very generous with their time. Gary, Tiff, Andrea, Kevin, Carlota, and Joie, you're always there to poke problems into a managable shape. Thank you so much. And my thanks also goes to Danny and Jes for the copy edits.

Digger the talking wombat is property of Ursula Vernon, who also puts on the name of T. Kingfisher to write amazing books and create stunning cover art. Thank you for the pirates!

Finally, I've taken some liberties with the Hohokam story presented in Chapter Twelve, and combined two different origin stories into the same one for the sake of brevity. If you are interested in reading more about the Hohokam, I recommend beginning with *The Short, Swift Time of Gods on Earth* by Donald Bahr et al (University of California Press, 1994).

K.B. Spangler lives in North Carolina with her husband and as many dogs she can sneak into the house without him noticing. She is the author and artist of A Girl and Her Fed, where Speedy, Hope Blackwell, Patrick Mulcahy, and the Agents of OACET are alive and well. The ghosts are well, too, thanks for asking. Additional information about these and other projects can be found at kbspangler.com.